BLC

A

Seduction

AND MURDER

A HOTEL BENTMOORE ROMANCE

SHELBY CROSS

To Vicki, my muse
To shadow, my inspiration
To Mockingbird Lane, my voice of reason
And, as always, to Husband

Special thanks to Shots, for his tutorial on
rope; to Tailstrike, for his tutorial on fire
flogging; and to Charlie, for his donated wit

For more information about The South Bay Spot,
please visit their website: www.thesouthbayspot.com

CHAPTER ONE

H E WAS READY FOR THE kick to the face. Blocking that one was easy.

But the knee to the ribs made him stumble back. He folded in, and held his gloved hand to his side.

"I thought you invited me here for a little workout," Brian said, panting. "I didn't realize you wanted to pummel me to a pulp."

"If this is what you call a pummeling, then you definitely need to work out more," came the reply. Inside the protective helmet, his sparring partner Justin made a face at him. "What happened, now that you're a family man, you've gone soft?"

That earned Justin a kick to the stomach, and he shut up after that.

Brian was taller than Justin, older, and a more seasoned boxer. But Justin had years of hard street fighting behind him, and stuck by his own set of rules, one of which was Fight Now, Recover Later. He absorbed Brian's blows without flinching, and immediately retaliated with a punch to the side of Brian's face.

"Hey, be careful with the face," Brian said, stepping

away and rubbing his jaw through the helmet padding. "Last time you left me with a swollen eye, Samantha wanted to come back here and scratch your face off."

"Stop being a baby," Justin said. But, taking the censure to heart, he stopped. The fight was over anyway.

Justin removed the gloves from his hands, dropped them to the floor, and pulled off the padded helmet from around his head. His dark hair remained plastered down to his skull. "I guess we're done," he said.

"Thank you," Brian grumbled.

"Speaking of baby, how's yours? Did you find out what it is yet?"

"Nope. We decided it should be a surprise," Brian said, removing his own protective gear as he spoke. He stopped and said, "Well, I decided. Samantha was all for finding out. It's driving her crazy. But I told her no asking the doctor, and no trying to peek at the ultrasounds. We'll find out together, in the deliver room."

Justin shook his head and said, "You're such a sadist."

"Indeed I am," Brian said. He smiled.

They both walked over to the counter and grabbed a couple bottles of Gatorade. Despite Justin's barbs, it had been a hard workout for both of them. Neither of them knew anyone else who could handle their level of fighting technique. At least with each other, they could both walk away in one piece, and not feel like they had to hold back like they did with other partners.

Over the last few months, despite their differences in ages—and personal opinions regarding certain matters—Justin and Brian had managed to become close friends. Brian knew things about Justin no one else did, and he lent a sympathetic ear.

But Brian's visits to Justin's house were becoming more and more sporadic, and Justin had a feeling they would stop completely once the baby arrived. Brian Sinclaire, renowned sadist and once famed Master of the Hotel Bentmoore, desired by bottoms and masochists from coast to coast, was about to become a family man. His wife, Samantha, was pregnant with their first child.

Justin would often rib Brian about his new lifestyle. He would also laud Brian for "getting out while the going was good," and leaving his old life behind.

Despite his change in lifestyle, Brian still kept himself in shape by going to the gym. Justin thought weight machines were a necessary evil—it was why he owned so many himself, right there in his own family room—but he also thought street fighting was a skill every man should have. He'd gotten into enough fights as a reckless teenager to know.

"So...you working on that piece for me?" Brian asked, returning his bottle of Gatorade to the counter.

"Yeah," Justin said, putting his own bottle down next to Brian's. "In fact, I just moved it from the garage to the workroom so I could put the finishing touches on it. You want to see?"

"Of course."

Justin led Brian down the hallway to the back bedroom. Originally designed as the master bedroom, it had been converted into one of Justin's workrooms.

His other workroom was the garage, where he worked on his bigger pieces; but here, Justin worked on the things that needed fine details and delicate handwork.

Right in the middle of the room, looking almost finished, was Justin's current masterpiece.

It was a padded table, cushioned with thick foam and black leather. It was lower than a standard BDSM table, but what made this one really unique was that the middle of it was completely cut out. It was a hollow rectangle, with a small padded square jutting out from the middle of the top, perfect for a head to rest on. The legs of the table were thick oak, and had already been stained and polished to a perfect shine. They were angled wide instead of straight down to give the table more support. Pen lines marked the sides of the table where metal rings and eyebolts would go for connecting chain and cuffs.

"Wow," Brian said, studying it with yearning in his eyes. "It's looking great, Justin. It's going to be perfect."

"Thanks."

"How soon will it be done?"

Justin laughed. "What, you haven't been able to whip your wife lately?"

"It's getting hard, you know," Brian said, solemn. "She can't lie down on her stomach, so she has to stand up, and she can't lean against the St. Andrew's Cross with her stomach in the way. It's getting difficult for her to keep standing that long at all, especially while I'm whipping her and she's off in subspace, and I can't let her fall." He scowled. "BDSM furniture is not built for the pregnant female."

"Maybe I should start a whole line," Justin said. "BDSM equipment for pregnant ladies."

"You'd make a hit," Brian said.

"I might," Justin nodded. "But I don't have time to think about it."

Brian gave him a level look. "Your brother keeping you busy?"

"Trowlege just called me yesterday. He put in an order for some new floggers."

"Hey, it's good for business," Brian said. "That can't be a bad thing."

"No, it's not." Justin sighed. "But I promised I'd finish this table for you by next week, and I will. That sounds okay?"

"That sounds great," Brian said. "Sam will be so happy."

"Good."

Justin was glad for his friend. Brian had left the Hotel Bentmoore to start a new life, and had ended up finding the woman of his dreams. He did not regret his time spent at the Hotel Bentmoore, nor his deep feelings of connection to the place.

If only Justin could say the same.

After Brian left, Justin showered, put on some old sweatpants, and got back to work on one of the floggers he was making for his brother. Well, he wasn't really making it for his *brother;* he was making it for the Hotel Bentmoore. But to Justin, the two were one and the same.

His cell phone, sitting in the corner of the wide table, began to ring. Justin knew that ringtone. He answered it anyway.

"Hello?"

"It's Mr. Trowlege, Sir."

"I know that, Trowlege," Justin said with a sigh. He had given up on getting Trowlege to stop calling him 'Sir' long ago. It was too engrained in the man's nature, Justin supposed. "Is there something I can do for you?"

Trowlege paused. "Your brother is wondering if we could add a few pieces to the order we put in yesterday, Sir."

"Depends," Justin said. "What does he have in mind?"

"Three more matching pairs of floggers...."

"That shouldn't be a problem."

"...And a double Queening Chair."

"A *double* Queening Chair," Justin said, already picturing it in his mind's eye. "Sounds interesting. Might take a little while, but if you send me the schematics, I can get that to him."

"We also need a new CBT chair, one that can hold at least four hundred thirty six pounds."

"*Four hundred thirty six* pounds?" Justin exclaimed. "Why so specific?"

"We have a troupe of acrobats coming through—"

"You know what, forget it, I don't want to know," Justin said. He squeezed the bridge of his nose. "When do you need that by?"

"Perhaps you should start on that one first, Sir."

"I see," Justin said, and pinched the bridge of his nose again. "Look, Trowlege, he can't expect me to have all of this done anytime soon. I do have other work to do—a shop to run."

"Your brother understands, Sir. He is wondering, though, how your search is going for hired help."

It was a long-standing issue that Justin did not have enough people working for him at his shop. In fact, he only had one other person working with him: his friend and co-owner of the store, Adam.

Adam was no stranger to the world of the Hotel Bentmoore, either. Like Justin, he had grown up inside it: his own brother was a host and Master of the Hotel Bentmoore. The Hotel Bentmoore was also where Adam had found his girlfriend and submissive, Khloe.

Adam and Justin both knew what it was like to straddle the line between the kink world and vanilla life. But while Adam maneuvered his way through both seamlessly, Justin still struggled with it.

It was one of the reasons why he had only recently relented to begin a search for a new employee, someone to work the front of the store while he and Adam were busy filling orders in the back. The two of them needed someone who could handle their *alternative* lifestyles. But the search was going slowly.

"I have ads and notices out in all the right places," Justin said. "It's just going to be hard finding someone who knows weapons, can deal with the customers, and wouldn't mind our back business."

"I could help, Sir. I could get back to you with

some recommendations."

"No, that's okay, Trowlege. We'll find someone ourselves." The last thing Justin wanted was one of his brother's spies planted in his own shop.

"Very well, Sir. But remember, we are here if you need anything."

"Oh yes, I know," Justin said dryly. "My brother is just a fount of support."

When was the last time he had spoken to his brother, anyway? Four months ago? No, five. Justin made a sound like a snort, and squeezed the bridge of his nose again.

Trowlege said, "I didn't mean to upset you, Sir. I apologize."

"No, it's okay, Trowlege." Another pinch. The skin between his eyebrows was starting to hurt. "Please tell Jonathan I will have the CBT chair ready for him as soon as possible, and will send the rest of the order as it gets done."

"I will tell Mr. Bentmoore right away, Sir. Thank you Sir."

"You're welcome Trowlege. Goodbye." Justin hung up the phone.

Only four pinches to the bridge of the nose. That wasn't so bad. Last night's conversation with Trowlege had awarded him six.

Justin went back to work on the flogger for a few hours. Then he went to his computer, opened up his email, and checked to see if he'd gotten any bites on his help-wanted ads. There was one response, but that was it. Justin wrote the guy back, asking to see a copy of his resume, and shut down the computer.

He wasn't too hopeful about his online search. In his opinion, the chances of getting lucky from an ad site were slim to none. But Adam insisted they try every avenue, so Justin was going along with it.

He brushed his teeth and got into bed.

As he drifted off to sleep, he began to picture the design for the CBT chair his brother had requested. It would need to be strong, but give a little...ash, not oak...and he would need to get more sandpaper....

As he drifted off to sleep, another picture began to form inside his head: that of his brother, the all-great-and-powerful Jonathan Bentmoore, owner (half owner—Justin still owned half of it, too) of the Hotel Bentmoore, getting tortured in a CBT chair.

The image didn't last very long; it was *too* evil, even for Justin.

But, fleeting as it was, it still made Justin smile.

CHAPTER TWO

THE NEXT DAY, JUSTIN WALKED into his store a half an hour early, only to find Adam already there. "Whoa, what time did you get here?" Justin asked.

"Early," Adam said. He gave Justin one of his charming, school-boy smiles. "Khloe woke up early, and decided to wake me up, too."

"I take it you didn't mind?"

"Oh, I minded. I punished her soundly for it." Adam's smile widened. "Then I felt better."

Justin had to laugh. "You two...."

He switched the sign on the front of the door from CLOSED to OPEN, unlocked it, and put a doorstopper against the corner. As soon as he did, a customer came striding through: a man who had obviously been waiting for them to open from some distance away.

"May I help you?" Adam asked, the swords and weapons displayed along the wall behind him becoming a backdrop.

"I'm not sure," the other man said, nervous. "I'm not sure what I'm looking for."

Adam smiled. "Well, if you're looking for a sword,

you have many to choose from," he said, waving his arm behind him. "Do you have a particular region of sword in mind? Or time period? We have everything dating from the medieval period until today. If you want something ancient Greek or Roman, we can get it for you, but it'll take a few days."

"No," the man said quietly. "I'm not interested in a sword."

"Oh," Adam said, confused. "A different type of weapon, then?"

"Yes, but I don't know what they're called...."

"A Sai?" Adam suggested. "A Jutte?" Adam frowned as the customer continued to shake his head, looking lost. "Can you tell me what it looks like, or what it's used for? Where you saw it?"

"It was, um, a set of...claws." The man's voice trailed to a whisper. "I saw them at a party." He looked down at the floor; his face grew beet red.

"At a party," Adam repeated. "Claws. Okay." His own voice dropped to a whisper. "Were they used in a *scene?*"

"A scene, yes...." The man looked around, ensuring there were no other customers in earshot; then he leaned into Adam's face and breathed, "They were these metal claws, worn over the fingers. A guy was using them to rake over a woman...."

"Ahh. I understand," Adam said. "We keep those kinds of weaponry in the back. My friend Justin here can help you." Adam's voice rose as he called over, "Justin? Do you have a minute?"

Justin, who had been watching the whole thing

from behind the counter, now came around to join them. "How can I help you?"

"This gentleman here is interested in some of the stuff we sell in the back," Adam said. "Claws, I believe."

Justin stared at the customer without smiling. After giving him a piercing look he said, "Follow me." He led the way into the back room, and the customer followed behind.

A short while later, the customer returned, holding a small box under his left arm. He paid and left the store quickly, looking excited.

"Another satisfied customer," Adam said, watching the man disappear down the street. Justin didn't smile, but Adam could tell from his demeanor he was pleased.

"Not as satisfied as he's going to be later," Justin said.

"I think you're right about that."

"He got the whole set of claws, all ten," Justin said. "Someone's going to end up with some lovely scratches."

Adam shook his head and said, "It's amazing to me how these people find us."

Justin shrugged. "I'm glad they do," he said. "It's nice knowing we can pay the bills."

"That's very true." Adam went silent for a moment. Then he said, "Listen, Justin, about coming in early...."

"Yes?" He had a feeling he knew what was coming.

"Would it be okay if I left half an hour early, too? Khloe thinks she can get the afternoon off. If I could just get home before the rush hour traffic...."

"It's fine, man," Justin cut in. Jonathan's new-and-improved order list flashed into his head, but Justin pushed the thought away. "Tell you what: if Khloe can get the whole afternoon off, why don't you take the afternoon, too. Spend the time with her. You guys need it."

"Are you sure?" Adam asked, hopeful. Between Adam's job at the shop, the evening classes he was taking to get his MBA, and Khloe's own busy schedule, Adam and Khloe were not spending as much time together as they wanted.

"Sure," Justin said. "No problem."

"Thanks. I'll owe you one...at least, until we can get someone else in here to cover for us. Then I won't have to owe you one," Adam said, smiling. "We'll just tell the new guy to work late. Any news on that, by the way?"

"I got one email last night. Some guy named Alex. I asked him to send over his resume, but he hasn't responded back yet."

"Only one?"

"Oh come on, Adam. How many guys do you know looking for full-time jobs have a passion for swords and weapons, and want to work in a store like this?"

"What's wrong with our store?"

"Nothing, if you're into it. But that's what I'm saying: you have to have a *passion* for it."

"We might get a walk-in," Adam suggested.

"All our walk-ins arc students, looking for temp-work after school," Justin said. "They wouldn't know the difference between a stiletto and a butter knife.

Face it, this search will take a while."

"True," Adam said. "But meanwhile, you and I both still need a break now and then." He thought about it for a minute and said, "Say, there's that Flesh Party coming up soon at The South Bay Spot. Khloe has no interest in going, but maybe Dawn does? You want to ask her?"

Justin turned away. "Dawn and I are no longer seeing each other for play dates," he said. "She just wants to be friends."

"I'm sorry," Adam said, contrite. "I didn't know. When did this happen?"

"Last week."

"It happened last week, and you didn't tell me?"

"I didn't think it was a big deal," Justin said.

Adam blinked at him. "That probably has something to do with why she ended things with you," he murmured. "Justin, we need to find you a woman."

"I have enough women to choose from, Adam."

"I didn't say women, I said *a woman*. That one woman who can flip your switch."

"My switch?"

"From Top to Dom."

Justin tensed. "I'm no one's Dom, Adam. You know that." He opened up one of the display cases and began to fiddle with some chain link, making a futile attempt to look busy.

"You're clearly not vanilla, either," Adam said, raising his voice. "You're more involved in the kink community than I am."

It was true that while Adam and Khloe were in a

Dominant/submissive relationship, they did not go out to kinky events and parties the way Justin did. Justin was a founding member of the local dungeon, The South Bay Spot, and he attended their play parties regularly.

"You're making it sound like I have to be either vanilla, or a Dom," Justin said. "Why does it have to be either/or? Why can't I be neither? The women I play with don't seem to care. They walk away from my scenes happy."

"Sure they do," Adam said. "And if *you* were satisfied with that, that'd be fine."

"But you don't think I'm happy."

"No, I don't."

"Last time I checked, it was the women who were ending things with me, not the other way around."

"Exactly," Adam said. "They're all breaking up with you, which means *you* are the problem."

"So tell me, oh great guru, what is my problem?"

Adam's eyes narrowed. "Khloe and I have talked about this. She thinks you have this *thing* inside you, this power, and it would make you a great Dom. Women sense it, and they want it, but you don't give it to them. All you're willing to do is Top them for a little while, but then you walk away. She says it's like a tease."

"Great, now you're talking about my psyche with your girlfriend."

"Hey, I think she's right. I think you would make a great Dom—for the right woman. But you're so caught up on the evil of labels, you use them like epithets. You're not willing to admit that maybe, just maybe, you could fit the bill."

"Maybe because I'm tired of feeling like I have to fit into a label," Justin said, his voice full of grit. "Top, Dom, Sadist, Master...you know, when I have a woman tied to a spanking bench or cuffed to a table, she's not thinking about what *label* I use for myself. All she's thinking about is what I'm going to do to her next—if she's able to think at all."

"And that's great *during* the scene. But what about *after* the scene?"

"I give good aftercare, Adam. You know that." Justin's face was beginning to turn stony, a sure sign his temper was up.

"That's not what I'm talking about, and you know it," Adam said, trying to keep his voice even. "I'm talking about the *relationship*. You take control of these women's heads in the dungeon, in the bedroom... but once you walk out the door, it's like you turn completely vanilla. Your whole dominant personality goes AWOL, like it's in hiding or something."

"Maybe you and Khloe are wrong," Adam said. "Maybe I don't have a dominant personality."

"You do," Adam said. "But you don't show it. And *that's* why you need the right woman."

"Fine. Whatever," Justin said, giving up before his temper exploded. "I'm going to get some work done in the backroom. Trowlege called me last night: he added to my brother's order."

"Seriously?"

"Yup. So you call me if you need me. I'm getting to work." He started walking toward the curtain that blocked off the hallway leading to the back of the store.

"Hey, I know what you need!" Adam called after him. "You need a woman who can turn your switch, *and* knows about swords. That'd be perfect."

"Yeah. Right," Justin retorted. "Like that'll happen."

"You never know," Adam said. "We might get lucky. Some hot vixen will walk off the street, desperate for a job and kinky as hell."

"Uh-huh. Some lush brunette with great tits who also happens to know sword fighting."

"Look, all I'm saying is, you never know."

"I know I have some orders to finish. Call me if any hot vixens walk in. I'll make sure to put her through her paces before I admire her tits." He disappeared into the back room.

A few hours went by. Justin got lost in his work as he always did, creating his kinky toys of hedonism.

A few hours later, Adam appeared in the doorway. He cleared his throat before he spoke.

"There's someone here to see you," he said. "Says she's interested in the job opening."

Justin looked up: Adam's voice sounded strange.

"I'll be right out," Justin said, furrowing his brows at Adam's curious tone. He laid the unfinished flogger on the table and followed Adam out.

As he came through the thick curtain, he called out, "So where is she—oh. Ah." His eyes caught and held on the woman standing in the middle of the room. "Hi."

She was a beauty, one of the most beautiful women Justin had ever seen: a gothic princess come to life. Her sable hair was thick, straight, and long—so long that even pulled up in a ponytail, her hair still fell to the middle of her back. Her eyes were dark, just a tint lighter than the thick lashes that framed them. Her lips were plump, perfectly curved, and glistened from a thin coat of blushing red lipstick. Or maybe she wore no lipstick...maybe her lips were wet because she had just licked them.

The thought of her running her wet tongue over those puffy lips made Justin's cock jump.

She was petite, but curved in all the right places. Her thin sweater covered her body well enough, but it could not disguise her high, full breasts, nor her reedy torso and narrow waist.

"May I help you?" Justin said, working hard to collect his thoughts. She had caught him off guard.

He recovered quickly...but he was thrown again when he got a whiff of her scent: lilac mixed with midnight breeze. He took in a deep breath of her, and his cock strained against his pants. God, he had to get himself under control.

"Yes, I'm here about the job?" She said. She pointed her thumb back, gesturing to the HELP WANTED sign taped to the window outside.

"I see," Justin said slowly, getting an inkling of what was really going on. "Well, the thing is, we're not hiring just anybody off the street," he said. "We're looking for someone with the right background, you know? The right knowledge."

"I understand. You want someone who knows her stuff," she said.

"Yes." He crossed his arms, giving her a shrewd look. She radiated confidence in her bearing and reply, which intrigued him, but not for the reasons she probably thought.

It was obvious to him now that Adam was playing some kind of trick on him. Adam probably saw her walking by the window, the exact image of the kind of girl Justin had just described—his fantasy woman—and had asked her inside.

It was Adam's idea of a joke.

There was no other explanation; there was no way a beautiful girl like her could have walked in off the street, knowing about weaponry, looking for a job. That would make her...well that would make her perfect. Exactly what he was looking for.

Exactly what *they* were looking for, he corrected himself. For the store.

But if she were kinky, too...

There was no way. No, this was Adam's idea of having some fun, that was all. But that was okay. Adam was only trying to be funny; Justin could play along.

He pointed to one of the swords mounted on the wall. "Can you tell me what kind of sword that is?"

"Which one, the katana or the wakizashi?"

Justin looked at her in surprise. Clearly, Adam had scripted her a little bit. "The katana," he replied. "What can you tell me about it?"

"It's been made to look like it's from the Meiji period, but—it's a replica. It's probably made in China. So is the wakizashi." She looked around. "It looks like most of the blades outside of the display cases are replicas and fakes. The only real ones I see are the ones behind glass. Everything else is either too modern, or too cheap."

Justin could hear Adam's sharp intake of breath, and turned to look at his friend.

Adam was now wearing an expression of surprised nervousness. Clearly, he had not been expecting the girl to insult their wares the way she just had. Maybe she didn't understand the gaffe she'd just committed, or maybe she was just trying to be cocky. Either way, by the look on Adam's face, she had veered away from the script, and it was time for the charade to end.

"I think my friend here would rather you stick to what he told you to say," Justin said. "Tell me, how many swords did he get you to memorize before he came and got me from the back? Probably no more than a few; he knows I always ask the same questions to all our walk-ins."

Her face pinched. "What are you talking about?"

"You think I'd be fooled by this little game?"

Next to him, Adam was shaking his head madly, but Justin ignored him.

"I'm sorry you got pulled into my friend's little prank," he said. "I must say, you certainly fill the bill of lush vixen. Nice tits, by the way."

"Excuse me?" Her voice grew sharp now. "Did you just compliment my *chest?*"

"What did Adam tell you to get you to play along in this little performance? That his poor lonely coworker needed to talk to a pretty girl? Did he offer you money?"

Her voice turned cold. "Look, I don't know what you think is going on here, but I came here about a job—"

"*He's* taken, you know," Justin said, pointing to Adam. "He has a girlfriend. Any flirting he did to get you in here was purely for effect. But I'm guessing you were easy enough to sway." He stepped up close to her, close enough to inhale her lilac scent and make her lean back. "You're cute, and the joke was funny, but it's over now."

Her face turned red. "This is not some kind of joke. I'm telling you—"

"Goddamnit, Adam, tell her it's enough already," Justin said, glancing at his friend, who was now wearing an expression of shocked horror. Unfortunately, Justin turned his eyes back to the woman before he registered what it might mean. "Look, here's a ten," he said, fishing into his wallet and holding out a bill. "Thanks for the amusement. It was fun." He held the ten out, waiting.

He had to wait a long moment for her to respond. She was too angry to speak.

"You filthy, disgusting, *pig,*" she hissed. "You arrogant chauvinist asshole *jerk*. I can't believe I just wasted an hour of my time—on two buses!—to get here. I can't believe last night I thought you were for real."

Justin's eyes grew piercing. "Last night? What the hell are you talking about?"

"You asked me for my resume! I came here to give it to you!" She pulled an envelope out of her back pocket and shook it at him.

Finally, Justin began to look uncertain. "I only

responded to one email last night. It was from some guy named Alex."

"I *am* Alex, you idiot!" She shouted. She looked around. "I hope whoever you find to work in this two-bit shop of yours smells like sewer and carries fleas. You're *sick*. The two of you—*sick*." She stuffed the envelope back in her pocket, turned around, grabbed the huge crème colored messenger bag she had left by the door, and left.

There was a moment of silence between the two men. Then Justin looked at Adam. "You didn't...?"

Adam shook his head. "No man, I didn't."

"Then she wasn't...."

"Nope."

"Shit."

"Yup."

Justin ran out of the store.

He found her making her way down Main Street at a brisk pace, holding her bag steady by her side. Swerving around the other people on the street, Justin ran in front of her and blocked her path.

"Look, I'm sorry for the shit I gave you back there. I thought my friend was playing a joke on me—"

"Get the fuck out of my way, you bastard, I have a bus to catch." She swerved around him with the speed and grace of a gazelle. He had to run another few feet to block her once more.

"Will you just listen for a minute? I thought my friend back there, Adam, was playing a practical joke on me. I didn't mean any disrespect. Believe me, I don't usually talk to women like that. I *like* women."

He stopped as he listened to himself. "Not that I would hire you because you're a beautiful woman," he said quickly. "I mean, you are beautiful, I'm not saying you're not, I'm just saying I would hire anyone, man or woman, if they had what we needed—"

"You mean a good pair of tits?"

"No, damn it, I didn't mean that...I'm sorry."

"Move aside, or I swear to God, I'll scream."

"Fine." He moved aside. But when she walked past him, he followed. She turned around.

"What the fuck are you following me for?"

"I'm not going to let you out of my sight until you accept my apology," he said. "I acted like an asshole back there, and I need you to forgive me."

She stared at him for a moment. "Fine, I forgive you! Just leave me alone!" She tried to walk faster away from him, but Justin kept up with her, staying a few feet behind. Finally, when the bus stop was in sight, she turned back around.

"What do I have to do to get you to stop following me?"

"Come back with me to the shop," he said. "Let me do the interview over. I'm not a jerk—let me prove it to you."

Her eyes narrowed. "Why should I?"

"Why should you...." Justin's face brightened—she was negotiating with him now, something he could recognize and handle full well—and he crossed his arms. "Well, let's think about it, shall we? If I *am* a chauvinistic asshole, you've only wasted another few minutes of your time. But if I'm not—and I'm *not*—

you can use this whole thing to your advantage. You've got me over a barrel now, you know. Even if I wouldn't have given you the job before, I'll be obligated to offer it to you now out of sheer guilt. You could probably even ask for double pay and I'd give it to you."

"I don't need any favors from you," she said, her voice cold. "If I get the job, it'll be on my merits alone."

"Fine," Justin said, looking at her shrewdly. "We'll do it your way: no special favors. But you have to let me redo the interview." His face turned pleading as she looked at him, unsure. "Please," he said. "Give me another chance." It was the closest he would come to begging.

"Fine," she said, scowling, as if she were already unhappy with her decision. But Justin grinned with relief.

"Come back to the shop," he said. "I have something to show you. If you're half as knowledgeable about swords as you said you are in your email, you'll get a kick out of it."

"This better not be some trick to pull out your dick," she called as she followed him back to the shop.

"No, I swear," he said, looking at her over his shoulder and trying hard not to laugh.

As he led her back to the shop, he couldn't stop the goofy grin spreading across his face. He had to cut that out...but damn, she really was too perfect for his own good. She was beautiful, confident, and quick, and if she was as knowledgeable about swords as she claimed, there was no way he could let her walk out of his store a second time.

How he was going to be able to work around her without constantly fighting off blue balls, he would have to figure out. But he *would* figure it out. He could get his treasonous dick under control.

When they entered the shop, they found Adam behind the counter, looking surprised to see them both.

"You came back," he said to her. "I'm glad you did." He jerked his head toward Justin. "He explain to you what happened?"

"Yeah, he explained it," she replied, putting her bag down with a plop. "And he promised to show me something cool. So where is it?"

"It's in the back room," Justin said.

"Uh, Justin, maybe you should bring it out here," Adam said quickly, giving his friend a laden look. "The back room is a little...cluttered."

"You're right," Justin replied, nodding. "Hold on one second, Alex. Adam, don't let her go anywhere."

A moment later, he returned holding what was obviously a long, heavy sword in his arms, wrapped in a soft blanket. "Adam, can you go lock the door and pull the shades down?" He said. "I don't want anyone walking in here while I have this out."

As Adam went to take care of the door and windows, Alex eased her body over, curious now what was under the blanket. Justin took on an air of satisfaction. His ploy had worked. He had her full attention.

The room grew quiet as Adam returned, and Justin carefully placed the bundle on the counter. All eyes looked down now as he pulled the covers away.

Alex's intake of breath was sharp and loud inside the

room. "It's a Masamune sword," she whispered. "No, wait...the style is a little different...Saeki Norishige?"

"Yes," Justin said, pleased. "A friend of mine is letting me take a look at it. He wanted me to confirm it's authentic, but now he's letting me keep it for a while, to study it."

"You have some nice friends," Alex replied softly, never taking her eyes off the sword. Justin watched the way her stare travelled up and down the length of it, looking at it lovingly. For some inexplicable reason, his chest swelled with satisfaction.

"Do you want to hold it?"

She looked up. "I—I couldn't. It's too valuable."

"You're not going to damage it just by picking it up. Go ahead. Who knows if you'll ever have another chance to hold a sword like this."

He moved back, giving her room. Alex grabbed the hilt with both hands and slowly picked up the sword.

For a moment, she just stared at it in her hands, getting a feel for the weight of it. But then she walked into the middle of the room, spread her legs, and began to swish the sword through the air, making tight figure eights. Adam looked like he was about to stop her, but Justin put his hand out and shook his head.

Alex began to do a beautiful, and obviously practiced, sword form. Her lithe body twisted and bent, leaned and thrust, and as she moved the sword inside her small circle of space, she looked as if she were vanquishing an invisible foe.

Adam and Justin watched in surprise and awe. The form was beautifully choreographed, and obviously difficult. They both knew enough about marital arts to know she was making the form look easier than it was. Her body was well trained.

"You know some marital arts?" Justin called out to her as she began another sword form.

"Yup," she answered without looking at either of them. "I started with Taekwondo, then moved on to Jiu-Jitsu. But then I wanted something different, so I took up Capoeira. After that, I went modern, and took up Krav Maga. That's where I am right now."

"I see," Justin said. He and Adam were staring at each other in surprise. "I don't know much about Krav Maga. Adam and I both take good old fashioned Karate."

"Hey, whatever works for you," she said. She finished up her form, stood up straight, and stared at the sword in her hands. "It really is a work of art," she said. She turned around and placed the sword back on the blanketed counter. "Thank you for letting me try it."

"Thank you for that beautiful presentation," he replied. "The sword is meant to be wielded, and you know how to wield it well."

"Thank you," she said, blushing becomingly. Justin cleared his throat and began to wrap the sword back up in the blanket. He could not meet her face, not before he got his dick under control again. Her innocent blush had ignited his blood.

"Adam, can you please put this away?" He said as he handed the sword over. Adam gave him a quizzical look, but took the sword. Once Adam was out of earshot, Justin crossed his arms. "So, the job," he said.

"You want it?"

She was quiet for a moment. "The back room—you obviously keep the nice stuff in there. Will I be able to work with that stuff, too?"

He frowned; her question had caught him off guard. "The stuff in the back room is...delicate," he said. "Not even Adam goes back there unless he has to. We'll keep you in front for now. After a while, if we think you can handle it...."

"I have to go through a probation period, huh?"

"You can think of it like that, yeah," he nodded.

"What are my hours going to be like? How much will I be making a week?"

"You'll be working about forty hours a week, but we'll be paying you a salary, not by the hour."

She took on a look of surprise. "Whoa. That's pretty generous of you."

"Not really," he said. "It means I'll have you at my beck and call, whenever I want you." He cleared his throat and tried to tamp down the flush creeping up his face. God, why did everything coming out of his mouth have to sound like an innuendo? "We sometimes keep odd hours," he added, "and I bring a lot of my work home. You might have to, too. What kind of computer do you have?"

"I don't." Justin looked at her in surprise, and she added, "I just moved here. My computer got left behind."

"Ahh. Well, we'll give you one of ours. That way you can get stuff done on the weekend without having to come in."

"I don't mind coming in."

"I wouldn't mind you coming either. Into the store, I mean."

"Uh-huh." She gave him a knowing grin.

Justin leaned his hand on the counter, looking embarrassed. "Look, I know this feels a little weird right now, after the way I treated you before. But give us a chance, and I promise you the weirdness will go away. Adam and I are good guys. You'll like us."

"You *are* weird," she said, "but that's okay. I like weird. I'm a little bit weird myself."

"Does that mean you'll take the job?"

She cocked her head, then shrugged. "Sure. Why not? It sounds like fun. If I don't like it—if I catch you staring at my tits too much—I can always quit."

"You won't. I won't." Adam came back through the curtains, and Justin asked him, "Can you get the employment paperwork for Alex? She's decided to give us a try." Turning back to her he said, "We'll need your social security number and all that. You know, for tax reasons."

"I get it." But she looked unsure.

Justin studied her. "We'll also need your address, and a bank account number if you want us to do direct deposit of your paycheck."

"I don't have an account set up yet," she answered quickly. "Like I said, I just moved here. Could you just cut me a paycheck instead?"

"Sure," Justin said smoothly. "We can do it that way if you want." An uncomfortable moment passed between them, as Justin got the strange feeling she was hiding something. But the moment was broken when Adam returned with the paperwork.

"Here you go," he said. "And welcome to the team. You have no idea how happy I am Justin's finally found someone who's up to his standards. Maybe now he can finally relax a little."

"Oh?" Alex said. "He's a workaholic, huh?"

"God yes. He needs to get out and play more."

Justin blurted, "You go out a lot for fun, Alex?"

He knew the question was inappropriate, but this time, he let the question stand.

"No," she said finally. "I don't go out that much. But when I do, I play pretty hard."

"Do you now." The two of them stared at each other, not saying anything. The tension built. Adam cleared his throat.

"I'll, um, I'll just take those papers from you when you're done filling them out," he said. "And welcome to the team, Alex."

"Thank you, Adam," she replied, looking straight at Justin's piercing eyes. "I think working here is going to be very…interesting."

CHAPTER THREE

T HEY GAVE ALEX—ALEXA WORTH, ACCORDING to her paperwork—a few days to watch and learn. Adam did most of the tutoring, showing her how to work the register, how to fill out an order, and basically, how to work the merchandise. Alex learned fast. Adam told Justin later, he got the impression Alex had worked in retail before; another bonus.

But there were a few things she needed to learn. "If you get a question you don't know the answer to, just ask me or Justin," Adam told her. "Don't get nervous, or the customer might think he can take advantage of you."

"Oh?" She asked, raising her brows. "You get a lot of customers who try to haggle on prices?"

"We do," he said. "You just got to be firm with them. Firm, but polite."

"I think I can handle that."

Adam smiled and said, "Just don't put a sword through anybody. That would be bad for business."

"Don't worry, Adam," she laughed. "I'll only spear the customers who try to compliment my tits." She made sure to raise her voice at the end, as Justin was just coming out of the back room.

"You shouldn't spear someone for speaking the truth," he said, his expression serious.

Over the past few days, Justin had gotten to know Alex well enough to know she was only ribbing him, and he thought she'd understand that he was only ribbing her back.

Or maybe not. Alex's cheeks blushed a rosy pink, and she looked down demurely. "Well," she murmured, unable to say more.

"It's about lunch time," Adam cut in, seeing her blushing cheeks. "You two want to go out? I can stay in this time."

The day before, Justin had stayed behind at the shop while Adam and Alex had gone out for lunch. They had brought Justin back a sandwich, and he'd eaten it in the backroom while he worked, trying to catch up on some orders.

But this time Justin was ready to take a break. "Sounds good to me," he said. "Alex, you want to go get something with me?"

"Sure," she said, looking at Adam. "But what do you want us to bring you back?"

"Justin knows what I like—just nothing with garlic or coconut."

"Allergies?"

"No, my girlfriend doesn't like me eating them. It affects the taste of my—"

"*We are going now,*" Justin said loudly, giving Adam a laden look. "Have fun holding down the fort. Bye."

"Bye," Adam replied, stifling a grin. Justin walked briskly out of the shop. Alex grabbed up her bag, hidden discreetly behind the counter, and ran to catch up.

They didn't walk around to the back of the store where Justin had his car parked. Instead, he began to stroll down Main Street. "I know a couple good places around the corner," he said, putting his hands in his pockets as he walked. "You want to check them out?"

"Sure," Alex replied. "This whole area's pretty nice."

"Oh yeah. Downtown Saratoga is really nice—and really expensive."

"So I've heard. It's pretty cool your shop's doing so well in an area like this."

"Well, it's not just because of the stuff we sell in the store. It's the stuff we sell online, and...."

"And?"

"Nothing," Justin said, regretting his words. He pointed across the street. "There's a good Mediterranean place. Want to try it?"

"Yeah, why not."

They hurried across the street, and Justin held the door open for her. When they got inside, he got the waiter's attention, and held up two fingers. The waiter showed them to a table, and Justin motioned Alex to sit first.

"My, how chivalrous," she said, sitting down with her bag between her feet. "Careful, or this might start to feel like a date."

He laughed, but couldn't meet her eyes. He had been thinking the exact same thing, and feeling inordinately pleased about it. Justin didn't like to put labels on things, or people—it was one big reason why he had never tried to label himself in the kink community—but if there was ever a thing as a perfect first date, this surely felt like the beginning of one.

Alex studied the menu. "Can you suggest something?" She asked. "Everything looks good to me."

"Well, let's start with what you like, and what you don't like," he said, taking on that reasonable tone of his. She suddenly looked flustered—now *that* was interesting. "Is there anything specific you'd shy away from?"

"I don't like anything too spicy," she said, peering at him above the menu. "And nothing too drippy. I don't want to get my shirt dirty."

"Nothing like spaghetti then, huh?"

"Right. Something that will stay on my fork...all the way to my mouth."

"Okay then," he said, clearing his throat and shifting a little in his seat. Every word out of her lips sounded suggestive inside his crude brain, and not for the first time, she was giving him a hard on. "Try the Mediterranean chicken salad," he said. "It's not spicy at all, and it should stay on your fork...all the way to your mouth."

As the waiter walked toward their table, Alex surprised Justin again by asking, "Can you order for me? You already know what I'm having."

"Um, sure," he said, taken aback. "Why?"

"Oh, it takes less time," she replied, averting her

eyes. She took his menu from him and placed it above her own.

After the food was ordered, the menus taken away, they had nothing to do but talk.

"So tell me about yourself," Justin said, leaning his elbows on the table.

Her eyes narrowed. "What do you want to know?"

"Well, for one thing, how did you end up with a name like Alex? Did your parents think you were going to be a boy?"

"No," she said, laughing. "It's short for my real name."

"I know. I read your paperwork."

"Oh." Her eyes dulled.

"Alexa is a beautiful name," Justin said quickly. "Sounds foreign."

"Well, I'm not foreign," she said. "Unless you call Los Angeles foreign."

"Jesus, Los Angeles is another planet," Justin said in mock horror. Alex laughed, making Justin stare at her in delight. He asked, "You ever go back to visit family?"

"Don't have any family left there," she said.

"Why not?" He asked. "They all move away?"

"No," she said. "My mom and stepdad died a while back. I never knew who my real father was, and I don't have any siblings, so...it's just me."

Justin's eyes widened. "I'm sorry, Alex. I didn't mean to overstep."

"No, it's okay," Alex replied. "I'm actually kind of surprised at myself for dumping all this on you." She looked somewhere far off to the left, nervous. "I don't usually just blurt out my life like that. I don't really talk to people about this stuff at all."

"In that case, I'm honored you find me so trustworthy," Justin said. He paused. "I guess we're both in the orphans club. My parents are dead, too."

"Oh?" She whispered. "How'd yours go?"

"Car accident. Stupid way to go. Yours?"

"My mom went first, from cancer. My stepdad died a few years ago: fire."

"I'm sorry, Alex," Justin said. It was the only thing he could think of to say.

"No, it's okay," she said again. "I'm over it. I mean, I loved my mom, but she was suffering a lot at the end, and it was time for her to go. My stepdad...he was a great guy and all that...a really great stepfather...but, you know...." She shrugged. "Things happen."

"Yes," Justin said. "They do."

The waiter brought them their food, and they sat in silence for a while, eating.

"Do you have any siblings?" She asked him after the awkwardness had passed. "Brothers? Sisters?"

"One older brother," he said.

"Must be nice, having some family around."

"Not really," Justin said. "He's my half-brother, and I never really knew him that well. After my parents died, he had me shipped off to boarding school. I only saw him on vacations and holidays."

"Jesus, Justin. I'm sorry."

"No, it's okay," it was his turn to say. He cleared the stiffness in his throat. "It's not like we ever had that much of a relationship anyway. He's a *lot* older than me—my mom married his dad when he was already almost an adult. I was kind of the second son of the second family. We don't even share the same last name."

Justin didn't point out it had been his own choice to start going by his mother's maiden name, Baker. Justin didn't want to be associated as a Bentmoore anymore, not with his brother acting as ruling head of the family.

"You think your brother resented you when you came along?" Alex asked.

"No, I don't think so," Justin said, giving it some thought. "I think he just didn't know what to do with me. He had his own life to live. He didn't need a kid in the way."

"You keep in touch with him at all?"

"Yeah, sure." It was true enough, he supposed. "He's one of our store's biggest customers."

"What? Why? He likes swords that much? He's a collector?"

"Something of a collector, yes," Justin said, swirling the water in his glass.

Her eyes narrowed. "Does this have something to do with what you keep in that back room of yours?"

"Maybe," Justin said, giving her a sly grin. He held up his glass as if making a toast, took a long gulp, and put the glass down flat. Then he gave her a wide, wicked smile.

Alex smiled back. *Two can play this game,* her eyes told him.

The waiter took their plates, but Justin made no

move to go. He didn't want this time with her to end. "So, Krav Maga," he said. "It's not a very common type of martial arts. What got you into it?"

"I travelled to Israel," she said. "A small Ethiopian man living on a kibbutz on the Jordanian border decided to take me under his wing."

"Israel?" Justin said, surprised. "What made you decide to go there?"

"I just felt like it," Alex said, curt. She began looking around the room again. "I've done a lot of travelling."

"Really? Where have you been?"

"Shouldn't we be getting back?" She cut her eyes back to him, and Justin saw a veil of wariness there that hadn't been there before. "Adam will be waiting for his food."

"Yeah…sure." His brows furrowed as he gazed at her, but she looked away again, unwilling to meet his eyes. He called the waiter over and handed him his credit card.

"Wait a minute, I have to pay for my food, too," Alex said, looking at him sharply.

"Don't worry about it, it's on me," Justin replied, waving her hand away.

Alex's face grew stony. "No, that's not okay. I pay for my own food. Otherwise this will really turn into…."

"Into a date?" He finished. "Tell you what: I'll pay this time, and you pay next time. Deal? That way it's not a date, it's just two friends taking each other out for lunch."

Slowly, she nodded. "Okay," she said, "that works. But I pay next time, Understand? No excuses."

"No excuses." The waiter came back with Justin's card and Adam's bag of food. Justin re-walleted his card and stood up. "Ready to go?"

"Yeah." She rose, pulling her bag up with her.

As she began to make her way out the restaurant, Justin's hand itched to press his palm into the small of her back. But that would have been too intimate a move, too much like something he would have done with a woman on a date.

He wished he could call this a date. It had certainly been the best time he'd had with a woman since...wow, he couldn't even remember.

And the sad thing was, he was remembering play dates, too.

For Justin, play dates meant BDSM and sex. His idea of "play" was still intimate, at least to a certain degree; sex always came with its own level of intimacy. But this time he'd spent with Alex felt far more precious. Justin realized he'd just shared with Alex more about himself than he'd shared with any other woman in years.

It felt good, talking to her. Comfortable. What pleased him was the thought that Alex had felt the same way—at least, up until the end. Then his questions had made her nervous, and she'd put her walls up.

He would break down those walls, he decided. He needed to put in the time and effort to get her to relax enough to trust him, but it would happen.

When they got back to the shop, Adam was very

pleased to see them.

"Well?" He asked. "Can I eat now?" His eyes lit up when he saw the food bag in Justin's hand. Justin gave it to him, and Adam disappeared with it into the back room.

Alex tilted her head and crossed her arms, watching Adam disappear around the corner. "Give me *some* idea here: when do I get to find out what's behind the curtain?"

"Eventually," Justin said, keeping his eyes averted. "When we think you can handle it."

"You'd be surprised what I can handle, you know."

"No doubt," he agreed good-naturedly. "All in good time, Alex. All in good time."

She was keeping her secrets. He had to keep his, too.

CHAPTER FOUR

J USTIN'S FIRST INKLING ALEX WAS perhaps not as vanilla as she seemed came about a week later, when the three of them—he, Adam, and Alex—were just getting ready to close down the shop. Before they could lock the door, a customer walked in, someone Justin and Adam knew all too well.

They scowled when they saw him.

He had been there three times before already; and each time, he had acted like an ass, asking all sorts of ridiculous questions and blustering over their prices before finally walking out without making a single purchase. But he was back now, and by the expression on his face, Justin knew he was going to behave just as badly.

As the guy walked by the counter, Adam moved to intercept, but Justin stopped him with an arm to his chest. Without saying a word, he motioned Adam to look across the room.

Alex, who had been busy polishing a glass showcase, was now coming to meet the man from their other side.

"May I help you, Sir?"

"You work here?"

"Yes, I do."

"No you don't."

Alex's lower lip dropped open. "Excuse me?"

"Let me clarify," the man said. "You may work here, but you can't possibly know anything about swords and weaponry. Go get someone who does." He jerked his thumb toward Justin and Adam, who remained by the counter and did not move.

Alex smiled, but a cold gleam came into her eyes. "I assure you, Sir, I know about all the items we sell here, and can answer all your questions."

"Oh, really?" The man said. "Then do you mind telling me why your prices are so high?" He pointed to a sword inside one of the showcases. "Just look at that! That sword is over a thousand dollars! It's nuts! You think you can charge whatever you want cause people don't know any better, but I know for a *fact* I can get that sword in San Francisco for one third the price!" His face reddened as his voice rose.

Alex's smile remained fixed, but her voice grew deadly soft. "You have seen *that* sword in San Francisco?" She said. "That exact one? For one third the price?"

"Yes!"

"Well then, Sir: I suggest you get yourself to San Francisco as fast as you can and buy it."

Confused, the man said, "What?"

"*That*," she said, jerking her finger at the display case, "is an original Homoyato sword. While they are not all that rare, they are almost never displayed out in the open, ready for sale. Most dealers only sell those swords by special order. So if you're sure what you saw in San Francisco is the *exact* same sword...."

"I know what I saw, young lady!"

"I do not doubt you know what you saw, Sir. But perhaps you would like to get a feel for the sword before you buy it? If you would allow me...."

Alex moved to the display case, opened it with her key, slid the glass across, and carefully removed the sword.

She held it up to the man's face. "Homoyato swords have a particular lightness to them," she said in a soft caress. "Since they are made with newer technology, their edges are more refined, but far less delicate."

She stepped into the middle of the room and spread her feet apart. Behind the counter, Adam began to grin.

Justin frowned.

Alex brought the sword down in a straight arc, slicing through the air with it.

"Since it is so light"—she cut through the space in front of her, making the surprised man step back, even though he was a good four feet away—"one might think"—she brought the sword behind her back and grabbed it with the other hand to make a quick stab—"that it is designed for a woman, or a child still learning the craft. But this is not so. A Homoyato sword in the right hands can be a silent and deadly weapon."

Alex swiveled on the balls of her toes and ripped the sword through the air in a straight curve—right at the neck of the customer, whose sharp intake of breath could be heard across the room.

Alex held the edge of the sword to the man's throat. He did not move. All the blood rushed from his face, and beads of sweat popped out across his forehead.

Before Justin or Adam could intervene, Alex pulled the sword away. With a quick twirl, it was laying inert across her palms, two inches away from the man's stunned eyes.

"Would you like to test it out yourself, Sir?"

The customer, pale and shaking, stumbled back. "No, that's okay," he stuttered. "I—I don't need to do that."

Alex went on the attack, matching his steps with her own. "You really should try it for yourself," she said, her voice thick and low. "I would hate for you to buy a sword you *think* is a Homoyato original, only to find out it's a fake. And I have a feeling the sword you saw in San Francisco must be a fake, because all Homoyato swords are numbered." With agile flicks of her wrists, she spun the sword around, held it downward, and pointed to the very edge of the handle. "You see Sir, right there?"

"Yes. Yes I see, thank you very much." The man tried desperately to step away, and ended up backing into another display case.

"Now, if you saw a number on that sword, and it truly is an original...and it really is one third the price...I suggest you go buy it. But perhaps you'd like to make sure." Her voice turned chilling. "Acting on impulse can often lead to regret, don't you agree?"

"Yes," the man said, his voice quivering. "Yes you're right. I'll...I'll check on that other sword again."

And with that, he ran out of the store.

As soon as the man was gone, Adam doubled over with laughter. But Justin looked at Alex shrewdly, a frown etched across his face. Alex saw Justin's look, and her own smile, so wide before, drifted away.

"You just took a big risk," Justin said.

"How so?"

"You could have hurt him."

"No," she said. "I couldn't have."

"How do you know?"

"I know my own skill."

His voice turned hard. "You might know your own skill, Alex, but you couldn't have known what *he* would have done. He might have moved in a way you weren't anticipating."

"I know my own skill," she repeated.

They stared at each other across the room.

Adam cleared his throat. "Well, I happen to think that was awesome," he said. "That guy deserved it. But it's time for me to get home, so...Justin, you mind closing up the shop?"

"No, I don't mind. You get home to Khloe," Justin said without averting his gaze from Alex's face. "I'll see you tomorrow."

"Yeah...sure. See you two tomorrow."

Adam gathered up his stuff and left without another word.

Justin's eyes narrowed on Alex's impassive expression. "Were you really that certain you weren't going to cut him?"

"I was."

"I don't know if I should be amazed at your skill, or your recklessness."

"My skill," she answered, her smile returning. "I'll amaze you with my recklessness another time."

Finally, Justin smiled. "Please don't," he said. "I don't think my nerves can take it."

Her eyes grew wide. "Were you really that nervous?"

"No," he said. "I knew you knew what you were doing."

Her brows creased. "Then why the censure?"

"I didn't know what *that* guy would do. Number one rule in fighting: Know Thy Opponent. He might've tried to attack you, and then I would have had to come to your rescue."

"Would you have?"

"Absolutely."

Alex's face blushed, but her eyes darted away, and Justin gained another new insight into her: Alex was not used to having people around to help her when she needed it.

"Look, I've got to go, too," she said. "I'm planning on going to check out a Krav Maga place tonight, and I have to catch a bus home."

"You don't have to catch a bus. I can drive you."

"No, that's okay," she said quickly. "I don't want to make you drive out of your way."

"It's no big deal."

"No." Her voice was firm. She came around the other side of the counter and bent down to grab her bag. "It's fine, really," she said.

But as she pulled out her bag, it fell, and some of

the contents came spilling out.

"Here, let me help you," Justin said.

"No, I got it—"

"It's okay—"

As Justin bent down to help, Alex was already stuffing everything back inside. Justin caught sight of a hair brush, a lipstick bottle, a blue hairband, a round blister pack of birth control pills, a strip of fabric that looked like part of a bra, and something silky that could have been wadded up sheer panties.

He looked farther down the floor: something had fallen that way, something that had *clinked* when it dropped.

His eyes widened as he reached for the shining rings of metal. As he stood up, he held the rings in the crook of his finger, giving Alex an unscrupulous look.

"Handcuffs?"

She stared at him, horrified. Then she tried to snatch the handcuffs out of his hand. "Give me those," she said.

Justin pulled his hand away before she could reach. "Now, now, don't be embarrassed," he said, avoiding Alex's desperate attempts to grab at the cuffs. "We're both adults here. It's not like I've never used handcuffs before."

"Give them back!" She yelled, reaching over his shoulder to try to swipe the handcuffs from his hold. Her face darkened from dusky pink to tomato red. Justin grinned in the face of her plight.

"The question is," he said, backwards-stepping away from her while she matched his movements in an angry dance, "who wears the cuffs? You...or whoever you're with?"

"Justin, stop it! Give them back!"

"Answer the question."

"No."

She swiped her foot under his leg; Justin had to catch his balance to prevent himself from falling face first to the floor. In that moment, Alex grabbed the cuffs back.

"That wasn't nice," she said as she turned away from him to stuff the cuffs back in her bag. Justin tried to smile at her, but she wouldn't look at him. It was then he realized, Alex wasn't playing around.

She really was angry.

"Alex, I'm sorry," he said, coming to stand next to her. She was done fixing her bag, but still wouldn't look at him. "I'm sorry," he repeated. "I didn't realize you'd be so sensitive about these things."

"These things?" Alex turned around to glare at him. "What 'these things'? What exactly do you think I do with the handcuffs?"

It was Justin's turn to fluster. "Well, I assume it's something, you know, kinky," he said.

"Maybe, maybe not," she answered back.

"Oh c'mon, Alex, nobody keeps handcuffs in their bag just because."

"Maybe I feel safer having them on me, did you ever think of that? Maybe I like knowing if someone attacked me, I'd have a way to keep their hands off me."

"Alex, have you ever been attacked before?" Justin asked, shocked.

"Just—just forget it," Alex said, pushing past him to get to the door. But before she could get her back to him, Justin caught a glimpse of her tear-filled eyes and trembling lip through the window reflection.

He felt like a cad.

"Alex, seriously, I'm sorry," he called.

She turned around. "I know," she said, trying to offer him a light-hearted grin, which only accentuated the misery etched across her face. "I'm sorry, too. I'm just...I'm messed up, Justin. You don't want to get to know me. Really. Let's just keep this an employer, employee relationship, okay? It'll be safer for everyone." She backed out of the door and hurried down the street.

A strange force rose up inside Justin, something new and potent, something he had never felt before: a need to help Alex.

It was a need to *protect* her, because it was obvious to him now, Alex was in some kind of pain, and needed someone to help save her from it.

Justin had never wanted to protect a woman before, not like this, not on such a deep, visceral level. The feeling was strange, but felt good. Bracing. Powerful.

Dominant.

How ironic the first woman he would feel like this toward would be the one woman who seemed to want nothing to do with him, and could probably take him down with one kick.

Justin had no doubt Alex could get a man into those handcuffs if she wanted to, with or without his consent. He wondered how many men had found themselves trapped in them before.

She won't be getting me in those, he thought. *No way.*

CHAPTER FIVE

THE NEXT DAY, ALEX WALKED into the shop with her usual smile, giving Justin only a cautionary look before going about her business as if nothing had happened between them the night before. Justin understood she wanted him to pretend last night had never happened, too. He decided his best course of action would be to play along.

The awkwardness between them simmered for a few hours, but slowly dissipated as the day wore on. Justin made it obvious he was trying to put Alex at ease by making lighthearted jokes, acting cheerful, and sending a smile her way every chance he got. In fact, his unusually chipper behavior began to puzzle Adam.

"Are you sick or something?" He asked.

Justin frowned. "No, why?"

"I've never seen you acting this happy. What the hell happened to you?"

"What, can't I act happy once in a while?"

"Not sober, no."

Justin scowled, aware Alex was watching. "Thanks a lot, man."

"Ah, there's the tense frown I'm used to," Adam

grinned. "All is right with the world again." He turned away before Justin could think of a sharp comeback.

Justin looked nervously at Alex, worried what she might be thinking, but she was smiling at both of them, and he relaxed.

The afternoon wore on into evening, until it was just about closing time. Alex was already locking up all the cabinets when the bell of the shop door dingled. Adam let out a sound of delight.

"Khloe," he said. "What are you doing here?" He went to give his submissive a tight hug and a light kiss on the cheek.

"I had to go to the bank, so I thought I'd come by, and see if we could all go out for dinner together," she said, passing her gaze toward Justin. When she saw Alex behind him, her eyes widened. "You must be Alex," she said, walking toward her with an outstretched hand. "I'm Khloe, Adam's su—ah, girlfriend. It's nice to meet you."

"It's nice to meet you too, Khloe. Adam's told me some very nice things about you."

As Justin watched, the two women took stock of each other, and for some reason he couldn't explain, he felt an inordinate sense of pride in Alex. Khloe was pretty, there was no doubt about that; with her long hair recently dyed a warm blonde, her pink lips, and her sparkling eyes, she could make any man pause in his tracks.

But Alex was another breed entirely. Where Khloe was innocent, Alex was sultry; where Khloe was modest and proper, Alex was mysterious, almost devious.

Khloe wore a short thin spring dress, belted to show off her curves, and a pair of high heels; Alex wore a t-shirt, jeans, and black converse sneakers, but had the look of a panther: dark, exotic, limber, and sleek.

Justin knew which woman Adam preferred. His own tastes were quite different.

Then he noticed Alex's eyes lingering on the gleaming metal fastened around Khloe's neck.

Khloe was wearing a thin metal collar, one with an invisible lock. It was designed to pass as a necklace. Khloe wore it in public all the time, and had never gotten so much as a second glance at it, at least none that Justin had been able to tell.

So why was Alex so fixated on it?

"I'm not against us all going out for dinner together," he announced to the room. "I know I'm hungry. Alex?"

Alex fidgeted on her feet. "Um, doesn't Adam want to go out with Khloe alone? I don't want to be a third wheel."

"You're not a third wheel, Alex," Adam answered. "If anyone is a third wheel, it's Justin here."

"Hey!"

"But he's welcome with us anytime." Adam laughed at Justin's glare.

Alex continued to hesitate. "I don't know," she said, as if trying to make a polite retreat. "I don't want to impose...."

"You're not imposing," Khloe said. "You're *invited*. Adam has told me so much about you, I wanted to say hi myself. I know what it's like to move to a new area and not know anyone. I thought maybe we could, you know," she shrugged, "talk."

"That...that sounds nice," Alex said, relenting. "Let me just go get my bag and freshen up, okay?"

"Sure."

Adam grabbed up Khloe and hugged her tight to his chest. Khloe giggled and swayed in his arms, and the two of them were lost in their own little world.

As Alex took her bag from behind the counter, she beckoned Justin to follow, and they walked to the other side of the room.

"Is it really okay if I go to dinner with them?" She whispered.

"Sure, why not?" Justin whispered back. "They invited you, didn't they?"

"I know, but they're a couple, and...."

"And?"

Her expression turned pained. "And, like I said yesterday, I don't want anyone to get the wrong idea about you and me. I don't want this to turn into a double date."

Justin's brows furrowed, as he realized the "anyone" in Alex's statement was referring to *him*. She didn't want him getting the wrong idea about her decision to join them.

"It won't be like that, okay?" He said. "We're just four friends going out for a meal together. Adam and Khloe are going as a couple, but that doesn't mean the two of us can't have a good time together with them as just friends, right?"

She thought about it for a moment; then her

expression relaxed. "You're right," she said. "There's no reason why we can't all go have a good time, as long as that's all it is: four friends going out, having a good time...as long as everyone understands."

"Believe me," Justin said crisply, "everyone understands. You can stop harping on it." His voice was sharp, sharper than he had intended, and Alex's face pinched, but he held his ground. "Are you ready to go? Do you need another minute to freshen up, or did you just say that to get me over here so you could clarify things?"

"I'm ready to go," Alex said, stiffening away from him. "We can leave if you want."

"Good."

They stepped away from the wall and saw Adam and Khloe still locked in each other's arms. "Let's go," Justin said, his low growl carrying across the room. Adam looked up at him over Khloe's head.

"Fine dude," he said, moving Khloe a step away from him while still keeping her close enough to press his hand into the small of her back. "We're ready."

As they made their way out of the shop, Khloe began to take her keys out of her purse, then stopped. "We shouldn't take three cars. That's just stupid." She looked at Adam. "Why don't you drive all of us? Your car is the biggest. Then you can drive us all back here, and we can go home separately."

"Fine by me," Adam said, pulling out his keys from his pocket and pressing his thumb pad into the keychain. Three cars down, a car cheeped.

Without hesitation, Khloe walked down, opened

the back door, and climbed into the second row of seats. "Sit back here with me, Alex," she called. "Let Justin sit up front next to Adam. You don't want to be sitting there when Adam is driving, believe me."

"Shut your mouth, woman," Adam said. He looked at Alex and said, "I am an excellent driver."

"Excellent if you're on the Indie 500," Khloe yelled.

Adam shot her an ill-boding glare and barked, "Be quiet, lady, or when we get home, I'll—"

"Adam," Justin interjected, passing his friend a warning look. Adam got the hint.

The rest of them climbed into the car.

As Adam began to drive, Justin peeked through his visor mirror at the two women sitting in the back. Khloe was unwittingly running her fingers up and down her collar, caressing it beneath her fingertips as she gazed out the window. A coy smile was turning up the corners of her mouth; she was obviously thinking of Adam's threat from before, wondering what promises it would hold for her later.

Alex was avidly watching Khloe fondling her collar.

But, sensing Justin's stare, she turned to meet his eyes through the mirror, gave him one of her unfathomable looks, and Justin quickly lifted the visor away.

They four people stuck to small talk after that. Well, Khloe, Adam, and Alex stuck to small talk... Justin just listened.

He listened to Alex.

He learned she spoke other languages, including French and German. He learned she had tried dyeing her hair before: blonde, red, and once, purple. He learned she loved elephants, and hated lilies.

He stored all these facts in a box inside his head labeled "Alex." The box was getting big, and taking on a life of its own; it was spilling over into other portions of his brain. But Justin didn't mind.

They arrived to the restaurant, and the waiter seated them quickly.

Adam made a point of holding the chair out for Khloe to sit down, but Justin made no such display of chivalry for Alex. If Alex wanted them to stick to friendship protocol, then that's what he would do.

The waiter took their drink orders and disappeared, leaving them to ponder the menus.

"Khloe, why don't you tell me how you and Adam met," Alex said as she studied the menu.

"Well, we first met in college," Khloe said, circling her hand around Adam's arm, who smiled in response. "But we didn't go out in the beginning. I was kind of messed up back then. We met up again later, after I had gotten myself straightened out a little. That's when we started dating."

"That's neat," Alex said, putting her own menu down and crossing her fingers together inside her hands. "Sounds like you just both needed to be at the right place at the right time. How come you didn't go out in college?"

"I was depressed," Khloe said lightly. "I was a cutter; I was cutting myself."

There was a pause of tense silence. Everyone waited to hear what Alex would say.

She peered at Khloe through half-lidded eyes. "You still cutting yourself?"

"God, no," Khloe said. "No, that's all behind me."

"That's good," Alex said, as if the matter were settled. "I'm glad you got better, and I'm glad you met Adam again when you did."

"Me too," Khloe laughed. "Thank God, I had help. I wouldn't have been able to solve my issues on my own."

"But you were past that by the time you met Adam, yes?"

"Mostly, yes."

"That's good," Alex said.

"Why?" Khloe asked, confused.

"Because a woman should never rely on a guy to take care of her or solve all her problems. That's no good," she said. "The best person you can rely on to help you is yourself."

"To a certain extent, I agree," Khloe nodded. "I had to be willing to accept the lessons others were trying to teach me so I *could* heal. That part was up to me."

Alex smiled, satisfied.

"But I don't think you should have to feel like it's *all* up to you," Khloe continued. "It's okay to have someone else looking out for you, someone who loves you, who you love in return. Adam certainly has helped me when he thought I was slipping. He keeps me grounded."

"That's definitely true," Adam murmured under his breath. Khloe playfully smacked his shoulder. Adam looked at her in mock severity, a bright sparkle in his eyes. "Watch what you do with that hand, woman," he said. "Remember, *you* don't get to hit *me*."

Khloe looked away demurely.

"Do *you* get to hit *her?*" Alex asked.

The mood around the table took a sudden turn. Alex's brows rose as she stared at Adam, waiting for a response. He was saved by the waiter, who came by at that exact moment to take their orders.

Justin thought the crisis had been averted, but his relief was short lived. It was Khloe's turn to order, but before she could open her mouth, Adam answered for her.

"She'll have the broccoli beef," he said. "And for dessert she'll have apple pie."

Khloe's look of dismay was apparent to all. Adam ignored it.

The waiter did not. "You don't want that?" He asked her in a fatherly voice. "I can get you something else. The orange chicken is very good tonight, and our dessert special is the cheesecake."

"Ooh, cheesecake!" Khloe exclaimed. "Adam, can I—"

"No," he said sternly. "Apple, or nothing. That's the choice I'm willing to give you."

The silence that followed was downright frosty. "I'll have the apple pie," Khloe said, her voice barely over a whisper. "Thank you very much."

The waiter left, looking curious, but not nosy enough to get involved.

Khloe passed Adam a sour look. Adam ignored that, too.

Justin looked at Alex to see what she was making of all this. She was passing her focus from Khloe to Adam and back again, looking like she was trying to make sense of what was going on.

But she didn't look concerned the way the waiter did, Justin realized. She didn't look like she was worried she was witnessing signs of an abusive relationship, a tyrannical boyfriend ordering his girlfriend around. No, she looked merely curious: like she was waiting to see what would happen next.

Justin desperately wanted to know what she was thinking, but as soon as she caught him looking at her, she slipped on that unflappable look of hers, and Justin couldn't tell what she was hiding inside her inquisitive mind.

The meal went on. Adam made a point of treating Khloe with great chivalry after that. Khloe accepted her food from the waiter without protest, and ate it all as if it was exactly what she would have ordered anyway.

Justin tried his best to keep to neutral topics, and Adam lent him a hand with his dry wit and dirty jokes until he had all four of them laughing hard enough to gain the attention of the surrounding tables.

At the end of the meal, Adam asked for separate checks. Justin assumed that would mean four separate bills, but he was wrong.

The waiter brought Adam one thick black billfold, and Justin another. Adam slipped his credit card into his billfold without even looking at it.

Alex opened up her purse. "How much is my share?" She asked Justin, looking through her wallet.

"I'll tell you later," he said, gliding his own credit card inside the plastic billfold.

She cleared her throat. Justin looked at her: she was gazing at him with knit brows and puckered lips. "I thought we agreed last time," she reminded him.

"Don't worry; I'll let you pay me back," he said. "I just don't want to do the math right now. You can pay me back tomorrow, I promise." When she continued to glare at him, he snapped, "Put your wallet away."

Both Adam's and Khloe's eyebrows rose at Justin's curt tone, but Justin wasn't paying them much attention; all his focus now was on Alex. Would she argue with him in front of everyone, and cause a scene? Or would she give in?

"Fine," she said, closing her wallet and putting it back in her bag. "But I'm not going to forget this. I'm paying you back tomorrow."

Justin only nodded. He was surprised she had acquiesced so easily; surprised, and pleased. It was a small accomplishment, but it was enough to fill his chest with a sense of heady triumph.

She had bended to his will. It was a small thing, granted; but if he could make her do it once, he could make her do it again. The thought flooded his veins with a spurt of hot lust.

They left the restaurant. Justin watched the way Adam grabbed Khloe's hand and entwined his fingers with hers as they walked. He wanted to hold Alex's hand like that, but dared not try.

What *would* she do if he tried, he wondered? Probably pull away. Maybe try to smack him. He'd have to tie her up first if he was going to have a chance at holding her hand without getting hurt, he decided.

The idea of Alex trussed up in rope made him grin.

"What are you smiling about?" Khloe asked him, looking back.

"Nothing," he said. "Why?"

"You just had a funny grin on your face."

Justin shook his head and shrugged, feeling his face grow hot.

When they got to the car, Khloe and Alex joined each other in the back seat once more.

"So you haven't told me what it's like, working for these two," Khloe said. "Do they run you ragged?"

"No, they don't run me ragged," Alex said. "In fact, they're going very light on me. I don't feel like I'm carrying my fair share of the work. I wouldn't mind them giving me more responsibilities."

"Oh really," Khloe replied. "This doesn't sound like our Justin at all." She leaned forward into the front row. "Justin, why are you going so easy on her?"

"I didn't realize I was," he said.

"Maybe he's going easy on you cause you're a girl," Khloe suggested, leaning back into her seat again. "Plus, you're pretty."

"Maybe," Alex said, her smile growing wider. Justin could feel the heat spreading under his collar. He knew they were both remembering the same thing: their first encounter at the shop, when he had admired her tits. "But you'd think I'd have earned his trust by now," Alex said.

"Why do you think he doesn't trust you?"

"Yeah, Alex, why do you think I don't trust you?" Justin asked from the front seat, twisting his body around to look at her in the back.

"You still haven't shown me your back room," she replied.

"Oh. Ah...." Khloe's voice trailed away. The silence that followed was oppressive, and stretched on for far too long.

"I take it you know what's in the back room," Alex said, staring at Khloe.

"Well, yes, I do, but I'm Adam's su—girlfriend," she stammered.

"So only *girlfriends* are allowed to see what's back there?"

"No, of course not, but you—you're—um—"

"I'm what?"

"Vanilla," Khloe blurted out, and covered her mouth with both hands as soon as the word was out.

"Excuse me?"

It felt to Justin like the car, so large and roomy before, was now closing in, as the mood went from oppressive to perilous.

"Khloe meant that, uh—"

"—She wants some vanilla ice cream," Adam finished loudly.

"Yes, that's what I meant," Khloe agreed. "I want some vanilla ice cream. Adam, do we still have vanilla ice cream at home?"

"I believe we do, sweetie," he said. "I'll try to go a little faster so you can have some."

"Thank you, honey." Khloe ended her statement

with a titter of nervous laughter. Justin cringed, wishing that, just this once, Khloe could do a better job of lying. But Khloe had never been a good liar; it was one of the reasons why Adam enjoyed her occasional attempts at bratty misbehavior so much.

They reached the store, and Justin hopped out of the car before Adam had even put it in park.

"C'mon," Justin said, opening the door for Alex. "Let's let these two go home and have their ice cream."

"I'm coming," Alex said, climbing out of the huge car, her bag over her shoulder. As soon as she was out, Justin slammed the door shut behind her, and Adam peeled away.

"Wow," Alex said, watching the car go down the road. "He sure was in a hurry to get her home for that ice cream."

"Yeah," Justin murmured. He felt a little sorry for Khloe. She was going to have a hard night ahead of her. Adam's punishments were often harsh, and Khloe had slipped up royally this time. Justin wondered when he'd be seeing Khloe sitting down again.

"So what's all this vanilla business?" Alex asked. Justin cringed, and all his sympathy for Khloe quickly dissipated.

"It doesn't matter," he said. "Just a stupid joke."

"You're not going to tell me, are you?"

He turned his head to look at her: she was pouting again. This time, her sultry look only fueled his frustration. "No," he said, "I'm not. It wasn't nice what she said, and for all I know, it's not true."

"You think what she said might not be true—but

you're still not willing to show me what's in the back room."

"No."

"Fine," she said. "Well, this was a nice evening, wasn't it? I'm going home." She hitched her heavy bag over her shoulder and began to walk away.

"Hey, wait a minute," he said. "How're you getting home?"

"I'm taking the bus. That's what I do, remember?"

"No, you're not," he said. "It's late, and it's dark. I'm giving you a ride."

Her eyes spat fire at him. "I can get home by myself, thank you very much," she said. "I don't need you looking out for me." She began to walk away once more.

He hurried the few steps to catch up with her, grabbed her shoulder, and spun her around. "Goddamnit, Alex, do you always have to be so fucking independent?"

He regretted the words as soon as they were out of his mouth…but damn it, they were true, and he was pissed off.

"Is that what I am? Independent?" She whispered. "Well yes, Mr. Boss Man, I guess I do need to be independent, since I am a woman on my own. Who else do I have to depend on?"

"You could depend on me," he said quietly, then added quickly, "and Adam, and Khloe, too. We could be your friends, people you can rely on."

"Oh yes, my friends," she said. "Except Khloe seems to have a bad opinion of me—I can't be sure, of course, since you won't explain the joke—and none of you are willing to tell me what the *fuck* it is you keep in that back room of yours." Her eyes glistened suspiciously. "Sounds like a bunch of people I can really trust to watch my back." She tried to turn around and walk away, but Justin grabbed her arm again. "Let go of me."

"I'm driving you home."

"No."

"I didn't ask you permission."

"Stop treating me like I can't take care of myself!"

"Stop acting like a child," he said, "and accept a favor when it's offered."

"I don't need your favor."

"Fine," he said, giving up. "Then do *me* a favor. Let me drive you home, so I don't have to follow you on the bus the entire way to your door. Cause I will if you don't let me drive you."

"You wouldn't!"

"You bet I would, Alex. I don't need to be worrying the whole night if you got home okay, and I will if I don't see you get to your door safely. So what's it going to be? You accept a ride, or do I follow you home?"

Her eyes softened, and the tiniest smile danced across her lips.

Justin was dumbfounded by the change in her. It made him wonder...could it be she was *happy* to have the choice taken out of her hands? Perhaps even grateful?

It was too much to hope....

"Fine, drive me home," she snapped, back to her obstinate self. "But you *cannot* come inside."

"Wouldn't have dreamed of it, babe," Justin muttered, getting out his car keys and unlocking the door with his keychain. "Get in the car."

"Yes, *Sir*," she quipped.

Justin smiled. *If you only knew how good that Sir sounds coming from your mouth*, he thought.

They got in the car, and Justin readied his finger on the GPS. "What's the address?"

"You don't have to bother putting it in. I'll just give you directions."

He looked at her through the corner of his eye. She was too ready to jump out of the car at the slightest wrong word. "Fine," he said, pulling his hand back from the GPS and resting it in his lap, fighting the urge to clench it into a fist. "Where to?"

"Go down the road and take a right."

The drive to her place was long, and the silence between them was punctuated only now and then by Alex's curt directions.

By the time Alex told him to slow down, Justin had managed to give things some thought...and seeing the evening from her point of view, he was feeling seven shades of guilt. They really had been rude to her, with all their secrets and innuendos.

Adam and Khloe certainly had an unconventional relationship, but who was to say Alex couldn't handle that? Was keeping her in the dark about the more sordid aspects of their lives really doing anyone any favors? Maybe she would be offended by their choices of lifestyle, but...maybe not. She had been offended by the way they had deceived her, and rightly so. Perhaps it was time to let her in on some of their secrets.

"This is the one," she said, pointing to a small blue duplex, circled almost completely by a tall wooden fence.

Justin slowed the car down to a stop in front of the door and killed the engine.

"Look, Alex, I want to apologize for tonight," he said. "We didn't mean to make you feel uncomfortable. Adam and Khloe just have a, uh, a unique relationship," he finished, feeling foolish.

"I get it," Alex whispered. "I just don't understand why nobody can be honest with me about what's going on."

"Because not everyone is accepting of their lifestyle, and some people think it's wrong...wait. You get it? Tell me exactly what you get," he said, feeling hope and panic mingle somewhere suspiciously close to his heart.

Alex sighed. "Khloe and Adam have a Dominant/submissive relationship. They are a kinky couple. She wears his collar." She trained her eyes on him, and Justin noticed they were as deep as the night sky. "I'm guessing they've had a D/s relationship for a while now. I'm also guessing you've known about it since it started."

"Yes, I have."

The relief he wanted to feel would not come. If she knew about D/s relationships and about what it meant to be kinky, then surely she could not condemn the concept, could she? But Alex was back to being her calm, collected self, intractable and mystifying. He could not detect a single emotion on her face, and it was driving him mad.

"Alex, how do you know about kink and D/s relationships?"

"I'm familiar with the dynamic," she said. "What about you?"

"I'm familiar, too."

"No, I mean, are you into those kinds of relationships, too?"

He scowled, wishing the question had not come up so soon. "Yeah, I am. But not like Adam and Khloe. I've never had a girl wear my collar before."

"But you're a Top."

"Why do you say so?"

"You said you've never had a girl wear your collar, with the understanding being, you're a Top—maybe even a Dom—but you've never taken a relationship to that level."

"What I am, is a man who hates labels," he said. "I like making women happy, making them satisfied, that's all."

"So you're a service Top?"

"No, I'm not that either," he said, frowning.

"Are you a Sadist?"

He gritted his teeth. "I like to please women who like to be hurt," he said, not wanting to scare her. "Is that a good enough answer?"

"You're a complicated one, aren't you?" She said, smiling. It was the first smile she had offered him all night, and it filled him with heightened awareness of the fact that her nipples were peaking through her sweater.

"I guess I am complicated," he said. "Do you have a problem with that?"

"I can handle complicated ones." Her grin grew wider.

"No, that's not what I meant," Justin said, throwing her words back at her. "I mean, can you handle that I hurt women?"

"Like you said, you only hurt women who like to be hurt."

"Yeah...."

"Then you're all about honoring consent. I like that. So yeah, I can handle it."

"Thank you," Justin said quietly. He shivered, feeling as if an electric current had run through him. "God, you have no idea how good it is to get this out in the open."

"Honesty works, Justin," Alex said. "And on that note, goodnight."

Alex stepped out of the car and shut the door behind her.

Justin quickly rolled down the window. "Hey, Alex?"

Alex turned around and bent down to peer at him. Gravity did its work on her sweater, pulling it down, revealing the creamy soft cleavage of her dangling breasts. Justin wondered if she knew what kind of picture she was presenting to him, and thought not. Probably not. Maybe yes? He mentally shook himself.

"What about you?" He asked.

"What about me?"

"Are you, you know...?"

"Am I what?"

"Kinky," he blurted. "You never really answered my question. How do you know about kink and D/s relationships? Have you ever been in one before?"

"Well, to answer your second question, no, I have never been in a D/s relationship before. But to answer your first question...yes, I am."

A pig wearing a leotard could have started dancing in front of the car at that point, and Justin wouldn't have been more surprised. "Really?" He asked. "Are you a Top, or bottom?"

"I guess I'm kind of like you, Justin," she said.

His stomach dropped. "A Top?"

"No, not a Top," she replied. Her lips curved, and her tongue came out, just the tip, to touch her upper lip. "Just someone who doesn't like labels," she said. She smiled at him, one of her captivating smiles that made Justin's breath catch.

Then she stood up and started walking away.

Justin decided not to push his luck by calling her back to ask her any more questions. He consoled himself with the sight of her pert ass cheeks swaying in her jeans as she walked down the driveway to the side fence gate.

She waved to him as she unlatched the gate, went through, and closed the door behind her.

Justin had to take a couple minutes to recover from the sweet unnerving she caused him. But once he got his pounding chest (and pounding prick) under control, he rolled out of the driveway and started on his way home.

Alex waited a few seconds after she heard Justin's car drive away. Then she quietly opened the gate she had just come through, looked up and down the street, slipped out, and slowly shut the gate behind her.
She started walking.

Thank goodness whoever lived in that house had not noticed what was going on outside their front door. They might have come out to ask what was going on in their driveway.

Alex looked at her watch, and started walking faster. She still had a ways to walk if she was to get herself home.

CHAPTER SIX

A S SOON AS ALEX WALKED in the store the next morning, before she even had time to put her bag down, Adam was hastening toward her.

"Alex, I want to apologize for Khloe's behavior last night," he said. "Mine, too. We were acting like a couple of obnoxious teenagers. It was very rude of us, and I'm sorry."

"When were you rude?" Alex asked innocently.

Adam began to fluster. "When we were being so cryptic about the back room, and when Khloe said...."

"When Khloe said...?"

"When Khloe was giving you a hard time," Adam finished.

"I don't remember Khloe giving me a hard time," Alex said. "I just remember her really, really wanting vanilla ice cream when she got home." Her tone had turned teasing. Justin knew he should step in and save Adam, but he was having too good a time watching his friend squirm.

"Yeah, she really wanted some ice cream, but, ah...."

"You can stop now, Adam," Justin finally interjected. "It seems our Alex is not as vanilla as we thought. She knows quite a bit about kink and the lifestyle."

"She does?" Adam said, giving him a wide-eyed look, then turning his stare on Alex. "You do?"

"A bit, yes," she said. She crossed her arms as if angry, but Justin could see the sparkle of laughter in her eyes. "I'm wondering why you assumed I'd have a problem with it."

"Because, ah, because, well, you know...."

"Alex, stop teasing him," Justin said. "He's drowning here."

"Oh, he knows I'm teasing," she said. "I'm just giving him a little back after what I got lost night. But he deserves it—don't you agree, Adam?"

"I guess so," he said. "But when you say you know about kink...what exactly do you know?"

"I know enough to know Khloe probably has a sore ass this morning. Am I right?"

"Yeah, you're right," Adam said, an evil gleam now entering his eyes. "Sore is not the word I'd use to describe it."

"What's the word you'd use?"

"Unusable," Adam replied. His grin turned lecherous.

Alex sighed and uncrossed her arms. "Well. I don't think that was necessary of you, but I'm not going to come between a Dom and his sub."

It was Adam's turn to look relieved. "So—you really do get it, don't you?" He asked.

"Yes, I really do get it," Alex replied. "And I'm fine with you and Justin living your lives any way you please. So can we get back to work now?"

"Yes! I mean, yeah, sure."

Justin could see the same surprise on Adam's face he had felt himself the night before, and he couldn't help laughing. "Relax, Adam," he said. "Alex is cool."

"As cool as vanilla ice cream," Alex chimed in.

Adam sighed. "I'm never going to live that one down, am I?"

"No," Alex and Justin replied in unison.

Adam gave them a lopsided scowl. "Justin, any special orders you want me to take care of?"

"Yeah, as a matter of fact, two...."

The morning got itself started on a much brighter note. Most of it was spent dealing with inventory and online orders.

They didn't get their first customer in until almost lunchtime: it was a guy wearing a pair of faded jeans and t-shirt that said I LOVE SANTA CRUZ. His hair looked disheveled, and he was sporting a five o'clock shadow on his face.

To Justin, he broadcasted one word: *tourist.* Justin didn't give tourists much thought; they didn't usually buy anything inside the store. Sometimes they would grab a business card and end up ordering stuff online, but they would never buy anything to take home with them. Tourists usually traveled by plane, and it was impossible to carry weapons inside baggage these days.

But there were always exceptions. Some travellers were not tourists at all, but business executives jaunting through Silicon Valley, making their million dollar deals. Often, those people were travelling on their private jets. For them, adding a rare sword to their posh art collections was the coup de grace of their trip, the ultimate souvenir…and there was no problem taking it on a private plane.

Justin had himself flown by private plane a few times. His brother had flown him home from boarding school on occasion on the Hotel Bentmoore's jet. During those times, Justin hadn't seen a reason to refuse. He had to admit, it was a much more comfortable and convenient way to travel. But since becoming his own man, he'd declined all his brother's offers to fly him home for a visit. Justin could find his own way home, if and when he wanted.

The new customer who had just walked in seemed to be very taken with Alex…a little too taken, Justin thought. After admiring her looks and her smile, he asked her where she hailed from.

"I'm American," she replied with a laugh. "Born and raised." She swept her dark tresses back, and a waft of her scent drifted across the room. Justin stopped what he was doing by the counter and watched the way the man ogled Alex.

"Really?" He asked. "This cannot be. You look far too elegant." He stepped closer to her, peering down towards her cleavage. "And what might your name be, sweet lady?"

"Is there something else I can help you find, Sir?" Justin cut in, coming around the corner of the counter in a swift stride.

The man turned around, stiff. He stared at Justin for a moment. "No," he said. "I was just looking around. But thank you very much. You have a neat store."

"You're welcome."

The customer smiled at Alex. "And thank you, sweet lady. It was a pleasure to meet you."

"You too. Come back anytime."

"I will, thank you." He glanced at Justin, his smile gone; then he left the store.

As soon as he was out the door, Justin turned to Alex with a frown.

"What?" She asked.

"Why'd you let him get so close to you?"

"I didn't see a problem," she said. "The guy was harmless."

Justin's brows furrowed as he crossed his arms. "You didn't get any sense of danger from him?"

"No, I didn't," Alex said. "I thought he was pretty nice, actually. But you got a bad vibe from him?"

"Yeah." Justin uncrossed his arms, feeling foolish.

More customers walked in off the street. This time, Justin helped them himself, and asked Alex to go clean some swords on display.

Adam was willing to stay late and help Justin close up—he reminded Justin he owed him one—and the two men argued for a moment, but Alex cut the argument short. "You get home to Khloe," she told Adam. "Pamper her a little bit. Make up for your behavior last night."

"What's to make up?" Adam asked. "Besides, I thought you knew: you don't get involved between a Dom and his sub."

"I'm not getting involved," she said. "This is just one woman sticking up for another." She grinned at him and said, "Buy her some rainbow sorbet on your way home. Tell her it's from me—cause not all of us like only vanilla."

Adam laughed. "First you tell me to make it up to her, then you ask me to do something that'll be sure to make her feel guilty."

"Yeah, well, who says I can't do both," Alex said. "Now go home. I think Justin wants to talk to me."

Justin was, indeed, standing behind the counter with his brows furrowed, silently waiting. His silence to Alex's remark only confirmed it. Adam gave him a shrewd look, then shrugged.

"Fine, I'm outa here," he said.

As soon as he was out the door, Alex turned to Justin and said, "So what's going on inside your mind? Is it still on that guy who came in before?"

"No," Justin said. "I've given this some thought, and I think...I think it's time I let you see what we keep in the back." His voice was heavy and low, the way it got when he was feeling particularly nervous... and right now, Justin was feeling extremely nervous. "I'm hoping, after you see the stuff, you won't quit."

"Is that what you're so worried about? That I'll quit?"

"Yeah," he said. "Or you'll run away screaming."

"I won't quit, and I won't run away screaming."

"Maybe not right away."

"Not at all," She said, shaking her head. "But once you show me this stuff, will there be an expectation that I'll let you use it on me?"

"Oh fuck no, Alex," Justin said, surprised. Then he

amended, "Unless you want me to, of course."

Alex only smiled. "So show me," she said. "All this buildup, this better be good."

Justin didn't answer. The thought had now occurred to him there was more than one way this could go wrong: Alex might be disappointed by what he showed her. She might be expecting something flashy, or big, or complicated. Justin didn't do complicated; he liked to keep his work simple, and let his care and precision show through the level of perfection he demanded from himself.

She might get scared and run...or she might get disappointed, and laugh in his face.

Things between them could get awkward.

She might never look at him the same way again.

So why was he doing this?

Because he was sick and tired of keeping the truth from her.

Justin swept back the curtain and stretched his arm out. "This way, my lady," he said, giving her a mock bow. Alex walked on through.

"Oh my," she said. She stepped further into the room, and Justin followed behind her. "Oh wow."

Every inch of wall space had a hook or peg on it, and from every hook and peg hung a flogger, paddle, or single-tailed whip. A small table sat in the corner, covered with knives, needles, awls, string, scraps of leather, and other tools half-hidden among the wreckage. A palm tree-shaped lamp was in the corner, bent in a perfect arch to illuminate the desk.

"You make this stuff," Alex said.

"Yes."

"And you sell it online."

"Yes. So what do you think?"

"Can I see something up close?"

"Um, sure. Which one?"

Alex pointed to a braided deer-hide flogger hanging from the wall, and Justin got it down for her. Alex held it up by the handle, getting a feel for the weight of it in her hand. Then she began to run the thick supple strands through her fingers. "It's so soft," she murmured. "Like velvet."

"It's deer hide," Justin said, pride coming through his voice.

Alex looked up at the wall. "There's another one exactly like it."

"They're a matching set," Justin explained. "A lot of people like to buy these things in pairs."

"Can you take that one down for me, too?"

Justin retrieved the sister flogger and handed it to Alex. She held up both now, as if looking for discrepancies.

"They're exactly the same," she said. "That's amazing."

"Thank you," Justin replied, feeling more relaxed.

"How do you do it?"

"With time and hard work, just like anything."

"How long have you been doing this?"

"Years."

Alex looked around the room. "This is more than just a hobby. This is a passion."

"Yeah, it is," Justin said, relieved he could detect

no censure in Alex's voice.

"And do you use all the tools you make?"

"No, actually, that's the funny part," Justin said. "I'm not that good with a whip, and I don't use paddles all that much. I use the tools God gave me." Alex gave him a quizzical look, and Justin held up his calloused hands, spreading his fingers wide. "Bare palm technique," he said, wiggling his fingers.

Alex laughed, blushed, and looked away. When she turned back around, she kept her eyes on the walls, still not looking at him, and Justin realized he had unnerved her somehow.

He had never seen Alex this unnerved before. It was fascinating.

"So you make these for people to buy. You must be amazing at it," she said, her voice tight.

"I like to think so, yes," Justin said, noting the restriction in her voice. "My customers like what I make enough to come back for more." He continued to study her, wondering what had brought on this sudden case of jitters, and what he could learn from it.

"And is this...it?" She said. "You make floggers, paddles, and whips?"

Justin frowned. "No, I make other stuff too, but I keep that stuff at home. There's not enough room here for it."

"Can you show me?" Now he could see the excitement dancing around the black light of her eyes. Her question had caught him off guard, but the answer was easy.

"Sure," he said, careful to keep his expression

neutral. He knew any smile he gave her now would just come out looking depraved, so he didn't bother to try. "I can take you over to my place if you want."

"Just to see the stuff you make."

"Just to see the stuff I make." He nodded. "I'll go close up shop. Give me five minutes."

Three and a half minutes later, they were in Justin's car, driving up Sixth street, and Justin was trying very hard not to go too fast. He couldn't believe his luck: Alex was not only okay with his trade, she admired it...and was now in his car, on her way to his house.

He would soon have her on his turf. In his lair, so to speak. What was he going to do with her once he got her there?

Damn it, had he left his dirty clothes on the bed?

The cemetery came into view. "You live next to a cemetery?" She asked.

"I do," Justin said. "A cemetery makes an excellent neighbor."

"Why is that?"

"No noise, and no one to complain," Justin said, grinning.

"I see," Alex said with a chuckle. "Can't stand noise, huh?"

"Well," he said, "I don't mind the noise coming from my *own* house, but I don't think my neighbors would feel the same way."

"And what exactly would they hear coming from your house?"

"Do you really want to know?"

"I...don't know," Alex said, turning her face to the

window. She was nervous again. Justin drove faster.

"This one's mine," he said, turning into his long driveway at the end of the street. Alex peered ahead, trying to make out the house in the darkened light.

"It's nice," she said. "Looks very old style."

"That's cause it is old," Justin said. "C'mon." He walked her to the front door, unlocked it, and led the way inside. Alex came through slowly.

"It's okay for you to come in," Justin said, switching on the light. "Nothing's going to bite you." *Not yet, anyway.*

"I'm just not used to going inside a guy's house," she said, looking around.

"It's a house, Alex," he said, trying to put her at ease. He started walking toward the kitchen. "You want something to eat? Drink?"

"Um, yeah, but maybe later. First, I'd really like to see what kind of stuff you work on at home."

"Sure. This way." He switched directions and led her across the kitchen to the garage door. As soon as he opened the side door, a cold rush of air drifted in, carrying with it the scent of leather and oil.

Justin walked down the two steps to the cement floor and turned on the light. He heard Alex make a noise in her throat as she took in the view: there, spread out to all four corners of the room, were his furniture pieces.

Padded spanking benches in differing levels of completion sat in one corner. Two tables sat in another. A torture wheel was propped up against the far wall, with two pliable leather cuffs already dangling from the sides. And right in the center of the room, looking imposing and regal, sat a queening chair, still in skeleton stage, but already revealing its future potential.

"Wow. You make all of these?" Alex asked, descending the steps and walking into the room. Justin couldn't tell if she was afraid, or just awed. Part of him wanted her completely relaxed.

Part of him wanted her terrified.

"This is what I do," he said. "What do you think?"

"This stuff looks expensive."

"It's not cheap, no," Justin said. "My work is good quality."

"I can tell." She walked up to the spanking bench, ran her finger down the soft leather side, and inhaled deeply through her nose. She closed her eyes and smiled. "It smells amazing."

"You like the smell of leather?"

"Oh yes." She took another deep breath as she turned to gaze at him over her shoulder, a dreamy look in her eyes. A plait of her hair fell in front of her shoulder, cascading over the curve of her left breast. "There's something very sensual about it, you know? Very...earthy," she said.

"Yeah," he agreed. He would have agreed to anything she'd just said. He could feel the blood pumping in his chest, his arms, his head...he watched the way she touched the bench, caressing it with her soft fingers and hazy eyes.

He wanted her to touch him that way.

No, he wanted to touch *her* that way. He wanted to cuff her down into that spanking bench and touch her to his heart's content. He would start out gentle, but then....

He cleared his throat. He had to get them both out of this room. "You want that food now?"

"Yeah," she said, straightening up. "Let's see what you've got."

"Not a lot, but enough to surprise you, maybe." He led the way back inside to the kitchen, and kept going until he reached the fridge.

Alex stopped by the counter, but Justin didn't turn around to look at her face. He couldn't, not yet—not until he got his blood lust under control.

Food. Food was a good distraction.

"I got some steaks I can put on the grill, and macaroni salad. Sounds good?"

"I guess." She was walking away from him now, following the path of the kitchen toward the family room. "Holy shit. You've got a whole workout room set up here."

Justin, realizing the food was going to wait a while longer, closed the fridge door. "Yeah, I don't like going to a gym all that much," he said, following her path into the room. "I do my workouts here at home."

Alex was busy looking over all his equipment. She took her time with the punching bag dangling from a hook on the ceiling, giving it a small push so it swayed. Then, to Justin's surprise, she took off her shoes, walked into the padded square in the center of the floor, and bounced on her toes, getting a feel for it.

"You invite your workout buddies here to grapple you?" She asked, bouncing on her feet a little harder now, giving the air a couple playful punches in his direction.

Not careless punches, though. Alex was responding to the feel of the room, an atmosphere designed to raise a person's heart rate and adrenaline.

"Sometimes," Justin said, studying her with furrowed brows. "Mostly just my friend Brian."

"No girls?"

"I don't invite girls to grapple," he said. "I invite them over for other reasons."

"Why don't you invite girls to grapple?"

"Girls aren't a fair fight for me," he said, giving her an honest answer. "I'd have to hold back, or worry about hurting them."

"What about me?" She asked. "I'm a girl. You think you'd hurt me?...Maybe I'd hurt you."

A clear challenge.

Justin, feeling the mood in the room suddenly change, slipped off his shoes and walked into the edge of the square. Alex stepped back to give him space.

They began to circle each other inside the padded square, holding each other's stare, sizing each other up. The electrical current running between them began to charge to dangerous levels.

"A fight with you would be fair," he said, his voice heavy. "But I'd still win, Alex. You have to admit that."

"Oh really, I have to admit that? Let's find out, shall we?" Stepping forward into the middle of the square, she spread her feet apart, balled her hands into fists, and raised them in front of her face.

Ready.

"Alex, you really better think about whether you want to do this," Justin said, giving her one last chance to bow out. "Cause this isn't a joke for me. I play for keeps."

"Oh?" Her fists came down. "How so? What do you get to keep if you win?"

"The knowledge that I pinned you; I beat you at your own challenge. I think that would be enough to last us both for a while."

He pulled his shirt out of his jeans, pulled it over his head, and flung it in the corner. He knew it was an underhanded trick, trying to distract her like that with his hard body, but as long as the trick worked, he didn't care.

And by the look on her face, it definitely had worked. Alex was responding to him in a purely physical way that had nothing to do with combat.

Crisscrossing his arms and bouncing on his toes a bit, he added, "but if that's not enough for you, we could up the stakes some more."

Alex put her fists back up. "What do you have in mind?" She asked, wary.

"If I win...." He pretended to give it some thought. "If I win, you have to tell me why you keep handcuffs in your bag."

"Done," she said. "And if I win?"

He paused. "If you win, what do you want?"

"If I win, you have to stop looking over my shoulder every time I'm helping a customer. It's getting annoying."

"Fine," he growled. "It really didn't matter what

you asked for. You won't win. I was just curious."

Her face grew sinister. "We'll see about that," she said.

"Yes, we will," he said. "I'm about to kick your ass, Alex."

He said it to make her afraid.

He needed her afraid. He needed her roused and tense, because a calm, focused Alex could very well beat him.

Justin threw the first punch. Alex easily deflected it, and laughed derisively. Her confidence was back, but only momentarily; Justin had purposely slowed his punch to distract her from the kick he was about to swing to her ass.

Alex didn't go flying, but she stumbled to the edge of the mats before she could catch herself.

"You'll pay for that one," she hissed, rounding on him.

"Come get me, babe," he replied.

The fight was on.

He threw a couple more mock punches, and she laughed; but her laughter was faked now, her own way to distract him while she took a moment to formulate a plan in her head.

Justin wouldn't give her time to make one. He swiped at her knees and had her on the ground before she knew it.

He made no move to pin her once she was down. But Alex didn't wait for him to change his mind: she twisted and bounded up quickly, kicking with both hips to gain momentum—and try to make contact between her leg and his chin.

He backed away. "You're still not taking this seriously," he said. "You're holding back. Don't."

She stopped. "Are you sure?" She asked. "I might really hurt you."

"And I might really hurt you," he replied. "But I want this to be a clean fight, so when I win, we both know I won fair and square."

"As if."

Justin had no idea what she meant by that; but before he could ask her, she stepped into his space, just close enough to jab at his midsection, and when he hopped away to dodge it, she swiveled back to kick him right under the ribs instead.

Justin didn't bend from the impact, as she was probably expecting him to do, but he did rub his side a little.

"Harsh," he said.

"You asked for it."

He came at her in earnest now, trying to grab her hands away and use his solid weight against her. But Alex was no novice. She anticipated all his tricks, and kept slithering away, knocking a few more jabs and kicks into him in the process.

She was mocking him.

Justin had enough. He sighed, put his hands down, and stood his ground.

"Why do you want to fight me, Alex?"

Her fists came down a few inches from the sides of her face. "What?"

"Did I do something to upset you?"

She stepped forward, unsure—and unguarded. "No, Justin, I was just—"

He didn't grab for her right away; in the back of his mind, he knew he might be too slow to catch her, and she wouldn't fall for the ruse twice. So he casually stepped around her, watched for his opening...and when his left side was just beyond her blind spot, he thrust out his foot, making a swipe at her legs.

This time, when Alex went down, Justin went down with her, pinning her to the floor.

"You've got ten second to get me off, Alex," he murmured into her face. "Go."

She was good; he'd give her that. She was almost out from under him before he managed to twist her body around to where she couldn't jab him in the stomach or kick him in the balls.

Alex fought hard, and she fought silently, with purpose...but to no avail. After five seconds, when she still hadn't given up, Justin stretched out her arm, bent her thumb back until he knew the pressure would be too much for her, and waited.

Alex howled—and tapped out.

Justin immediately got off her, rolled away to rest on his back, and propped himself up on his elbows.

"Told you," he said.

He was breathing hard, his chest heaving, his head beaded with sweat.

He was nervous. He got the feeling he had just been tested, and now that he'd beaten her, he wondered if he'd passed Alex's test—or not.

"You made me tap out," she whispered. "But I can

still pin you down."

"You don't have the strength, Alex. Face it, I'm bigger than you."

Alex didn't answer him. For a moment, she stared into his face, her own veiled expression revealing nothing of what was going on inside her mind. Justin was about to ask her—

But before he could, she swung a leg over his lap, and straddled his hips.

"Alex? What are you doing?"

"Pinning you," she said. "If you want me off, you'll have to push me off. But I don't think you do."

She leaned in and kissed him hard on the mouth. Her lips were soft, moist, and enslaving.

She pulled away. "I'll give you to the count of three," she whispered. "One...."

"Alex, I don't think this is fair."

She kissed him again, grinding her groin into his lap, and Justin grabbed her hips with both hands to hold her steady.

Alex pulled away once more. "Two...."

"Alex, if this is your idea of a harmless fun—"

She pushed her whole body against his, and Justin fell down hard on his back, grabbing the back of her head with both hands so their lips would not break. Alex's body shifted, and Justin tried to hold her still. She pushed up to sit straight across his groin, her hair tumbling around her head in wispy disarray, and smiled down at him.

"Three," she said. "I win."

"Goddamnit, Alex, this was not part of the deal."

"Au contraire," she said. "There was no deal. Only the challenge—and the wager." She leaned down, and when he tried to reach up and grab her head to pull it in for another kiss, she stretched his arms above his head until his hands were circling the bar of the weight machine behind him.

She could not hold his hands there—not by physical force, anyway. They both knew she lacked the sheer strength she needed to do that. But what she lacked in strength, she made up for in sensual allure. Justin, captivated by the drawing power of her eyes, held his arms still above his head even after Alex pulled her hands away. He grabbed the bar of the weight machine and gripped it tight, afraid to do anything that would ruin the moment and make Alex get off him.

"Good," she said, sitting up and smiling. She tipped her head back and arched her body in a perfect curve, pressing her breasts against the confines of her shirt. She dipped so far back, she had to lean her hands on his legs behind her.

She whipped her head back up, stopping only two inches from his face. Justin could feel the heat coming off her body, smell her scent...he gripped the metal bar tighter.

Her lips came around to his ear, and Justin could feel her soft breath against his neck. "You're right about one thing," she murmured. "You did win the fight. So I'll share the truth with you. Close your eyes."

Justin, who was not really paying attention but would do anything to keep her across his lap, closed his eyes.

He opened them again when he felt the snap of metal around his wrists and heard the click.

Alex had handcuffed him to the bar of the weight machine.

"Alex, what the hell?" Justin tried to pull his hands away, feeling foolish for trying even as he did so. There was no way he'd be getting out of the handcuffs.

How had he gotten himself into this? "Ok, joke's over, Alex," he said. "Uncuff me."

"Are you sure you want me to?" Alex was kissing his forehead now, his chin, moving on to his chest... moving down, down....

"Fuck, Alex, seriously," Justin got out. His hands rattled the cuffs again.

Alex got up onto her feet. She stepped back, but stayed closed enough for him to see her fully.

She began to undress.

"Alex, this is not how I pictured the first time I fuck you."

"But you did picture it," she teased. She had taken off her shirt, and was now slipping off her bra.

Justin's eyes couldn't move. As her bra fell away, revealing her heavy, perfectly rounded breasts, his mouth went dry. Her breasts were just as beautiful as he'd thought they would be. Creamy dark areolae. Thick fat nipples. High-crested tips. Her breasts would be a handful...if he could just get his hands free....

"Justin? How did you picture it?"

Justin raised his eyes to her face, and found her smiling at him in a knowing way that galled him.

"I imagined us in my bedroom, on my bed, with

neither of us cuffed to anything," he said.

Her eyes narrowed. "Oh? You really never pictured me cuffed to anything?"

"Well, you maybe. Not me."

"Because you're the Top, so you get to do all the cuffing?"

"You told me you're not a Top, Alex," he reminded her, suddenly worried. If he found out they weren't compatible now...but he couldn't help himself from becoming transfixed by the way her breasts moved as she spoke.

"That's true, I'm not a Top," she admitted. "But I also told you I'm like you—I don't fit any one label. So here's where it comes down to the test."

"What test?"

Alex began to unzip her pants. As she opened the hem and began to pull them down her hips, she said: "Are you willing to switch roles with me tonight, just a little, just for a while, if it gets you what you want? Are you willing to let me Top you if it means you get...me?"

She stepped out of her jeans and panties, kicked them away, and stood up straight and proud before him in all her naked glory. "How badly do you want me, Justin?"

Her stomach was flat below her breasts: smooth, lean, and supple. A thin line split her muscles beneath the skin. Her arms were lean, too, ropey with muscle and well defined. Her thighs widened at her rounded hips, showing off her womanly curves.

Justin was itching to get his hands on those hips.

But he couldn't, not cuffed down the way he was.

Alex began to lower herself to her knees. Justin bent his legs up to give her space.

"I can uncuff you, if you want," she said. "But then I'll get dressed and go home. Is that what you want?"

Justin couldn't speak. He couldn't articulate speech as Alex began to unfasten his pants, grab them by the hem together with his underwear, and yank them down his lap. His cock sprang free, long and hard.

"Or I could climb on top of you, and give us both the ride we've been waiting for."

She pulled his clothes off his feet, rolled them into a ball, and tossed them in the same direction as hers. But she didn't move closer to him then, didn't straddle his hips as Justin was aching for her to do. She just knelt by his feet, balancing her butt on her heels.

"So what's it going to be, Justin? I uncuff you, or...not?"

"Get over here," he growled.

Alex's smile was wide and adorable. Justin realized she really had been afraid his need to act the Top would be greater than his need for her.

There were many Tops who were like that, Justin knew. There were Doms whose inherent need to control every scene overruled their ability to succumb to a lady's desire if that meant giving up control. Those were men who could not have sex if their power did not hold sway.

Justin wasn't like that. He was no bottom, to be sure; he would not submit to Alex as a normal part of their relationship. But he could defer to her kink once in a while, if that's what she needed to feel satisfied.

And it was clear she needed this from him right now. She had said it straight out: if he demanded she uncuff him, she would get dressed and go home.

There was no way in hell Justin was going to let that happen.

But he didn't have to worry. His answer was all the catalyst Alex needed to push down his legs and straddle them. She grabbed his cock, squeezing it hard enough to get a gasp out of the agitated man.

"You have a nice dick," she said. "Has anyone ever told you that?"

"Yes," he said. "But it's nice to hear it coming out of your mouth."

"Do you want to feel it coming from my mouth, too?"

"Fuck, Alex, if you don't slow down, I'm going to come right now," he said. Alex stopped pumping her hand up and down his wide shaft, giving him a look of surprise.

"Really? I thought you'd have more control than that."

"I usually do, but I'm not normally the one handcuffed."

"Ah, I see," she said, contemplative. "So let's see how far I can take this. You're clean, right?"

"Yeah. Got the blood work to prove it."

"Me too. So…enjoy the new experience."

"Alex, please—"

His voice stopped when he felt her hot mouth around his throbbing cock. Alex had taken his entire length in her mouth in one lunge, all the way down the shaft. He could feel her lips pressing against his balls.

"Oh fuck, Alex." She had pulled his cock down her throat, swallowing him up whole, sending shivers of ecstasy down his prick and up his spine. The suction was incredible, as was the pressure of her lips.

She held him against the bridge of her mouth, and her tongue came out below his shaft to lick and lap at his balls. Justin leaned back and groaned, feeling helpless against the onslaught of pleasure.

He opened his eyes again when he felt the cold air against his cock. Alex had broken their connection long enough to move up his hips. He watched with half-lidded eyes as she sat up on her knees, aimed his cock with perfect precision, and sat down on it—slowly.

Her pussy was just as hot and tight as her mouth, and Justin groaned once more.

This time, Alex groaned with him.

"Move forward," he ordered. "Give me your tits." He couldn't help the command in his voice—he was still a Top—but Alex didn't seem to mind. She smiled and leaned forward, and Justin took one plump swollen nipple in his mouth. He'd always had a secret belief that large areolae tasted better, and Alex's breasts did not dispel his theory. He sucked her nipple in hard, and bit down when Alex tried to pull away.

He was cuffed down...but he would still take control where he could.

Alex began to grind her hips back and forth, rolling against him in hypnotic, rippling waves. Justin watched her move over him, enthralled, holding her nipple between his teeth every time she began to arch back too far. She moaned and gasped as his tongue swirled around her engorged nipple.

As she began to move faster, she grabbed his head with both hands and pulled it into her chest, shifting over to give him access to her other breast. Justin released his cage-like hold on her nipple only long enough to trap the other one between his teeth. He began to work it like he had its sister, biting, licking, and sucking.

Soon, Alex began to bounce atop his lap, sliding his slick cock in and out of her gripping cunt. Justin bent his knees up, trying to keep her sitting straight, and Alex pressed her hands against his chest to brace herself.

He could tell by the strain on her face she was about to come. He lifted her with his hips, ground his groin against her slick flesh, and slammed back down. His balls tightened, and his prick went completely rigid. He was about to come himself.

In the last minute, he decided to run his own little experiment: he locked his mouth right around the edge of her nipple and bit down, hard.

Alex came with a howl, shrieking into the sky.

Her clenching, pounding pussy began to pulse along his entire cock, and Justin couldn't hold out anymore: he let go. His cock jumped inside her hot gripping cunt, spurting his come all the way up her womb.

Alex collapsed across his chest. Justin didn't mind. She felt right there.

But after a few minutes, she climbed off him, and walked away to find her jeans. He watched her pick them up, find her back pocket, and reach in with two fingers to pull out a key.

Without a word, she knelt beside him and unlocked the handcuffs.

"Thank you," he said, rubbing his wrists. They had red marks were the metal bands had dug into his flesh.

"For unlocking you, or for everything else?"

He grinned at her teasing tone. She sat down next to him, but when he reached a hand out to pull her into the crook of his arm, she pulled away.

"What, I don't get any aftercare?" He said. "I need reassurance, you know." He was trying to be funny, but Alex didn't look amused. Her smile faded.

"I'm really not a Top, you know," she said quietly. "I don't want you to think, because I did this—" she held up the handcuffs by the crook of her finger—"I'm some kind of secret Domme. I really do usually like men who can take control. I just needed our first time to be…this." She threw the cuffs into the pile of their clothes. "I'm sorry if I upset you."

"What the hell?" Justin didn't like the guilt or uncertainty he saw on her face, and what was worse, he had no idea what had suddenly brought on either. "Alex, what could possibly make you think I'm upset? I know you're not a Domme. I also know this was a hot fuckin' scene. *I'm* feeling damn satisfied. Aren't you?"

"Yeah, but…" she turned her face away, weighing her next words, and Justin gave her time to gather her resolve. "I owe you the truth about the cuffs, so here's the truth: you're the first person I've ever used them on. I keep them in my purse because they make me feel safe."

"Safe, how?"

"I don't know. See, that's the stupid part. I know I'll never have a use for them, but they make me feel safer just by being in my bag. They make me feel more in control."

"And that's what you need? Control?"

Her eyes went wide, and her cheeks turned red. "I...yes, sometimes," she whispered. "But not all the time. Not if I don't have to." She covered her face with her hands, then brushed her hair away. "I know this makes no sense."

"It makes perfect sense." He sat up, moved in closer, and put his arm around her; and this time, she did not pull away. "You know what you need, and you go after it."

"Some men have a hard time understanding," she said. "I'm not a Domme, I'm not a switch, but I'm not 100% sub, either."

"I think what you are is amazing," he said. "You don't feel the need to fit inside someone else's idea of who you should be. You're honest and direct."

"Not really, Justin," she said, looking at him with that impassive stare of hers, the one Justin was beginning to realize she only used when she was feeling a surge of emotion she did not want to reveal.

"No? How so?"

"You want me to be honest? During our fight, I held back."

"You held back...why?" Understanding dawned. "So you would lose," he whispered. "You never wanted to win."

"No. I wanted you."

"You didn't feel that way before," he reminded her. "You made it very clear you didn't want us to be more than just friends, if that."

"Yeah, well, I changed my mind."

"Why?"

"Because," she shrugged her shoulder. "You're cute."

"I'm cute, huh?"

"Yeah."

Justin sprung up, grabbed Alex by the hand, pulled her up, and slung her over his shoulder. Alex let out a short shriek.

"I am cute," he agreed as he began to carry her through the kitchen. "I also think it's my turn."

"Justin! Where are you taking me?"

"To bed. We're going to do this my way now."

He carried her down the hall, through his bedroom door, flung her on his bed, and immediately pounced on her to get her nipple back in his mouth.

They did not leave the room for a long, long time.

Justin was surprised when Alex argued with him about him giving her a ride home.

"What did you think, I was just going to hand you some cab fare?" He asked, raising his voice at her.

"I don't need you to pay for it," she snapped. Lowering her voice she added, "I just don't want to put you out. You're already home. You don't need to go out again just to take me."

"I'm driving you home, Alex, and that's it, so just shut up about it."

"God you can be such an asshole!"

"I don't think this constitutes as asshole behavior," he said, trying to sound reasonable now that she wasn't flat-out refusing his offer. "And you lost our match, remember? I get to keep trying to protect you."

She grumbled a bit more after that, but the smile just under the surface of her lips kept breaking through, and Justin stopped worrying.

When they got to Alex's house, Justin saw all the front windows were lit up, and the back gate was open.

"You left your lights on all day?" He asked her, putting the car in park.

"I guess I did," she said, looking at the house. "Thanks for the nice time." She began to climb out of the car.

"Hey, wait, Alex."

She turned around: "Yeah?"

She looked as if she was afraid of what he was about to say, so Justin decided to keep it light. "I had a good time too," he said. "I'll see you tomorrow."

"See you tomorrow." She walked through the open gate.

Justin waited to see if she would close the gate behind her, but she didn't. He put the car in reverse and peeled out anyway. Now that she was home, Alex could take care of herself.

When he was halfway down the block, he caught sight of something shiny on the floor, reflecting in the light of the passing streetlamps. Justin slowed down, and looked.

It was a cellphone. It had dropped out of Alex's bag, he realized.

Justin made a tight U-turn in the middle of the street and began to coast back to Alex's house. Alex's bag, and its contents, were very important to her; he did not want her wondering where something had gone.

But to his surprise, as he drove up the street, he saw a lone figure walking at a clipped pace in the same direction, about a hundred yards ahead.

Justin would know those legs and that hair anywhere. It was Alex.

Why was she walking away from her house?

He was already rolling down his window, about to yell out as soon as he was close enough to get her attention, when Alex turned the next corner.

She was going somewhere with purpose...and she was going fast.

Where the hell was she going?

A bad feeling was beginning to ball up somewhere low in Justin's belly. He slowed to a crawl, staying well behind her, while keeping her clear in his view.

Alex didn't look back. He managed to follow her down half a dozen blocks, keeping her in his sight without her once turning around.

After about fifteen minutes, Alex finally slowed. They entered a townhouse complex. It looked upscale and modern, but the alleys were narrow and poorly lit. Alex went into one of the lined alleys, pulled out a key, and walked up to a door with a large letter "D" on it.

She unlocked the door and went inside.

Seeing that, Justin wheeled the car to the curb, put it in park, killed the engine, turned off the lights, and sat.

This was Alex's place. Not that house on the other side of the neighborhood, not the place she had shown him before.

She had lied to him about her address. Why?

And what else was she lying about?

CHAPTER SEVEN

ALEX CAME INTO THE STORE the next morning all bright and smiling.

Her smile faded when she saw Justin's face. She slowed as she approached the counter where he stood. As she pulled her bag away from her shoulder and pushed it under the counter, Justin continued to stare at her, eyes fuming.

"Jesus, Justin, what the hell happened to you?" She finally asked.

"Oh, don't get all scared," Adam said, coming out from behind the curtain. "This is actually Justin's normal expression. He's just been hiding it from you. You should feel honored he feels so comfortable around you now he can show you his *real* face."

Adam laughed at his own joke, but Alex did not. She stared back at Justin, clearly growing annoyed.

"Are you going to tell me what's really going on?" She snapped.

"I could ask you the same thing," he said.

"Nothing's going on with me," she said. "I'm fine. I thought we both had a good time last night."

"Last night? What happened last night?"

Adam asked.

Neither of them replied.

"Were you okay once you got home?" Justin asked her, his voice deceptively calm. "No, I don't know, *induced guilt?*"

"I don't feel guilty about anything we did," Alex said. Then, cautiously: "Do you?"

"No," Justin replied. "I did nothing that would make me feel guilty."

"I didn't do anything that would make me feel guilty, either."

"Oh, really?"

"Is this about me throwing the fight? Are you mad about that?"

Justin slowly shook his head, his face turning stern. "You and I have unfinished business," he said. "But now is not the time. There are some unopened boxes in the back. Please inventory them."

Adam horned in, "So she has free access to the backroom stuff now? You showed her last night—"

"Now is not the time, Adam," Justin said. "Let's get to work."

The day dragged. Justin spent a good chunk of the day working in the back, away from both Adam and Alex. For lunch, he asked Adam to pick him up a sandwich, and ate it in the backroom by himself.

When he came out to talk to Adam, he wouldn't look at Alex at all.

Adam tried to coax Alex to talk about whatever it was that had happened after he'd gone home the night before, but Alex was her usual tight-lipped self. She wouldn't tell Adam anything except "go ask the boss."

By closing time, Alex looked just as mad as Justin did. Adam, sensing the battlefield was about to get bloody, made a quick escape.

Justin came out of the backroom as soon as he heard Adam leave.

"Get your things," he said. "You're coming home with me."

"Why?" She asked. "And why are you so angry with me? What did I do?"

"Just get your fucking bag," he said. "Unless you're afraid."

"I'm not afraid of you, Justin Baker," she said. "You want a repeat of last night, that's fine with me. I've got my handcuffs in my bag."

"Whatever you want to bring with you, Alex," he said, giving her a cold smile that made the hairs on the back of her neck stand up, "is fine with me. Just get it and let's go."

Alex got her bag from under the register, beginning to wonder for the first time if going with Justin back to his place was a bad idea. But she realized she didn't really have a choice. She had to know why Justin was so angry with her.

Justin drove to his house in silence, and Alex, sitting next to him, did not try to engage him in conversation anymore. She had a feeling whatever it was that was bugging him, she would find out soon enough.

Once they were inside his house, he still wouldn't talk to her. Anxiety began to fill her chest, making her heart beat faster. She didn't like it.

"You mind telling me now what's going on?" She said, her ire sharp in her voice.

"In the family room," he said, motioning her that way. When she didn't move, he walked past her. Alex followed, feeling her need to know overshadowing any sense of fear or dread. Alex liked to be in control—most of the time—and she couldn't control what she didn't know.

When she got to the family room, Justin was already standing in the middle of the square pad, shoes off, shirt off. His arms were at his sides, but his back was stiff, and he watched her come into the room with narrow, unblinking eyes. Eyes like a vulture, she thought.

"You didn't fight fair with me last night," he said. "I'm beginning to think you've never fought fair with me."

"What is that supposed to mean?"

"You and I are going to spar again, and this time, you're going to give me your all. You'll need to, because the stakes are going to be much higher."

Her own eyes narrowed to match his. "What kind of stakes are we talking about?"

He shook his head. "Not telling you yet. You have to fight to find out."

"That's not fair, Justin," she said. "I should get to know what I'm fighting for."

"So should I," he murmured, giving her a piercing look that made her skin tighten all over her body. "That's the point. We fight, I win, and you give me what I demand."

"You expect me to agree to give in without knowing

what your demand is?"

"That's the deal."

"What if you win and I don't give in?"

"I trust you enough not to renege on a deal once you agree to it." He tilted his head and said quietly, "Should I not?"

She crossed her arms, letting out a rumble of frustration. "What if I win?" She said. "What do I get?"

"You won't win."

She believed him. "Then why should I fight? Why shouldn't I just go home?"

"Because, Alex," Justin said, "if you do, there is no chance for us anymore. I have a feeling you thought— just like me—that last night was the beginning of something real between us. But if you walk out now, all that goes away. You will be my employee, and I will be your boss, but that'll be it."

"What the fuck, Justin?" Alex could feel the heat threatening in the back of her eyes. "What is going on with you? Why are you being like this?"

"Fight me, and find out," he said. "Or don't. It's up to you."

Alex had no choice. She could not walk away from a fight, and she certainly could not walk away from finding out what was really going on in Justin's head. And because she wasn't the kind of person to lie to herself for long, she also knew she had to fight to save her relationship with Justin.

Over the last couple weeks, she had stopped resisting the power he had over her, and after last night, she knew it was too late to pretend she could keep Justin at arm's length. He was there, in her head, in her quiet thoughts, in her spaces between. Justin was something special. She would not walk away so easily.

Not this time.

Her silence gave him his answer, and Justin gave her a single nod. Then, to her confusion, he began to take off his pants.

"What are you doing?"

"You saw it all last night, right?" He flung his pants over the weight machine. "The pants restrict my movements."

He made no move to take off his boxers, thank God. It was hard enough keeping her thoughts together at the sight of Justin standing there feet apart, arms crossed, eyes glowing with anger. They glowed just that way last night, when they were staring at her in passion.

Two could play at this game. Crossing her arms around her, Alex began to lift her t-shirt off her head, feeling her hair pull away from her neck and cascade down her back once the shirt was off.

As Justin watched, Alex unfastened her pants and peeled them off her rounded hips. She shimmied them down to her ankles, and when they were a pool around her feet, she kicked them across the floor.

"Should I take off my bra, too? Make it fair?"

"Up to you, Alex."

She had been hoping to see some kind of passion in his eyes, but there was nothing there, nothing but anger and hurt. Only the slight bulge in his boxers was any indication her nakedness was getting to him in any way...but not enough to distract him from whatever it was he was trying to get out of her from this brawl, she thought.

She balled up her fists and spread her feet. "Let's go," she said.

Justin put his arms up, shielding his face, and began to stalk her in their tight space. He did not say another word. They were both silent after that, focusing all their attention on each other.

Alex threw the first punch. Justin blocked it with his arm—hard. The impact made Alex's arm ache, but she ignored it. She threw another punch. This time, Justin grabbed it, twisted her arm around, and threw her to the ground. He gave her time to get up, but his lips pressed into a hard line, and his expression said clearly: *stop fucking around.*

So she did. Alex came at him with everything she had, starting with a swift kick to the chest.

The kick knocked the wind out of him, but Alex gave him no time to recover. She punched him in the ribs, making his lungs spasm up, and before he could get his breath back, she slammed her heel into his stomach, twisting to jab him with her foot again.

Alex had fought a lot of people in her life. She had known, from the beginning of this fight, that her best bet was to keep Justin on the defensive, force him to react to her attacks, so he couldn't get in any of his own.

She thought if she could just get in one more good solid kick, Justin would be in trouble. She could wrestle him to the ground, go after his pressure points, and make him tap out.

But Justin didn't need any recovery time between her kicks. Acting on the instinct of a practiced fighter, he flung out his arm, blocked her foot, and swung it high. Alex was unbalanced just long enough for him to get in his own punch to her side.

That one hurt like a son of a bitch.

In her moment of shock, he grabbed her by the hair, pulled her toward him, flung her to the ground...and slapped her on the ass.

"Hey!" She cried. She rose up on her hands, but Justin dug his fingers into her hair and pulled it tight to keep her still. He slapped her ass again, right beneath the hem of her underwear. A crimson outline of his hand began to form across her skin.

Alex reached her hand behind her head to try to pry his fingers away from her hair. "That's not fair!" She cried.

"When have you ever fought fair?" Justin growled into her ear.

He pulled her hair tighter. Alex howled. Justin slapped her ass again, hard enough that she would have been pushed forward if he hadn't been grabbing her hair.

Justin began to pepper her ass with hard, resounding slaps. Alex wiggled and shrieked, trying desperately to disengage his fingers from her scalp.

"You lied to me yesterday," he said, raising his voice above the steady stream of smacks. "You've been lying to me all along."

"What are you fucking talking about?" She yelled. She tried to kick back with her heels, but Justin just shifted away and spanked her harder.

"You don't live in that house," he said. "I saw you walk home—to your *real* home. Why have you been lying to me this whole time?"

For a second, Alex stopped her struggling, and in her shock, her grip on his fingers loosened. Justin took the opportunity to pull her into a more secure position across his lap and pin her hips down before he started spanking her ass again.

"Do you know how concerned I was when I realized you walked home the other night, when I thought I had safely dropped you off at home?" He yelled. Her panties were beginning to shift across her ass, and Justin decided they were in the way. In one fluid movement, he yanked them down across her knees.

"Justin, stop it!" Alex cried.

"No," he said, bringing his palm down against her bare ass hard enough to sting his own hand. Alex screamed. "You deserve this for lying to me."

"You can't just spank me like a—like a—"

"Like a bad girl?" Justin's hand rose and fell in quick succession, pounding away at Alex's blushing butt, making her thighs quiver and her hips shake. She didn't know it, but in her struggle to get away, she was rubbing her crotch against his leg. Justin could feel her moist heat, radiating from her core. "Bad girls deserve to get a spanking, and that's what you'll get!"

"I am not a bad girl!" She screamed.

There was something in her tone, a shrill desperation that made Justin stop his hand mid-air. Alex propelled her body sideways, hard, determined to get away, and

Justin let go of her hair so it wouldn't get ripped out of her skull; she was that determined.

She quickly made it to her feet, and Justin did the same. As she retreated away from him, she pulled up her panties. "I am not a bad girl!" She cried again. Justin was shocked to see tears pooling in her eyes. "You take that back!"

Justin, keeping his distance now, paused to study her. Some drastic change had happened inside Alex: she was more than just hurt by his choice of words, he realized. Alex was suffering in a way Justin, for the life of him, could not have foreseen. He had triggered something within her he had not meant to.

It was time for damage control.

"I take it back," he said, using a flat voice meant to calm her down. "You're not a bad girl."

"I'm not," she whined. Her voice quivered, and a single hot tear began to fall down her left cheek. She wiped it away with the pad of her thumb. "I'm not. You don't even know me. You don't even know me, Justin!"

"You're right. I don't know you," Justin said. "So let's just sit down and talk about this."

"You didn't ask me here to talk, you asked me here to fight, so you could spank me!" She hollered at him. Her face was pale, and her fingers were trembling. "But I'm not a bad girl!"

Justin put his hands out in a placating motion. "I'm sorry I said that," he said. "You're not a bad girl. I was angry. I should control my anger better."

"Yes, you should!" Her voice cracked. Justin realized with alarm that Alex was very close to sobbing.

He said, "Please, Alex, just calm down. I'm sorry, okay? Let's go sit down in the kitchen and talk about this."

"No." She put both her hands to her face and did a sweeping motion across her cheeks, looking pitiful and forlorn. "You wanted a fight, so we're going to fight. And this time, I'm going to aim much lower!"

"Alex, I'm not going to fight you when you're like this."

"Oh yes you are, or you'll be sorry!" To Justin, she sounded like a child having a tantrum. "I didn't want to hurt you before, but I do now!"

"I know," Justin said, trying to sound like a voice of reason in the face of Alex's anguish. "If you want, later, you can tie me down and do your worst. But right now, you need to calm down."

"I don't have to take your orders!" Alex shrieked. "You're not my Dom!" Her words were cut off by a wild and reckless punch.

Justin easily deflected it. "Calm down, Alex," he said again, colder this time. "This isn't like you."

"How do you know what's like me, you—" she threw another punch, and Justin deflected it again. He made no move to keep his hands up to defend himself. Alex's punches were careless and sloppy, and he had no trouble intercepting them mid-swing to fling them away.

As her throws got more and more frantic, Justin began to simply duck from side to side, weaving his head away, keeping his hands at his sides. It would have been funny if Alex had not been so angry.

She was crying out her rage as she swung. Her face was a blurry mask of tears.

When she threw a particularly wild punch, Justin ducked far to the right, trying to create some space between them. But Alex went with him, and Justin realized he had ducked too far: he was now standing directly in front of the weight machine. If he dodged to avoid Alex's fist now, she might very well hit the machine, and break her knuckles in the process.

"Alex, wait," Justin said, raising his hands now to try to push her away. Alex's eyes narrowed into hard slits. "Don't—"

Alex's swing cut him off. There was no time to think: if he moved his head, the trajectory of her punch would put her hand right in the path of the cold hard metal of the weight machine pole behind him.

There was nothing else to be done. Justin took the punch.

The right side of his face exploded in pain. His eyes blurred, and his vision dimmed. He stumbled back, trying to collect his balance, and fell right over the bench press beside him. As he tumbled down, his shoulder caught on a piece of hard metal, and Justin felt the skin tear open.

He came to a stop by the side of the bench press, dazed, his face throbbing, his shoulder sending up icy jolts of pain. For a moment, he just lay there, stunned. By the look on Alex's face staring down at him, she was just as stunned as he was.

"Oh my God, Justin, are you okay?" She finally said, standing over his supine body.

"Yeah, I think so," he said, making a grimace. He brought his hand to his jaw and slowly moved it from side to side, but stopped quickly. "Ow."

"Fuck, Justin, I'm so sorry...." Alex put her hands out to touch him, but stopped, afraid. "Your shoulder."

He turned his head to try to look at it. "How bad is it?"

"It's lacerated. You're bleeding."

"Do I need stitches?"

"I don't think so, but—oh God, Justin. I'm so sorry."

"Why? You meant to hit me." He got up slowly, bent at the waist, and spit blood between his feet. "You got my cheek good."

"Your shoulder...."

Justin tried to see the damage, but couldn't get a good look at anything but the blood dripping down his arm. Letting out a curse under his breath, he began to walk down the hall to the bathroom, and Alex followed behind.

"It's not that bad," he said, leaning toward the medicine cabinet mirror to get a closer look. "I've had worse. You hit hard, though."

Alex stood in the doorway, watching him examine himself.

Justin slid open the medicine cabinet, took out some supplies, lined them up across the counter, and began to clean up his wounds. Alex watched him work without saying a word.

Once his shoulder was bandaged up, he checked his face in the mirror again, and gingerly poked at his cheek. It was swelling, but not much.

"This is going to look like a sonofabitch by tomorrow," he said, like it was no big deal. "At least I still have all my teeth."

"Justin, I...."

"Wait." He began to put all the supplies back in the cabinet. Only when that was done did he say, "Let's go in the kitchen and talk. Do you want to put some clothes on?"

Alex looked down at herself and gave him a fleeting smile, realizing she was still wearing nothing but her underwear. "No," she said. "I'm good if you're good."

"Oh, I'm good, Alex, believe me," he said, giving her a wolfish grin that looked lopsided with all the swelling on his face. Alex grinned back, but almost immediately, it was gone.

"I hurt you." Her voice was thick with contrition.

"Yes, you did," he agreed. "I hurt you, too. Let's go talk." He motioned her forward, and she led the way back to the kitchen. When they got there, he pointed for her to sit in the closest chair, and Alex sat.

Justin got them both a couple of drinks from the fridge and slid into the chair next to her, watching Alex's eyes move back and forth from his shoulder to his cheek. She wore an expression of dismay.

Justin took a swig of his drink and said, "Let me start. I apologize for the way I acted. I shouldn't have taken the liberty to spank you the way I did."

"No, you shouldn't have," she said softly. "But I guess I deserved it." She still would not look in his eyes; all her focus was on the swollen side of his face. "And you were right, I did lie to you."

Justin took another swallow of his drink. "Are you going to tell me why now?"

"Let me ask you something first," she said. "My punch to your face. You could've avoided it."

"No, I couldn't."

"Yes, you could have. You dodged all my other ones."

"If I had moved away, your hand would've hit the weight machine."

She looked down at the table, quiet. "Thank you," she whispered.

"Don't thank me, you were only reacting to what I said. Which is another thing I'd like to ask you about—after you tell me why you lied to me."

She grew quiet again. "A wise man once told me, never a question unless you're ready for any answer. If you ask me, Justin, I will tell you. But the answer might not be what you want to hear."

He took a minute to digest that. "I want to know," he said. "I want to know everything about you."

So she told him.

"My name isn't Alexa Worth," she said. "It's Alexandra Wellington." She said it like it was supposed to mean something to him.

As luck would have it, it did. "Wellington...of Wellington Enterprises?" He asked, his voice raised in shock.

"Yes," she said. "What do you know of it?"

"I know it's huge," he said, "and has connections

around the globe. Your family is pretty powerful."

"Not my family, Justin," she said. "Just me. I *am* Wellington Enterprises. I am the only Wellington left."

Justin's eyes widened, and he leaned back in his chair. "Holy shit, Alex," he whispered. "Holy...."

"Yeah," she sighed. "You begin to understand why I don't want people knowing who I am?"

Justin let out a sound that came out like a high-pitched hiccup, leaned forward, and put his palms flat on the table. "If you're Alexandra Wellington, what are you doing here? Why are you working in my store? Why aren't you in some, I don't know, mansion somewhere, with servants and shit?"

Alex put both hands around her drink, but didn't lift it to her mouth. Justin studied her hands, and realized she was holding the drink to keep them from shaking. "So you know Wellington Enterprises...but you don't know about what happened to me," she said.

"No," Justin said, lowering his own voice to match hers. "Should I?"

"It was all over the news a few years ago."

"What was?"

"I was, um...I was kind of kidnapped."

"Kidnapped?"

She nodded, looking down at the table. "Some guys were after a ransom from my stepfather."

There was a moment of silence. Then Justin said, "But you got out okay, right? I mean, they didn't hurt you, did they?"

"No. They didn't hurt me." There was a pause before she added, "But my stepfather, Joshua...he was killed."

Justin stared at her still form, the dark shine of her hair, the gentle slope of her shoulders, the deep sadness in her eyes. "Alex, I'm so sorry," he said. "I had no idea." He wanted desperately to touch her, but held back. "Did they catch the ones who did this?"

"Oh yes," she said. "The feds had tracked them down to the cabin where they were keeping me. They surrounded the house, but Joshua had gotten inside by then. Things went a little crazy...my stepfather got shot, the house caught fire, and I...."

"You escaped."

"Yeah. I escaped." She let out a shaky sigh. "After Joshua's memorial service, I handed all control of the company to the new president, and I left. It was either that, or live like a prisoner, trapped inside a circle of guards and fences. Living in a mansion is nice, Justin, but when you can't leave because you're afraid someone's going to kill you, it starts to feel a hell of a lot like a prison." She looked so desolate, her skin pale, her face drawn, her eyes haunted.

"So you walked away from all of it? The company, the money...?"

"Well." Her cheeks flushed, and she finally took a swallow of her drink. "I didn't *completely* walk away. I still have access to some of the trusts."

"Wellington Trust...." Something about the name stirred his recollection, whisking up some old memory he couldn't quite place. It nagged at him in a disturbing way, and Justin didn't like it.

Alex picked up her drink to take another swallow,

BLOOD AND DESIRE, SEDUCTION AND MURDER:

but she tipped it back too fast, and some of it spilled down her chest. She flinched and pulled the drink away, holding her chin with her other hand.

"Ugh," she said, giving him a half-hearted laugh and looking down at herself. "I'm all wet."

"Here, let me get that." Justin got up to get a paper towel, but instead of handing it to her, he began to wipe down her chest himself. "So that's why you're living this simple life, working in odds and ends stores?" He continued to rub the paper towel softly across her skin. "You're on the run?"

"I'm not on the run. I'm just, uh...Justin, I think I'm dry now."

"I want to be sure."

He began to circle her breasts with the paper towel, sliding it along the outside curves, holding it steady as it grazed her nipple over the bra.

"I'm not running," she said, her voice coming out hoarse and strained. "I'm just taking a very long sabbatical. I needed to get away."

Her voice trailed off as Justin continued to skim over her skin with the paper towel, until her nipples hardened under the bra. "Justin, I'm sure you've gotten it all," she said, growing breathless.

"I know." Justin didn't stop, and Alex made no move to stop him. He began to knead her breasts through her bra and the paper towel. Alex's breathing grew more labored as her chest heaved against his palms.

"I know we have a lot more to talk about," he said. "But right now, I'd really like to fuck you. Would that be okay?" He let his nail catch on her nipple through the thin cotton, and Alex groaned.

"Yes, please," she whispered. "That would very much be okay."

"Good."

He hoisted her to her feet, picked her up, and carried her down the hall in a cradle hold. Alex giggled.

"You know, so far, not once have I had to walk myself to your bed," she said. "If this is going to become a pattern, I think I'm going to like it."

"We'll see," Justin said, grinning.

Alex was beginning to see herself in Justin's bed as part of a pattern, a regular thing, Justin realized.

He didn't mind. Not at all.

Much later: "So is it going to get weird between us, now that you know? Are you going to fire me?"

She had asked the question out of nowhere, just as Justin was slipping on a clean black t-shirt. He stopped pulling it over his head to stare at her.

"No I'm not going to fire you," he said. "Why would you even suggest such a thing?"

"I don't know." She glanced out his window, then looked back again. "I've never had to tell anybody who I am before. Now that you know I come from money, are you going to treat me differently?"

"No," he said. "You're still the woman I hired. I don't care where you come from."

She smiled. "You're still not going to admit you hired me because of my tits, are you?"

"Nope." He sat down on the edge of the bed to put

on his shoes. "Now go get your bag, and I'll drive you home—your real home."

"Yes, Sir."

She said it playfully, but it triggered something in Justin's brain.

"Alex."

She turned around. "Yes?"

"You still haven't forgiven me for spanking you."

"That's because I'm not sure I do."

"Oh?" He stopped slipping on his other shoe.

"I don't think there's anything I need to forgive," she said. "I think...I think you earned the right."

"I did, did I?" He stood up and walked over to her until she had to look up to meet his eyes. "For this one time, or for all future circumstances?"

"For the future, too." She blushed. "I think... yes." Her face turned crimson red, and she looked down, embarrassed.

Justin cupped her cheek in his palm and forced her face up.

"Are you giving me permission to punish you when necessary?" He asked. He needed this to be absolutely clear, with no confusion or ambiguity that could come back to bite him in the ass later on. He needed to know she understood what she was suggesting, because if she did, he would agree to it wholeheartedly. "Alex, are you giving me that kind of authority over you?"

"Yes. Within reason," she added quickly. "I mean, we'll have to talk about parameters and limits, stuff like that. But I think I can trust you in that kind of position over me." She looked down again as she mumbled, so low he could barely hear her: "Unless that's not what you want."

"Not what I...Alexandra Wellington, that is exactly what I want." He forced her head up with both hands this time, and held her face still as he looked into her eyes. "I have wanted it for a long time, in case you couldn't tell."

"I don't want to talk about boundaries and things like that right now," she said, caught up in his stare. "I want to get used to the idea. I've never had a man in this kind of position over me before."

He noticed the vocabulary she used, or lack thereof. "So you don't want to call me your Dom?"

"No," she said, trying to shake her head, and smiling when he wouldn't let her. "I don't like labels either, remember? I'd rather worry about titles later."

"Whatever you say, Alex." He kissed her then, not gently, because the rush of power she had just granted him felt too good to make it gentle. God, he had wanted this for so fucking long, more than he realized until just that moment. "Now go get your bag, and make it quick," he said, turning her around and slapping her on the ass to get her moving.

She sashayed away, swaying her hips to tease him. But she looked over her shoulder long enough to repeat, in a voice low enough to jolt his senses: "Yes, Sir."

He didn't have to ask her for directions this time; he remembered exactly where her apartment was. He put the car in park, but left the engine on.

"I'll see you tomorrow Alex," he said. He made no move to kiss her, afraid she wouldn't want him to.

But Alex leaned her face in to kiss him herself. Justin fought his inner beast and kept his hands on the steering wheel instead of grabbing her head and crushing her mouth with his own. Her lips felt swollen against his mouth, probably bruised from all their kissing, and her breath was as sweet as baby's breath.

She pulled away. "I'll see you tomorrow, Justin," she answered back. She got out of the car. Justin watched her go inside, gave her a minute to lock her door, and drove away.

She had called him Justin, not Sir, but that was okay. She had called him Sir before; she would call him that again.

Often.

Justin drove home, smiling all the way. When he got home, he went straight to his computer, clicked onto his search engine, and typed in: "Alexandra Wellington."

As he began to read, his smile evaporated, and it did not return.

CHAPTER EIGHT

THE WEATHER BEGAN TO GROW cold. It was a harbinger of things to come.

It started out with an early morning chill. Every day, the chill creeped a little further into the day, until people finally began to understand that summer was truly over, and it was time to get out the coats.

Justin liked the cold air of the morning. He found it bracing. It made his morning runs just a little bit easier.

He had always liked taking his morning runs alone. It was his time to think and reflect, to plan out his day and prioritize his to-do list. But since Alex had become a significant part of his life, he'd made it an open invitation for her to come join him.

Alex never did, because by morning, she was always gone from his house. She spent most evenings with Justin now, but as soon as it started to get late, she would insist on going back to her place.

Only once had she invited Justin inside her own apartment. Justin had gotten the feeling she had only done it out of a sense of duty, to show him she had nothing to hide. But seeing the apartment with his own eyes, Justin could understand why Alex wouldn't want to spend so much time there: the place was downright dreary.

There were no pictures on the walls, no personal touches, nothing to make Justin feel like Alex had spent any time making this her home. The furniture looked cheap and used; even the cutlery looked like she had bought them at a thrift store.

There was nothing there Alex would mind leaving behind, Justin realized.

He was beginning to understand just what kind of life Alex led.

She would travel from place to place, but never get too comfortable, never set down roots. When things got difficult, when things got boring—hell, when the weather changed—she would grab her bag and move on. She was like a migrating bird, only she never returned to the same place twice. It was the reason why she was so well travelled.

Alex never stayed in one place long enough to make it feel like home.

She never mentioned any past relationships, either vanilla or kinky. Justin was beginning to wonder if he was her first serious relationship. He was okay with that; he didn't mind being the first. The problem was, he was beginning to realize he wouldn't mind being the last, either.

He was in deep.

New Relationship Energy, or NRE: that was what they called it in the kink community. That feeling one got at the beginning of any new relationship, a new power exchange, when everything was fresh, exciting, and titillating.

Negotiations had to be made. Limits had to be decided, then clarified, then re-decided. Play had to be conducted. Techniques had to be honed.

And mistakes had to be made. But that was part of it; part of the learning process.

Justin was learning about Alex in stages. It was a slow process, punctuated now and then by deep breakthroughs. She often held back until she couldn't anymore, and then something inside her would give in, and she would surrender to him in the most beautiful and tender of ways.

The raw Alex—the carnal, sensual, inner Alex—was not the brazen beast Justin had been half-expecting. This secret part of Alex, when stripped away of all fears and insecurities, was gentle, calm, and felt a terrible need to surrender.

But it had been interred for so long, buried deep down under a veil of defiance and fortitude, it didn't know how to emerge on its own. Justin was trying to coax it out, bit by bit, and make it stay out a little longer each time.

It was an intense process, deeply intimate, one Justin took more seriously than anything he had in his life.

He wondered how much Alex understood what was going on. It was possible she was not willing to admit to herself what he was doing, how deep into her psyche he was trying to go. But she had to have had some idea, and she wasn't running away in terror, so...there was that.

Adam was beginning to notice the change in Justin and Alex's relationship, the deeper bond between the two of them, but he diplomatically stayed off the subject. Only once did he ask Justin about it, the day after Justin learned who Alex really was.

"So I guess you two patched things up?" He had asked.

"Yeah, we're okay," Justin had answered. "We're good."

"Good."

That was all.

It was obvious Adam had been hoping for more details, but Justin had not given him any; nor had he elaborated on his relationship with Alex since then. Justin and Adam had been best friends since college, and had shared some of their most innermost secrets, but about Alex, Justin would say nothing. Not what he thought of her, not where he hoped the relationship was going...and certainly not who Alex really was.

Alex and Justin had decided that no one, not even Adam and Khloe, could know Alex's true identity. It was safer that way, Alex said; and after what he'd read about her, Justin had to agree.

It was harrowing stuff.

Alex had been kidnapped, held up in an old cabin, and kept there for three days before the kidnappers had finally contacted her stepfather, the great Joshua Wellington, to demand the ransom money.

Joshua had not told the FBI about the phone call; he tried to deliver the ransom money to the kidnappers himself. But the Feds had followed him to the cabin when he'd tried to make the drop-off.

Law enforcement had circled the cabin. When the kidnappers got wind of their presence, a loud fight broke out inside. Shots were fired.

Then the fire broke out. Alex had managed to escape.

Her stepfather was not so lucky.

Alex had not told Justin anything about what happened to her during the three days she was kept prisoner. It made him wonder...but he didn't ask.

Online websites told him her mother had died the year before the abduction. Alex had gone a little wild after her mother's death, travelling around on her family's credit, meeting up with the wrong people, and basically, creating gossip-fodder for the tabloids wherever she went.

But she'd calmed down, cleaned up her act, and had started to get serious about her role at Wellington Enterprises.

Then the abduction.

After that, she'd disappeared.

According to the websites, nobody had seen Alexandra Wellington since Joshua's memorial. The new president of Wellington Enterprises, Peter Ames, now held power to make day-to-day decisions; Alexandra was "MIA."

Three years she'd been running. That was a long time. It made Justin wonder: would she someday go back?

Or would she run again? Run from him?

Those kinds of questions filled him with queasy

uncertainty, but he veered his mind away from them. She was here now, in his life, in his bed, and he would take each day at a time.

It was easy for him to do that, because each day with Alex felt better than the last. There were no surprise contentions, no brewing clashes that made Justin worry they were a mismatch. The two of them *fit.*

Adam, watching their relationship develop at a brisk pace, finally felt the need to say something.

"She's your submissive now," he said. It was more a statement than a question.

"For want of a better word," Justin replied.

"What is that supposed to mean?"

"It means one of the many awesome things about Alex is that, like me, she has a disdain for labels. She's given me certain authority over her, but we're still having fun working out the details."

"But having 'certain authority over her' would still mean having veto power over most of her decisions, and punishing her when she doesn't listen, am I right?"

"Yeah, that would be correct."

"Justin, be careful."

"Why?"

"This woman works for you. She is your employee. If things go bad between you two, she can really fuck you up."

Justin frowned. It only took him a moment to realize Adam's fears were ridiculous: Alex had no reason to go after him, even if things between them went sour. She would do anything to avoid a scandal; the last thing she'd want to see is her name reappear in public. No, she wouldn't try to take some sort of revenge on Justin…she'd just run.

But Justin could hardly tell Adam that.

So he said, "I think things between us are working out. Don't you?"

"Yes," Adam had to agree. "I just don't want this to blow up in your face later."

"Tell you what, Adam: if you ever think things are going wrong, I give you cart blanche permission to tell me."

Adam had not looked happy with the arrangement, but he'd kept his mouth shut after that, mainly because he couldn't deny that it *was* working out between Justin and Alex, and he wanted to see his friend happy.

Alex, for her part, kept doing her job as she had always done, completing her duties as told. Justin might have made the occasional innuendo about his new power over her from time to time, but he never crossed any line; he never let their personal relationship pervert their professional one. Alex didn't, either.

It was like they had two separate lives, one in the shop, and one out of it.

But they were good together. With the sexual tension kept at bay, and everything (everything except Alex's true identity) now out in the open, Justin could focus on why he had needed Alex in the shop in the first place: to get orders out faster. And they *were* getting orders out faster, no one could deny that.

Even Justin's brother Jonathan remarked on it—or rather, he ordered Trowlege to.

"We were surprised to get our completed order so

quickly," Trowlege told Justin over the phone. "Are you sure they are to the specifications we asked for?"

"Did Jonathan say they weren't?"

"Your brother did not say so, he only said he was surprised we got the complete order in the time frame we did."

"If Jonathan wants to actually ask me a question, or has a complaint, he can call me up and tell me himself," Justin replied, annoyed. "As for the order, he doesn't have to worry. The merchandise is as good as always, exactly as requested. I just have more help in the shop now, so I was able to finish the order faster."

"It makes sense then. This person working for you—anyone we might know?"

"No, Trowlege, no one you might know," Justin answered with a sigh. "Nobody my brother can use to spy on me."

"Your brother would never spy on you, Sir," Trowlege said. "He is just concerned for your welfare. He wants you to be happy."

"Yeah, sure. Well, goodbye, Trowlege. It was nice talking to you."

But before Justin could hang up, Trowlege kept talking. "If I may say so, Sir...I would like to see you happy, too. It pains me that you and your brother do not have the relationship your father hoped for."

The comment caught Justin off guard. His vocal cords thickened as he said, "You're the closest thing to family I have, Trowlege."

"Sir, your brother is your family."

"Then maybe you should remind him of that."

"I do, Sir. I'm reminding you, too. It's never too late, you know."

"I know, Trowlege." Justin sighed. He moved his hand up to squeeze the bridge of his nose, but stopped. "Tell my brother...tell Jonathan I say hi."

"Thank you, Sir," Trowlege said, pleased. "And good luck with your new employee. Perhaps soon, you could come home and visit us at the Hotel Bentmoore. We would love to see you."

Justin had gotten off quickly after that. The thought of returning home and seeing his brother sitting at his father's desk, the same desk where Justin had once played at his father's feet, filled him with nauseating bitterness.

But he had much more pleasant things to think about. Things like getting Alex naked and horny.

In fact, he had something big planned for that night. It was a surprise for Alex; one he hoped would drive her wild, and also reinforce his power over her.

He was taking her to his favorite dungeon, The South Bay Spot, for some play.

Justin was a known regular at The South Bay Spot. Very rarely did he walk in alone. He would usually negotiate future play dates with other women while he was there. It was how the game was played; at least, it was how he played. No confusion, no regrets, no implication he was there for anything other than play.

Alex was his exception.

Tonight, for the first time, he would be walking into the place with a woman on his arm he considered his girlfriend—and in many ways, his sub. Tonight, he would not be coasting the place, searching for future possible play dates; tonight, all his attention would be on his Alex.

He would be pushing her resistance to the breaking point, and doing it in a setting she wasn't used to. It was possible things would not go as planned. Justin couldn't see how things could go *wrong*; he thought he knew Alex well enough by now to be able to tell if she couldn't process things. It might get rough, yes, but she'd handle it.

He was kind of hoping she'd give him a wild ride.

Also for the first time, Brian would be visiting The South Bay Spot. Brian's more usual dungeon of habit was Club Sade, up in San Francisco; but since Samantha got pregnant, he was going out a lot less in general. Brian no longer felt the pull to drive up to the city for some play, not when he could stay home and play with his wife.

Justin had been nagging Brian for a while now to check out the newest dungeon in town, and when Brian had heard Alex would be accompanying Justin tonight, he'd relented.

Justin had a feeling Brian was coming not just to check out The South Bay Spot, but to check out Alex, too. Justin wondered how much Brian saw and heard would end up being reported back to Jonathan.

It didn't matter. Justin didn't care what his brother heard about Alex. Jonathan's opinion of his girlfriend was completely irrelevant to him—and that was a first, too.

Justin and Alex's plan was to stay late at the shop,

finish up some paperwork, and then leave for The South Bay Spot together, directly from the store. Adam was off for the night at one of his MBA classes, so Justin had the shop, and Alex, to himself.

He couldn't help exploiting the situation just a little. An hour after closing time, when all the doors were locked and the window curtains drawn, he called Alex into the back room.

Alex came in holding a broom in her hands. "What?" She asked. "I still have to sweep."

"Look." In his wide calloused hands, Justin held up a large shoebox. He tilted the top towards her, but the contents were still covered with tissue paper.

"What is it?" Alex asked, eyeing the box cautiously and trying to peer through the paper. Justin peeled the paper away so she could see inside.

It was a pair of long, black, BDSM ballet boots.

The boots themselves were patent leather, glossy and slick. The stiletto heels were a wicked 7" high, thin and pointy; the square toes did not bend at all. Black laces crisscrossed the front, all the way up, and ended at the edge of the ankle hem.

Such boots were not made for walking, but for kinky torture. The wearer would be forced to "walk" on her toes; balancing would be next to impossible.

Alex eyed the shoes with curiosity, and, Justin thought, a hint of delight. "You bought those for me?" She asked.

"Yup," Justin replied. "Try them on."

"Right now?"

"Yes, right now. I need to know if they'll fit

for tonight."

"Tonight?" Her voice became a high-pitched strangle. "You want me to wear them tonight?"

"Not the whole time," Justin said, pleased by her reaction. "Just for a certain part of it."

Alex's eyebrows narrowed as she stared at the shoes. "Seriously?"

"Yes, seriously." Justin's voice grew harder. "Now try them on."

Alex rolled her eyes and gave Justin a look that told him clearly she didn't like what was going on, but she'd do it anyway. Justin grinned. He'd had no doubt she'd go along with this. She wouldn't be able to help herself.

Alex sat down on the floor right where she stood. She pushed off her shoes with her feet, and Justin handed her the box.

"You checked my shoes to see my size," Alex stated, pulling the ballet boots out from the tissue paper.

"Yes," Justin admitted, trying hard to restrain his chuckle. Alex was now studying the boots like they were sleeping vipers, about to wake up and bite her.

She held up one of the boots with both hands, loosened up the laces, stretched the opening as wide as it would go, and eased her foot in.

"This—this sucks," she said, stretching out her leg. Justin laughed.

"I thought it would," he said. "Put the other one on."

Alex laced up the other boot, tying it as best she could with both feet pointed out before her.

"Try to stand up," Justin said.

Alex tried to hoist herself up...and fell back on her ass. Justin had to give her a hand up and keep her steady until she could balance herself for a few minutes on her toes. Alex wobbled and lurched, looking panicked. She could not straighten her knees at all.

Justin had never seen her so unsure of herself on her feet before. He thought it was charming.

"Justin, please do not tell me you will make me walk around in these boots at the dungeon tonight," Alex cried, teetering dangerously to the right.

"No, I'm not," Justin said, pulling her back by the arm and holding her straight. "There will be no walking required while you're wearing these boots."

"Then what are you going to do?"

"You'll see," he said. "Go ahead and take them off. I just wanted to make sure they fit."

She looked down at her feet. "This is what you call a fit?"

"That, babe, is what I call a perfect fit," he said. "You look beautiful in them, by the way. Very sexy. Now take them off. I'll go get your bag."

"You're beginning to worry me, Justin."

"Good."

They arrived at The South Bay Spot half an hour after the party started, just when things were heating up.

It was *literally* heating up; all the people in the room were creating a swirling kiln of body heat. But that was okay. People were going to get into various stages of undress soon. Then the heat would feel nice.

Justin and Alex were dressed comparatively casual for the party. He wore a black button-down shirt and blue jeans, while she wore a simple white t-shirt and black denim skirt.

Alex's t-shirt was slim-fitting, and tight around the chest; it stretched across her breasts and hinted at her lacy cotton bra beneath. Her skirt was short, ending at the thighs, and revealed her long, slender legs.

Her shoes were flat. Justin had granted her permission to wear them, even though a pair of heels would have displayed her coltish legs better. But considering what he was going to force her into later, he decided she deserved a respite now.

Alex wore her hair loose, and it flowed down her back like glossy obsidian. She had applied very little makeup to her face, but her eyes sparkled under the light, and her thick lips, done up in her signature red lipstick, glistened. As she walked further into the room, her eyes widened at all the people and equipment, and her lips parted just enough to show a row of even, white teeth.

She looked beautiful, delicious, and sexy as hell.

She was his.

Justin stuffed Alex's bag into one of the lockers, located next to the social-slash-aftercare area, and locked it down tight. He was also carrying a bag, but didn't leave it in the locker next to Alex's. He would need his later.

People studied Alex as the two of them walked by. Justin could not blame them for their captivation, but he did not stop to say hi. Instead, he kept his hand on the small of her back, pushing her forward, leading them directly to the piece of equipment he was looking for.

But when he saw Adam in his path, he stopped.

"Hey," Justin said, getting Adam's attention, which was focused somewhere towards the bar. "I thought you had class tonight."

"Hey, Justin, Alex," Adam said. "Class was cancelled: professor's sick. So Khloe and I decided we'd come here."

"Where's Khloe?"

"Over there, getting us drinks."

"Well, I'm glad to see you here. You can watch my scene with Alex."

"He bought me ballet boots," Alex chimed in.

Adam glanced at the large black nylon bag resting over Justin's shoulder. "What else did you bring?" He asked Justin.

"You'll have to watch and find out," Justin said. "I'm not telling Alex anything."

"Sounds fun," Adam said. "But I have to wait for Khloe. Are you starting your scene right now?"

"If I can get the piece of furniture I need."

"Which one?"

"I'm putting Alex in the chair."

"The chair?" Alex piped up. "What chair?"

"You'll see," Justin replied. "I hope I see you soon, Adam. Oh, and listen: Brian is also supposed to come tonight. If you see him, can you tell him where to find me?"

"Sure. Is Samantha coming, too?"

"I'm not sure."

"You're not afraid Brian will report your girlfriend back to your brother?"

"Oh, I'm sure he'll do that, I just don't give a damn."

"That's a change."

"See you soon, Adam," Justin said, refusing to get sucked into a conversation about his brother just then. He smiled and pushed Alex on.

When they were a short distance away, Alex asked him, "What was all that about your brother?"

"Oh, Brian used to work for him," Justin said. "It's kind of how we met in the first place."

"He worked for your *brother?* Doesn't that make things awkward between you two?"

"No, not really. It's like one big happy family over there." *One I was never really part of.* The thought lit a spark of anger, but he quickly tamped it down.

"What kind of business does your brother run, anyway?" Alex asked.

"We can talk about that later," Justin said. He pointed her to the other end of the floor. "Right now, I want you there."

She tried to look across the room, but it was hard to see beyond the small groups of people blocking her view. Weaving her head from side to side, she finally caught a glimpse of it. "That's the chair?"

"That's the chair," Justin said. "Let's go claim it so nobody else takes it, and then we'll get you undressed."

For the first time, she looked afraid. "Just what do you have planned, Justin?"

"You'll see." He gave her another small push. "Go."

The chair sat by itself in a corner of the room, parallel to the wall. Stately and imperial, it had thick mahogany armrests, and claw legs to match. The seat and back were well padded, covered over in black leather. The cushioning looked sleek, but firm. The back of the chair rose a good three feet, making it look especially tall and imposing.

It looked like a throne well suited for a king, befitting a royal estate somewhere, or perhaps a museum; certainly not a BDSM dungeon. Yet here it sat, empty...waiting.

They walked straight to it, sidelining all the people, and as Justin walked, his bag grew a little heavier over his shoulder with each step. Finally, when they were right next to the chair, Justin dropped the bag beside it, thereby claiming the chair as their own, at least for a little while.

Justin looked Alex right in her eyes and said, "Get naked."

"What, right now?"

"Right now."

"Justin, we just walked in, I—"

"We talked about this, Alex. Tonight, you follow my lead, and there will be no half measures. You either make a conscious commitment now to follow through to the end, or we don't start the scene at all. What's it going to be?"

"If you would just give me some idea of what you're going to do...."

"No." He shook his head, never letting his eyes waver away from hers. "Do you trust me to give you a scene you'll enjoy, and remember with pride?"

"Yes...."

"Then show me how much you want this. Listen to me: get undressed."

Justin waited. He knew this moment was his greatest hurdle. If she backed out now, the whole scene would be lost. But if she agreed, and undressed before him in this room full of people, there would be no way for her to halt the action later. Her pride and her dignity would not permit it.

Of course, once he had her in subspace, she would have no control over anything—not time, not space, not where she was or what he was doing. Nothing at all.

After a few tense seconds, she gave him a tight shallow nod, and looked down at his feet. "Okay," she said, her voice shaking.

"Okay? What do you say, Alex?"

"Yes...yes, Sir." Her voice was barely above a whisper, but he heard her, and he grinned.

"That's my girl," he said. "Now go ahead. Take off your clothes."

She began to strip before him. He knew it was not shame that slowed her, or the eyes of the many people around her who were now sensing a scene about to unfold. It was the uncertainty, the fear of the unknown; the lack of control, and deep beneath that, the dilemma of faith—how much faith she had in him.

He would not let her down.

First came her shirt. She crossed her arms and lifted the flimsy fabric high above her head, peeling it away from her body. Her hair, caught in the fabric, fell back down her back as she pulled the shirt off her arms.

Then came her skirt. Alex unzipped it from the side and pulled it down her shapely legs.

Next came the bra. Justin held his breath as Alex slowly lifted her hands to hook two fingers in each shoulder strap. Slowly, taking deep ragged breaths, Alex peeled the straps down her arms. She lifted her elbows out of the straps, never taking her eyes off his as she did. Once the straps dangled down her arms, she reached around, unclasped the strap from behind her back, and pulled the bra away.

The gathering crowd gasped.

Alex's enormous breasts, freed from their bondage, dipped down her chest, but only a little. The areolas crinkled, and the dark thick nipples stiffened in the room air. They looked proud and gorgeous.

Alex folded her bra in two and lay it down on her growing pile of clothes. Then she slipped off her shoes, and left them beside the pile.

The last thing to go were her panties. Cobalt blue, sheer and flimsy, they clung to her perfect curves like a second skin. But they concealed her exquisite body from view, and now, Justin wanted them gone.

Alex took a deep intake of breath, closed her eyes, and slid her hands between her skin and the delicate silk of her underwear. As she moved her hands down her supple, sleek skin, the hem of her underwear went with them, until her flimsy silk panties dropped silently around her feet.

The crowd buzzed with approval.

Justin cupped her cheek with his palm. "I'm proud

of you," he said.

"Thank you." Her eyes grew softer as she stared at him, smiling. Her lips parted, and her face relaxed. She was happy she had pleased him.

She was beginning her journey into complete surrender.

"Close your eyes," Justin said. "Keep them closed."

Her brows shot up, and her expression turned anxious, but she closed her eyes. As soon as she did, Justin unzipped his bag.

Right at the top was the first thing he would need: a blindfold. Made of thick soft leather, it would prevent Alex from seeing anything in the room, even light through her eyelids.

He slipped the blindfold over her eyes, and Alex's lips parted further as she sucked in a sharp, shivering breath. Her arms remained at her sides, but they twitched with nervousness.

Then Justin helped her into the chair. Even knowing it was directly behind her, Alex still moved clumsily, and jerked when her knees hit the edge. She sat down slowly, as if afraid of what she would feel.

She had reason to fear, but not yet...not quite yet.

Next to come out of the bag were the boots. The crowd murmured as Justin pulled the devilish shoes out of the box. He could hear their reaction, but did not respond. All his attention now was on Alex and their scene.

He put the shoes on her himself, ordering her to lift her legs and point her toes so he could slip them on her feet. Alex squeezed the ends of the armrests as she felt

Justin lace up the boots. Because she was sitting, she could keep her weight off her toes, but just the angle of her feet inside the shoes made her calf muscles strain and her back stiffen.

Now Justin went back to the bag and began to pull out varying chords of rope. The rope was thick jute, soft, surprisingly pliable, and dyed a deep red. Justin had dyed the rope himself to make sure the tone and hue would come out exactly right.

He used it now to tie Alex's ankles to the chair.

Alex had to sit up and straighten her back so Justin could get the knots the way he wanted them. She clenched the armrests, but sat still as told.

It was time for the final arrangements. "Stand up," Justin said.

Alex's head darted this way and that, and her mouth opened into a perfect O, as if she couldn't believe the words she had just heard.

"Stand up," Justin repeated.

He waited. The crowd waited with him.

Slowly, heaving with effort, Alex rose from the chair to stand on her toes. Her ankles, tied to the legs of the chair as they were, kept her knees and thighs spread open. She put her arms out to balance herself in her precarious position.

"You can put your hands on the armrests behind you for balance if you want," Justin said. "Just don't sit down...not yet."

"You'll let me soon?"

"Soon." Of course, by then, she wouldn't want to—but she had no idea of that yet.

Justin went back to the bag and got out his most fiendish implement yet. When the crowd saw it, their rumbles grew louder, and Justin heard more than a few long, woeful "ooh"s.

Alex, hearing their babble, turned her head from side to side, trying to make out the words. But the crowd, for its part, revealed no secrets.

Justin held up a clear glass buttplug, five inches long, and a beastly four inches wide. Thick and completely unforgiving, it would stretch her ass to the fullest.

The handle was ingeniously crafted to have two holes on each side, and those holes now had two leather straps dangling from both ends. Coming around the chair, Justin placed the buttplug right in the middle of the seat, reached underneath, and tied the straps under the chair. He pulled the straps down tight enough to make the plug press into the cushion.

Now Justin reached back into his bag and got out a bottle of lubricant. He began to squeeze a dollop of the slippery lube onto the tip of the plug, rubbing the oily liquid all around the shaft.

Alex could sense Justin was doing *something* behind her, but she could have no idea what, and with all her attention focused on keeping herself balanced, Justin knew she would have little thought left to guess.

Working quickly now, Justin went back to the bag one final time, and got out his last toy: a five stranded, black, heavy rubber flogger. The strands were thick and short, perfect for striking in close quarters, and the handle fit inside Justin's hand perfectly.

It was designed to. He had made the flogger himself.

Justin leaned in until his lips were almost touching Alex's ear. He could hear her soft heavy breathing, feel the nervousness radiating off her smooth satiny skin, and felt his blood hum.

"We're going to start now, Alex."

Her breathing grew more labored, more ragged. Justin lifted his hand to trace a single finger down her chest and around the round curve of her breast. It zeroed in on her nipple. Alex flinched and let out a high-pitched wheeze.

"Relax." Justin rested his hand on her shoulder and looked into her blindfolded face. "We've not even started the game yet."

"What game?"

"A game I call Safeword or Surrender."

Alex's lips pressed. "And how do you play this game, Safeword or Surrender?"

"There are many variations," Justin said. "But the rules right now are very simple: I'm going to flog your breasts until you sit down."

"Can't I just sit down now?"

Justin smiled at her hopeful tone. "Believe me, Alex, you don't want to sit down."

"Why not?"

"Because this is a game of endurance. I want to see how long you can last on your feet while I flog your breasts."

"But once I sit down, you'll stop?"

"Yes. Once you sit down, I'll stop."

"This doesn't seem like a game that will last for

very long."

"Oh it will. For one thing because once you sit, I'm going to make you come."

Alex sucked in her breath. One of the things she had mentioned to Justin in passing was her fear of coming in public. Apparently he had remembered.

"Is that how it is," she said, her voice full of newfound grit. "If I surrender, you get to do whatever you want to me."

"Kitten, I already get to do whatever I want to you," he said with a chuckle. "In case you haven't noticed, you're the one tied to the chair." He could tell she was annoyed, and it sparked his amusement.

"You think I'll go down so easy?" She asked.

"No," Justin said. "I think you'll be standing here for a good long while. I think I'll be working my arm off to get you to sit that pretty ass of yours down. The question is, how long will it take you to surrender to the inevitable?"

"It's not inevitable. Even if I sit, that doesn't mean you can get me to come," she said.

He leaned his lips back to her ear. "But we both know I can," he whispered. "You'll hold out, and struggle not to come...but in the end, all your work will just make you come harder. You'll be screaming as you come, Alex, and there's not a damn thing you can do about it." He pulled back just in time to see her lips purse in fury.

"Are you going to flog me or not?" She taunted him. "Get to it. We're going to be here all night."

Oh I don't think so, babe, he thought to himself.

I'm about to send your ass to the moon in that chair.

He stepped back, got into position...and swung the flogger in a perfect slant across her right breast. Alex cried out and grabbed one of the armrests behind her to steady herself.

The crowd strummed.

Justin began to swing the flogger across Alex's breasts in perfect figure 8s, flicking the handle down as the strands brushed against her nipples. Alex set off a series of tiny shrieks every time the strands made contact with her skin; she started jerking, twisting, and teetering on the edge of the chair.

But she did not beg him to stop. She was determined now to suffer this torture for as long as it took to win Justin's little "game."

Her skin quickly reddened, and her breasts began to swell. The skin across her heavy globes grew taut and mottled. Her nipples fattened and hardened, as if reaching through the air for more of Justin's exquisite torment.

Justin obliged. The flogging went on.

Alex's cries grew louder as she began to shift subtly on her feet. First she would lean on one foot, then the other....She was forced to work hard not to lose her balance completely. The rope around her ankles wouldn't allow her to lift her knees. And all the while, Justin continued to flog her breasts.

She began to crouch down on the chair.

"Are you trying to sit, Alex?" Justin called.

Her body jerked up, straight and tall.

Justin began to flog her harder now, putting some

weight into the blows. The strands ached and burned across a wider swath of chest and breast.

Alex whined.

The crowd began to squeeze in, waiting, knowing what was bound to come.

Alex swayed her head back and forth, flailing. She twisted and writhed, trying to find some means to escape the pain on her feet and breasts, but could not. Justin was no expert flogger, but he was more than qualified to beat a woman tied to a chair.

She was nearing her breaking point: Justin could sense it. Alex was quiet now, yielding to the strikes of the flogger, her supple body rippling and undulating in tandem with the strands flying through the air.

She began to lower herself down to the chair.

The crowd held its breath as one.

She squealed and jacked up when her butt touched the plug. "What the hell?" She yelped.

"Oh I forgot to tell you, I put a butt plug on the chair," Justin said, letting up on the flogger just long enough to tell her. "You'll be sitting on that when you come."

Alex's brows rose high over the blindfold, and her mouth opened in shock. "You—you didn't—"

"I did."

"Justin, please, I—"

"You have two options now, Alex. Surrender, or Safeword."

"I can't!"

"You can't what?"

She sucked in her breath and let out a frantic choke

when he hit her again with the flogger. "I won't be able to come this way!"

"That's what you think," he said. "I happen to know otherwise. But we'll just have to wait until you sit down so I can prove it to you."

"There is no way I am sitting on that thing!"

"You will, babe. You can't last forever."

She said nothing to that.

The flogging continued.

Now that his secret weapon was revealed, Justin began to shift tactics a little. He stopped waving his wide figure 8s, and began to slash the flogger from side to side, straight across both her breasts.

He knew Alex would hate that. He'd done it to her once before, and she'd made plain her displeasure then. Justin had tucked away that piece of knowledge for later use; he would now use it to his complete advantage.

Justin knew Alex was afraid; it was obvious in every quiver of her flesh, in the very scent wafting from her pores. But he also knew her fear was not directed at *him*. It was her fear of surrendering herself to his will—of giving up control, completely, in this crowded public room—that was stopping her from giving in. It was that fear he would have to conquer if he was going to win this little game.

Justin *would* win. There was no doubt in his mind about that. But he wanted Alex to enjoy his winnings, too.

Alex's knees began to bend. Justin immediately changed course with the flogger, swinging it up her breasts instead of across. The strands cracked as they smacked into her flesh. The tips grazed her nipples as they made their upward flight.

Alex whined.

Justin knew that whine: it meant Alex was giving in.

Gripping the armrests tight, she began to lower her ass down to the chair.

Justin was careful to keep up his steady rhythm on her breasts. He did not want to rush her, but did not want her to think he was letting up, either. He would continue to beat her breasts until her butt was firmly down.

Bending gingerly, Alex lowered her ass down…and sat on the edge of the chair.

Justin's reaction was swift and solid: he swung the flogger straight up between her legs, right into the moist lips of her pussy.

Alex screamed and jumped back up on her smarting toes.

"On the butt plug, Alex," Justin growled. Alex began to let out a series of plaintive wails.

"Please, Justin!"

"You can do it, babe. I'm giving you time, but you *will* do it."

"Justin…."

"Surrender or Safeword."

She wouldn't safeword. She had too much pride. And really, when it came right down to it, this was exactly what she wanted: to be forced to surrender.

It was the only way she could.

This time, when Alex began to bend back again, she aimed her smooth curved haunches directed over the center of the chair. She lowered herself down...

Down...

Her ass touched the plug.

That's it babe, Justin thought. *Just keep going.*

Alex's face around the blindfold was a mask of pain and fury as her body continued to sink. She let out a grievous cry, and Justin knew the plug must have breached her most sensitive sphincter.

The head of the plug was in. It was now starting to stretch her ass wide.

Alex tried to go slow; she even tried lifting herself back up a couple times. But with her ankles roped down, and her toes already tortured from all her standing, it was impossible for her to remain on her feet. She was trapped.

She shrieked, hollered, and cried...and finally, after a hair-raising scream...she sat.

The soft curves of her bottom touched leather, and she sank into the cushions with a moan. Her body relaxed, and her head bent down in defeat.

The crowd murmured in appreciation.

Alex didn't react; she didn't hear it. She was too deep in subspace now, lost in her own foggy world of humble surrender.

Justin was watching her carefully, looking for any sign of true distress. He knew how defenseless she was like this, how vulnerable, and it was his job to protect her. It was a demonstration of her trust in him, that she would allow herself to lose control like this, and he took his responsibility seriously.

But he could not help himself from taunting her a

little bit.

He knelt beside her shaking, sweating body and said, "You see babe? I told you you'd do it."

She was incapable of answering. He smoothed her sweaty hair away from her bent neck, admiring her sleek beauty and her softly chiseled lines. He knew he could do anything to her at this point, and she would not try to stop him. She had submitted control of herself to him completely.

But Justin had made a promise, and now, it was time to keep it.

Shifting over to kneel on one knee by her side, he reached his fingers between her legs. Alex released a single-toned "Ah."

His fingers slipped between her pussy lips. Her cunt was wet and slick. He stretched her cunt lips wide with his hand and slowly, oh so slowly, began to rub.

At first, Alex did not respond. She was too overwhelmed, engulfed by the heady sensations coursing through her body. Her mind was submerged in the dark sea of subspace.

Justin began to rub harder, pressing his fingers into her hot, wet flesh.

Alex's breathing quickened, and her head snapped up.

Justin's eyes remained fixed on her face.

"That's it, Alex," he whispered. "Feel it." He rubbed faster.

Alex groaned. Her fingers clasped both edges of the armrests. Her back arched.

Justin continued to rub. "C'mon, sweetheart," he

whispered. His finger pads found her swollen rubbery clit, and he fondled it with soft circles. Alex's groans grew deeper.

Without thinking, she rocked her ass against the chair...and cried out.

"Gently now," he said. "Gently." He kept up his sensual, lazy kneading of her cunt and clit, and waited. Her face relaxed as her pain waned, but her need to move could not be denied, and she began to rock again, this time undulating at the waist. Her thighs grinded against leather as she tried to press against his fingers.

Justin complied with her silent request by sinking his fingers into her cunt with each downward rub.

His hand moved faster. Alex rocked harder. The pain in her ass had disappeared in her waves of pleasure, and now, she was trying desperately to get herself off.

Justin smiled as he pistoned his fingers in and out of her sopping wet cunt. Her clit was completely hard now, erect between her folds, and he let it slide between his squeezing fingers with each stroke of his hand.

Alex began to hop her butt up and down the chair, rolling her upper body like a belly dancer, frantically trying to come—but at the same time, not come.

"Come," Justin ordered. "Now, Alex."

His words were the final straw. Alex came with a scream, her whole upper body leaning forward in the chair. Her howl of pain and pleasure did not abate until all breath was completely gone from her lungs.

The crowd remained silent, stunned by the breathtaking ending. Then they began to quietly cheer.

Only when Justin was sure she had ridden the crest of her orgasm to its end did he stop rubbing her clit. His hand came away dripping. Before her breathing could return to normal, he was already pulling off her shoes.

"Oh my god," she panted. "Oh my god." It was the only sentence she could seem to manage.

He cupped her sweaty face in his dry palm. "You okay?"

"Yeah." She put her fingers to her face, then stopped. "Am I allowed to take off the blindfold now?"

"Yes." He helped her pull it off her stringy hair. It caught a little, but she didn't flinch. Beneath the blindfold, her face was a mess of perspiration and smudged mascara. Her eyes narrowed in the light of the room.

Justin, not for the first time, noted how endearing she looked after succumbing to his control. "I'm staying right here," he said, so she wouldn't get scared. "I'm just going to be putting things away. You sit and relax, and when you're ready, I'll help you off the chair."

"Help me off...?" Realization dawned, and her eyes grew wide. "The plug. Oh Jesus."

"He's not going to help you, but I am. Now just relax. Give your body some time to calm down. It'll hurt more if you don't."

"Okay." She was still swimming through subspace, and would acquiesce to anything he said.

Justin cleared the space up quickly. He was not paying any attention to the onlookers, but he knew someone was bound to be waiting for the chair by now. Equipment and space inside the dungeon were in constant demand.

But he would not rush Alex. Only once she was ready did he move over to stand before her.

"Okay," he said, meeting her eyes. "I want you start getting up—slowly. Don't use the armrests for support. Use me."

She gripped his hands, started to pull herself up, stopped, and sat back down. "Oh. Ow."

"It's going to hurt some, Alex. No stopping that. Just go slow."

She tried to pull up again. "Oh fuck, I can't, it hurts."

"You can't stay in the chair forever. C'mon. Get up." He hardened his voice, making it an order, and Alex began to pull up, using his hands for balance.

"Oh ow ow *ow* OW—" Her voice rose and fell as the plug popped free of her aching, burning asshole. She stood up completely, but still needed Justin to balance herself on her feet.

"Better?"

"It feels good to be out of those boots," she said, smiling blissfully as she swayed on her feet.

"Over here now." He led her to the corner next to the chair and lowered her down to the floor. "Sit."

"Mmm." She lay down, curled herself into a tight little ball, closed her eyes, and lay still. She reminded Justin of a sleeping kitten. He went back to his bag, got out a thin sheet, and covered her with it. Only then did he begin cleaning the chair with disinfectant and packing up the rest of his stuff.

When he was done, he gave her shoulder a little

shake. "Alex, it's time to go."

Her eyes opened, glassy and dilated. "Mmm?"

"Time to go, babe. I'll help you get dressed."

She let him dress her like a child, holding her arms out for the sleeves and lifting her feet for her panties and skirt.

As soon as Alex was back on her feet, Justin began to pull her away by the elbow, and another couple stepped forward to claim the chair. It was then Justin got a good look around, and realized how crowded the dungeon had become. There was a full crowd tonight.

He led her toward the aftercare area, and caught sight of Adam and Khloe sitting on one of the sofas.

"Hey Adam," he called.

"Justin," Adam called back. His eyes moved over to Alex, and he took in her dreamy smile and shuffling feet. "Looks like someone had fun," he said, lowering his voice as Justin and Alex drew closer.

"She's a little high right now," Justin said. "Can I plant her next to you while I go get her something to drink?"

"Sure." Adam scooted over one way, Khloe scooted the other, and Justin plopped Alex right down between them. She was beginning to recover a bit; her eyes held more focus, and she smiled at Adam next to her. But she was still dazed.

"You had a good scene, Alex? Your bottom sore?" Adam asked. Alex scowled at him. Adam laughed.

"So you did see some of our scene," Justin said.

"Yeah, we caught the beginning," Adam replied. "But then Brian showed up, and asked me to show him around the place, so we moved on."

Justin looked around. "Where is Brian, anyway? I wanted to introduce him to Alex."

"He's around here somewhere...." Adam pointed across the room. "There, next to the bar."

"Thanks."

Justin walked over to the bar, came up behind Brian's back, and said, "Hi Brian."

Brian turned around. "Hi Justin," he said quietly, his voice reserved. "How are you?"

"I'm fine," Justin replied, struck by Brian's wary demeanor. Usually Brian was the warm and welcoming type; he would offer Justin a big smile and a huge bear hug, not this cautious, guarded hello. "How are you?"

"Fine," Brian said in turn.

When Brian said no more, Justin asked him, "Are you enjoying the dungeon?"

"It's nice. Good location, good people...." He kept nodding his head, but his voice trailed away.

"That's nice," Justin said, at a loss for words. "Um, listen, I'm here with Alex. I was wondering if you'd like to come say hello?"

"I saw you two playing together earlier, in the chair."

"Yeah, it was a great scene. So if you'd like to come over...?"

Brian looked across the room to where Alex sat.

"She probably doesn't need to be meeting new people right now," he said. "She won't remember meeting me anyway; she's too high. You should take her home and give her aftercare." He turned back to the bar and leaned against the counter on both elbows.

Justin, dumbstruck, could only stare at him. "I guess you're right," he said. "Maybe next time."

"Yes, maybe next time."

"It was good to see you, Brian."

"You too. Tell Alexandra I said hi."

Justin had taken three steps before he stopped. He turned around. "You know her," he said, his voice sharp.

"What are you talking about?" Brian said; but he wouldn't meet Justin's eyes.

"I never told you Alexandra's name."

"It was a lucky guess."

"No, it wasn't, not the way you said it. You know her." His teeth clenched. "Tell me."

"I don't know her. There's nothing to tell."

"Maybe you don't *know* her, but you know *of* her. Brian, *tell me*."

"I can't!" Brian's voice rose. With that one simple statement, all pretenses fell away. "I can't," he repeated. "You understand, Justin? I...can't." His face was full of sympathy.

"Yes," Justin whispered. "I understand." His whole body felt frozen, numb with shock, but he recovered quickly. "How long?"

"What?"

"How long was she a client of the Hotel Bentmoore? Is she still?"

"Justin, I—"

"How long, Brian?"

"You'll have to ask your brother."

Brian pushed away from the counter and moved to leave; but then he stopped, sighed, and looked over his shoulder at Justin's stricken face. "I'm sorry Justin," he said. "I wish I could tell you more, but I can't. I've said too much already." He began to walk away.

All Justin could do was stand there and watch him go, feeling like an idiot.

The ride back to Alex's apartment was quiet, which was perfect for Justin; he needed time to think. Alex needed time to recover from their scene, and clear her bloodstream from the endorphin hit. She was still a little trippy, but almost back to normal.

One of the many things Justin found so incredible about Alex was that she needed such little recovery time after a scene. She was not what one would call a typical submissive, by any stretch of the imagination—which made her surrender to Justin all the more precious.

But because her brain was still on coast, she failed to notice Justin's thoughts were miles away, too. They sat in silence, with Alex looking out the window, languid and happy, and Justin watching the road, pensive, but still attentive to Alex's every movement.

"I can't believe you planned that whole scene," she whispered, amazed. "I can't believe it."

"You liked it though."

"Yes. Holy shit, yes." Her eyes blazed with radiant light.

"I have to confess, that scene wasn't my original idea," Justin admitted. "I've seen it played out before."

"You have?"

"Yes, with a couple of my friends of mine, Loyd and Judy. Only their scene did not end so well."

"Oh? What happened?"

"Judy responds to that kind of stimuli a little differently than you do. She's more, um, frisky. And she didn't have a buttplug grounding her to the chair, either. So when she started to come, she rocked the chair so much...she ended up tipping over the side."

Alex's eyes rounded. "You can't be serious."

"I am. Poor Judy went down," Justin laughed. "It wasn't funny at the time, but it is now."

"Was she okay?"

"Yeah, she was fine. It brought the scene to an end, though. A *crashing* end, I guess you could say." Alex giggled, and Justin smiled. "I didn't want to risk that with you, so I used the butt plug. I had a feeling you wouldn't be rocking that hard with a plug stuffed up your ass."

"How thoughtful of you, Sir."

"Yeah, well, I'm a nice guy." They both laughed at that.

He pulled up next to her door, killed the engine, and turned his head to study her. "So how are you feeling?"

"I'm good," she said. "Happy."

"Your ass hurts?"

She giggled again. Alex was always more giggly after a trip to subspace. "Yes, a little. But I don't think I'll get an apology out of you for that one."

"No, you won't." His head tilted as he inquired, "Would you want one?"

"No." She looked down at her lap, then back up at him, her eyes clear and true. "You told me I would thank you for that scene. I do. It was amazing, Justin; just perfect. So thank you."

Her mouth closed softly, just enough for her lips to touch, and Justin could see every delicate line on her plump lips. He reached over, grabbed her by the back of the head, pulled her in, and kissed her hard.

He broke away a few minutes later and said, "Look, I can't leave you like this. You're still recovering from the scene."

She smiled. "I'll be fine, Justin. You know me."

"But this scene was different. You may still go through subdrop."

"I'm a big girl. If I feel like I'm starting subdrop, I'll call you."

"At least let me go inside with you and make sure you get in okay."

"You can make sure I get in okay from here," she said. "And I know you: once you get inside, you'll want to stay the night."

"Would that be so bad?"

She sighed at his hurt tone. "No, but I just really want to go to sleep. I'll be fine, Justin. I'll see you tomorrow." She unlatched the door and began to get out.

"Promise me you'll call if you feel any sign of subdrop," Justin said, watching her exit the car with a worried frown. "Or if you need anything at all. Or if you just need to say hi."

"I will," she said, smiling again, looking half

asleep on her feet. "Goodnight."

"Goodnight babe."

He watched her enter her apartment and shut the door. As soon as she was safely inside, he left. He had the whole ride home to think.

The problem was, he didn't know *what* to think. His encounter with Brian kept replaying in his head.

At some point, Alex had been a guest at the Hotel Bentmoore; that much was made plain. But Brian couldn't tell Justin anymore than that. It had been a major gaffe on his part to reveal that much. The Hotel Bentmoore guaranteed their guests secrecy and anonymity.

Had Alex been a longtime guest at the hotel? Did she go there often? Did she meet a lot of hosts? Did she have a favorite?

Did any of it matter?

Justin was curious, but only in a superficial, nosy sort of way. He wanted to know what Alex had gotten out of her visits, but he wasn't bothered she had been a guest there.

No, what bothered Justin was just how close Alex was to his world, his past...his home. Because no matter how much Justin resented it some times, he knew the Hotel Bentmoore was the closest thing to a home he had. It was the one place he could always return to, despite his brother's presence, no matter what.

And now, to find out Alex had been a guest there....

If she knew just how connected he was to the Hotel Bentmoore, would she see him any differently?

But why would she?

Then why wasn't he telling her?

The questions in his mind kept turning in his head as he drove. Finally, he turned into his own driveway, turned off the car, took a breath, and decided to stop thinking about all of it, at least until morning. It was hard for him to think clearly: he needed time to recover from their scene, too.

He reached over to get his cell phone from the charger, saw the screen, and felt his chest lock.

In the time it had taken him to drive home, he had missed seven phone calls, all from Alex.

Justin had turned off his cell phone ringer when they'd entered The South Bay Spot, as per dungeon rules, but he had forgotten to turn the ringer back on once they'd gotten out of the place.

He punched in her number quickly, cursing his own stupidity.

"Alex, it's me—"

"Justin, please come, please." Her voice was wracked with sobs. "Somebody's broken into my apartment."

When he got to Alex's apartment, he found her sitting outside, huddled against the wall, her bag by her feet, her face buried between her knees. Even from the car, Justin could see she was shaking.

Justin called her name as he got out of the car. Alex ran to him, and Justin grabbed her in his arms.

"Are you okay? Did anybody hurt you?"

"No," she said, her voice muffled against his chest.

"Did you hear anything? See anyone?"

She pulled away and shook her head. "No. Nobody."

"You didn't go inside, did you?"

"Of course I went inside. That's how I knew someone broke in."

"Did you *leave* as soon as you realized?" When she stared at him, confused, he said, "Alex, whoever broke into your apartment could have still been *in there*. You could have been *hurt*."

"I didn't think of that."

"Goddamnit, Alex."

"You weren't here! You weren't answering your phone! I didn't know what to do!" She began to cry again.

"I'm sorry," Justin said, feeling like a jerk. He grabbed her up again and held her tight. "You're right. My phone was on silence. I should have been more careful, too." He stepped back from her enough to peer inside the door. "We should call the police."

"Justin, no. If we call the police, they'll have to file a report, and I'll have to give them my name and everything. Then they'll know who I am and where I live. People might find me."

"But Alex—"

"Nothing was taken, so the police won't make this a priority anyway. It wouldn't be worth their time."

"Nothing was taken?"

"No...even if they did, I wouldn't care. All my important stuff is in my bag."

Justin eyed her bag, sitting on the ground. "I'm going inside to look around."

"Don't do that! You said they could still be in there!"

"I need to know. Stay here, away from the door. If anyone comes running out, *don't try to stop them*. Just let them go."

She gave him a shaky nod, and Justin went in.

He looked around, and frowned. There was not a thing out of place. Everything looked exactly as it had the last time he had been there.

He went to Alex's bedroom, and found all the drawers shut, the bed made. The closet door was slid open a couple inches; he slid it open wider, and found Alex's meager set of clothes hanging straight and even across the pole. He went back to the drawer chest, opened one of the drawers, and saw all her socks neatly balled and laid flat across the drawer floor.

On his way out of the apartment, he took a peek inside the bathroom, just to be thorough, and found it exactly as he knew it would be: clean, tidy, with not a speck out of place.

Alex was back to crouching huddled against the wall outside, biting one of her nails, looking petrified.

"Everything looks fine," he said. Then, delicately, he added, "There doesn't seem to be anything out of place, Alex. Are you sure someone was inside?"

"Yes, I'm sure. You think I don't know my own apartment?" Her voice rose to a yell. "You think I'd be this afraid for nothing?"

"No, of course not." Justin's brows creased as he thought. "C'mon. You're coming over to my place."

"What about *my* place?"

"You can't sleep here anymore. You won't feel safe." He grabbed her bag, pulled it over his shoulder, and held out his hand. "Let's go."

She held back. "I...."

"Wasn't this the idea when you called me? Didn't you want me to take care of you?"

Her eyes widened, and she hugged herself around the chest. "Yeah, I guess so."

"Then let's go." He stretched out his hand to her. Slowly, she took it. As soon as she did, he pulled her forward, and didn't let go of her hand again until she was inside his car.

As they drove away, Justin took a last look at her place. There was no sign of forced entry, no indication of a break in at all. The narrow alley was quiet except for the muted sound of a TV coming through an open window from somewhere down the street.

CHAPTER NINE

"**H**OW IS SHE DOING?" ADAM'S voice came out like a whisper of breath.

"She's still antsy," Justin replied in the same muffled tone. "She's trying to hide it, but I can tell."

"We can all tell."

They both continued to count the money in the register, doing a passable job of looking completely absorbed in what they were doing. Alex was in the back room, cleaning up some of the mess Justin had left behind that morning, but they had no idea when she'd be walking out.

The day before, Justin had decided it was time to tell Adam (and by extension, Khloe) who Alex really was, and what was going on. Alex had been right from the start: honesty was the best policy.

Justin had not asked Alex's permission to tell Adam, nor her forgiveness; he had simply stated his intentions. But Alex had not voiced any disapproval. Then again, she had not been saying much of anything.

Adam had been surprisingly okay learning the truth about Alexandra. In fact, he seemed relieved her abstruse history now made sense.

He asked Justin now, "Is she going to stay with you for a while?"

"That's my plan," Justin replied. He could only hope he could persuade Alex to keep going along with it.

It had been two nights since the break in, and since then, Alex had been sleeping at Justin's place. It was clear she appreciated his help, and for the most part, liked being in his house. But every morning, she would still press him to let her move to a hotel.

Justin had no idea why. Maybe she was afraid he didn't really want her there, that he was only putting up with her out of obligation? He was doing everything he could to dispel her of that notion. If he thought he could get away with it, he'd convince Alex to move in with him permanently. Now that he had her there, he didn't want her to leave.

"I just don't understand why she didn't want to call the police," Adam said, looking completely focused on the pile of tens he was returning back to the register.

"Whoever broke into her place didn't take anything valuable," Justin replied, a little on edge from the question. "She couldn't report anything missing. What would've the police done?"

"I don't know. Take prints?" Adam suggested. "I mean, why *not* call the police? Isn't that the normal thing to do when someone breaks into your apartment?"

Justin just shrugged.

"Just seems weird to me," Adam finished, slipping the stack of bills back in the register slot.

Justin frowned. "I'm handling this, okay Adam? Don't give Alex a hard time."

"I won't," Adam said. "I just—"

A customer walked into the shop, cutting off the conversation.

The guy was tall, about as tall as Brian by Justin's guess. He was wearing pressed pants and a polo shirt, not exactly executive wear, but well dressed all the same. His greying hair gave away his age, and his wide cheekbones and slanted eyes gave away his Asian descent. He carried himself with a certain assurance Justin couldn't put his finger on exactly, but it made him pay attention to the man.

The new customer looked around the entire shop in a single, poised perusal. That calm look around gave Justin a certain insight into the man, and his brain lit up with one word: *Cop.*

Finally, after a few moments assessing his surroundings, the man turned his gaze to Justin and Adam.

"May I help you?" Justin asked, his tone more aggressive than he'd intended.

"I'm looking for someone," the man said. There was no trace of an accent. "A young woman."

"We get a lot of young women in here. What does this one look like?"

"Medium height, long dark hair—unless she's cut it." He gave them an embarrassed smile. "The truth is, I haven't seen her for a while—"

"HOSHI!"

Alex had come running out of the back room, her

dark hair flying behind her, and she now ran into the man's arms, standing up on her tiptoes to hug him desperately around the neck.

"Alexandra," the man said, enveloping her in his arms. He held her against him, and they swayed a little in their locked embrace. "You're okay."

"I'm okay, Hoshi," Alex said, pulling away to look up at him, smiling, her eyes brimming with tears. "I'm so happy to see you."

All them quickly decided it was time to go out for a drink. Adam offered to keep fort at the shop, but gave Justin a look that told him very clearly, *tell me everything when you get back.*

They walked down the tree-lined street, Justin, Alex, and the new man, Hoshi. Justin led the way, while the other two walked behind him, arm in arm. Justin could hear them laughing and talking behind his back, but he couldn't make out what they were saying. He was annoyed.

He veered them into the first coffee shop they came to.

When he turned around to ask Alex what she wanted, he was chagrined to see Hoshi already on his way up to the counter to order for her. Justin joined him in line, and got more annoyed when Hoshi paid for all three of their coffees.

While Justin was busy standing next to Hoshi in line, sizing him up, Alex had found them an empty table in the corner. The two men came over and sat down with the coffees in their hands. Hoshi carried Alex's.

As they went through the process of adding sugar and whatnot to their coffees, Justin was able to surreptitiously study Hoshi. But it was soon apparent to Justin that Hoshi was just as confused about the situation as Justin was. Hoshi kept looking at Justin like he was surprised to see him there.

Hoshi got in the first line of questioning. "So, Justin, tell me about yourself. You run the store back there?"

"I own it, along with the other guy, Adam."

"Ahh. I was very impressed with all the swords and weapons. They looked very, um...."

"Real?"

"I was looking for something more like *deadly*, but yeah, real works too." He offered Justin an open smile, and Justin let his face relax.

"That's the number one question we get when we have people walk in off the streets," Justin said. "'Are these things *real?*'"

All three of them laughed, easing the tension...a little. Then it was Justin's turn to ask a question. "So how do you and Alex know each other?"

Alex turned revering eyes on Hoshi and said, "Hoshi saved my life."

Justin's brows rose, and he looked at the other man in surprise. Hoshi was not looking at him, he was looking at Alex; but he seemed just as surprised by Alex's answer as Justin was.

Alex continued, "Hoshi pulled me away from the fire that killed my stepfather. He looked after me for a while after that."

"You didn't let me help you much," Hoshi said, embarrassed. "You were pretty self-reliant."

"Hoshi, I wouldn't be here if it wasn't for you," Alex said. She looked at him with her wide, adoring eyes, and Hoshi nodded.

"Why were you there that day at all, Hoshi?" Justin cut in, feeling left out of the loop and not liking it, at all.

"I guess I can explain," he said, glancing at Alex for confirmation before leaning in. He said, in a single statement: "I'm former FBI."

Justin gave him a nod, finally understanding. *Not cop, but close enough*, he thought.

Hoshi continued, "I was assigned to Alexandra's case—but I guess she told you all about that?" He glanced at Alex for confirmation again, but she was busy sipping from her coffee cup.

"She told me," Justin stated. There was an awkward pause; Alex was playing with her coffee cup lid, refusing to look at either of them. "I guess the two of you kept in touch after that?"

"Off and on," Hoshi replied.

Another awkward pause. Justin asked, "So what brings you here? Just a visit?"

Hoshi looked at Alex. When she didn't stop him from answering, he said, "I got a call the other night from Alex. She sounded like she needed help. I came."

"I called you back and told you I'm fine," Alex said softly. "You didn't have to come."

"I had to see for myself," he chided her. "You

sounded bad. I wasn't sure if you'd even still be here." He gave Justin a cold stare then, and told Alex, "Now that I'm here, why don't you stay with me, at my hotel? I'm sure my suite is nicer than whatever hovel you've holed yourself up in. You can take the bed, I don't mind the couch."

"I'm staying at Justin's place."

Hoshi leaned back in surprise. "Are you now," he said.

"Yes, she is," Justin said. "But you're welcome to come over and check the place out if you want. Make sure it's not that bad of a hovel. Any friend of Alex's is a friend of mine."

The two men stared at each other across the table, like two poker players betting the odds on their cards. Justin thought he had the stronger hand, though. After all, he had Alex.

Didn't he?

"Justin! Alex!"

All three of them looked up to see who it was calling them from across the room.

Khloe, looking fetching in a polka-dot frilly dress and matching red beret, strode over to them from the coffee shop door. It was obvious she had just been walking by, headed to the store, and had managed to catch sight of them through the clear glass window.

She had on her usual pink-cheeked smile, but her smile faded as she took in the expressions of the three people sitting around the table.

She stopped. "Am I interrupting something?"

"Khloe," Justin said, "I was just getting introduced

to Alex's friend here. Adam is at the store if you were headed that way." He was polite, but laid the hint on thick.

Khloe's focus scooted between them, holding now and then on Hoshi, who looked back at her with a pleasant smile, but offered no words of greeting. Finally, she said, "Yeah, I think I'll go find Adam. I'll see you guys later. Bye."

But before Khloe could turn around, Alex piped up with, "Khloe, *where* did you *get* that hat?" She sounded remarkably like a teenage girl; to Justin, very un-Alex like.

"Oh, this?" Khloe took the beret off her head and twirled it on her finger, her smile returning. "I just got it at the boutique store a few doors down. Isn't it cute?"

"It is *so* cute. Can you show me where you got it?" Before Justin knew what she was about, Alex had risen from her chair, walked around the table, and grabbed Khloe's hand.

"Um, sure," Khloe said, looking at Justin. "They have the same one in blue, and in black—"

"Awesome, let's go." Alex hooked her arm around Khloe's, and began to steer her back out of the coffee shop. Hoshi and Justin could only watch in surprise as Alex pulled Khloe toward the exit.

"Uh, Alex?" Hoshi called.

"I'll be back in a few," Alex answered back over her shoulder. "You two get better acquainted while I'm gone." She dragged Khloe away, arm in arm, and they were gone.

"I guess she wanted us to talk," Justin said, giving Hoshi an unguarded look of speculation.

"I guess so." Then, to Justin's surprise, Hoshi leaned back in his chair and smiled. "You must be someone really special," he said.

Justin's brows furrowed as he said, "How do you know?"

"Alex has never introduced me to any one of her friends before. She's never cared that much about them to take the time. She must really like you."

Justin, feeling much more relaxed now, accepted Hoshi's discerning words with a nod. "I really like her, too," he said. "Alex is one of a kind."

"Indeed she is." Hoshi drummed his fingers on the table, looking as if he was debating what to say, and Justin waited. "She told you about her past, I take it," he said.

"Yes," Justin said. "Most of it, anyway. I looked up the rest online."

"So you know about the kidnapping, and about her stepfather, Joshua."

"Yes."

Hoshi looked down at the tabletop. "You only think you know, Justin," he said quietly. "There's a lot that never made it in the papers."

"I know."

"You do?"

"There were too many holes in the story, too many missing pieces. But Alex won't talk about it with me. Has she ever talked about it with you?"

"No." Hoshi took a long sip of his coffee.

BLOOD AND DESIRE, SEDUCTION AND MURDER:

Justin waited for him to put his cup down. Then he asked, "Is it normal for an FBI agent to get so close to a person in one of their cases?"

Hoshi nodded his head, not to answer the question, but to convey he understood where it was coming from. "The Wellington case was my last one on the job," he said. "Back then, my career was my entire life. I had no family, no friends. The moment I saw Alex come running out of that burning cabin, I...." He paused. "Alex was alone, I was alone...so I took care of her. I did the best I could; the best she would let me, anyway. Back then, she didn't trust anyone very much. But I was an outsider, so she trusted me."

"What do you mean?"

"I think Alex was worried there were other people involved in her kidnapping, people she knew. She shut out everyone from her former life after that."

"Was she right to be worried?"

Hoshi was quiet for a moment. "What do you think?"

"I think nothing I read online makes any sense," Justin said. "Three random guys who know nothing about high society or the banking world, manage to swipe Alex off the street, under everyone's nose? How'd they know where to find her? And why did they wait three days to ask for the ransom? The whole thing sounds suspicious...but they almost got away with it."

"Almost." Hoshi's eyes were cold glints under the overhead lamp. "They might've succeeded if they hadn't waited the three days to demand the ransom. Joshua would've paid the money, and that would've been it."

"Are you sure?" Justin said. "Would they have just let her go?"

There was another long pause. Then, softly, Hoshi sighed. "No," he said. "They had no plans to let her go. There were gas canisters in the back of the cabin. It's why it blew up the way it did. They were waiting to get their money, and once they did, they were going to blow the place up...with her inside."

"Jesus."

"At the time, the whole thing didn't make sense to me, either," Hoshi said. "I tried to get answers, but everything led to a dead end. We had no leads: the cabin was burned to the ground, all the DNA evidence was destroyed, the kidnappers were dead, and everything seemed to indicate they were acting alone."

"Everything except your gut instinct."

"Except my gut instinct," Hoshi concurred. "But we had no evidence, and everyone wanted the case closed, including Alexandra."

"Really?" Justin said, surprised. "I would think she'd want to know if someone else had been in on the plot."

"That would have been my thought, too," Hoshi said. "But she asked me not to push it. She was staying with me then, recovering, and she was so weak, so... quiet. Not the Alexandra you see today."

"It's hard to imagine her like that."

"I don't have to imagine. I saw it." His face drew in as he remembered. "When they released her from the hospital, they told me physically, she was fine. But I tried to convince her to get some psychological help.

She told me she just needed to get away for a while." He looked down as he swirled the last dregs in his coffee cup. "I guess she was right, because she did go away for a while, and when I saw her again, she seemed better."

Something in the back of Justin's brain triggered, and he sat up straight. "Huh. Sounds like she knew where to go to get the help she needed," he said, trying to sound casual.

"I guess so."

"I wouldn't mind knowing a place like that. Any idea where she went?"

"Some hotel out in Nevada," Hoshi said, in a tone that told Justin he found the whole thing confusing. "It wasn't a short stay, either. She spent quite a few weeks there. She's gone back a few times since then, too. The place must be good for her...but why she would feel the need to fly all the way to some hotel out in the middle of nowhere to get that kind of service, I have no idea."

Justin walked back to the café table slowly, holding a fresh cup of coffee in his hand. He had no appetite for it; what he really wanted now was a nice cold glass of Jack Daniels. But the few minutes at the counter ordering his coffee had given him a chance to collect himself, and by the time he returned to the table, he was doing a remarkable job of duplicating Alex's neutral, passive expression that revealed nothing.

Hoshi's brows creased as he watched Justin sit

down; it was obvious he was trying to figure out what was going on inside Justin's head.

"Let me ask you something," Hoshi finally said. "Two nights ago, when Alex called me: what was going on?"

Justin was slow to answer. "She says her apartment was broken into," he said, giving Hoshi a quick rundown of that night, leaving out where they had been earlier and why. "Since then, she's been staying with me."

"You tell me her apartment was broken into, but you say it like you don't believe it."

Justin's lips tightened. "The door wasn't messed with. Nothing inside looked out of place. But she was sure someone had been in there, so...."

"She was terrified the first time she called me, Justin," Hoshi said. "But then she called me back a few minutes later, much calmer, and said someone was coming to get her. I take it that person was you."

"Yeah." Justin leaned his head in. "I should've been the person she called first. She *did* try to call me first. But my ringer was off." He was furious with himself, more furious than he had been before, because now he knew Alex had felt desperate enough to call Hoshi, God knew how many miles away, when she couldn't reach him.

In her moment of panic, she had given up on Justin, and it was his own fault.

"She's staying with you now," Hoshi said.

"Yeah." Justin looked up, and was surprised to see Hoshi staring at him in wonder. "What?"

"Justin, I don't know if you realize what a big deal it is that she's staying with you. She would never agree to do that unless she felt something for you, something real. So I have to ask you: what do you feel for her? Is this just your idea of having a good time?"

"This is the real deal for me, too, Hoshi," Justin said. "I haven't told Alex yet, but I think I love her."

Hoshi crossed his arms and said, "That's good. That's good." He looked away for a moment, looked back, and said, "She'll need to know she has your love if she's ever going to trust you completely, Justin."

"I know. I'm working on it."

"No, I don't think you understand." Hoshi's voice lowered as he gazed at Justin across the table. "Some things about what happened to Alexandra during those three days—the fire, the kidnapping—she hasn't even shared with me. It's why she's been running for so long; it's why she hasn't been able to let it go. A part of Alexandra is still running from that cabin, Justin, and until she finds someone to trust with the truth, she will *always* be running."

CHAPTER TEN

"Y OU'RE NOT MAD, ARE YOU?"
Justin heard the question from his spot in the bathroom where he was just finishing brushing his teeth. He was almost ready for bed.

Alex was in the other room, lying on his bed, stretched out on top of his soft down blanket, waiting for him.

They had been lying down in that bed for the last half hour, watching TV together, and Alex had not said one word to him of any significance. He had asked her how her day went with Hoshi after he'd gone back to the shop without her, and she'd replied, "good." That was all.

Only now, when he was out of the room with his back turned away to her, did she reveal the question that was really on her mind. She'd probably been wondering about it since they got home.

Goddamnit, why couldn't she ever be direct with him?

"Why would I be mad at you?" Justin called back, feigning ignorance.

"I spent the afternoon with Hoshi without asking you if I could first. I kind of abandoned you. You were a good sport about it."

Justin splashed some water on his face, dried it off with the hanging towel, and turned around to look at Alex through the open doorway. She was lying on her stomach now, propped up on her elbows, staring at him. Her flawless breasts were resting on the sheet, half hidden by her arms. Her long beautiful hair lay in a plait down her back, coming to a stop at the dip of her arched spine, where her soft round butt cheeks, barely concealed under her gauzy panties, began to slope upward. Her legs stretched together in a straight line across the length of the bed, and her feet were resting on her pillow.

"Get your feet off your pillow," Justin ordered. Alex quickly complied. Justin came around the bed and lay down on his side while Alex turned herself around to look at him.

"So are you mad?" She repeated, coming to rest on her side, facing him.

"No I'm not mad," Justin said, crossing his arms under his head and staring up at the ceiling. "I understand your need for time with him, and he needed time with you. He needed to make sure you're okay."

"I'm glad you understand," she said, kissing his cheek. Justin pulled a hand out from under his head to pull her into the crook of his arm.

"*Are* you okay, Alex?" Justin asked her, looking into her face.

"I guess so," she said, looking down at his chest

and running her fingers through the soft hairs there. "I'm just...you know."

"No, I don't know, because you won't tell me." He picked up her chin with his fingers and forced her eyes up. "You think someone was in your apartment—"

"There *was* someone in my apartment."

"Okay, but they didn't take anything. Nothing is missing. You're safe now, in my house, and nothing is going to hurt you," he smiled, "except me. But you're still all anxious. You have been for the last few days. So why don't you tell me what has you worried so much, so I can worry for you. Or at least, with you."

She pushed against him now to pull away, but Justin held onto her tight, not letting her create any distance between them, and she scowled.

"Talk to me, Alex," Justin pressed, using his hard, demanding, Dominant voice—he was getting more and more accustomed to using that voice. "Tell me what's going on inside your head."

"Nothing. I was just shaken up by the break in, that's all."

"Goddamnit, Alex, why won't you tell me?" He mounted his body atop hers and trapped her under him with his elbows so she couldn't get away. "What secrets do you have buried in there?" He whispered, closing his eyes and leaning his head down to kiss her forehead. "What are you so afraid of?"

"I'm not afraid of anything," she said. Before Justin could open his eyes, Alex had flipped them both over with a limber jujitsu move Justin should have anticipated, considering he'd taught her the move himself. "I can take care of myself," Alex proclaimed against his mouth, pushing her hands down on Justin's outstretched wrists to hold them still.

"Can you now," Justin said, enjoying her satisfied, impish smile looking down at him from above.

He flicked his wrists around and grabbed onto Alex's hands, making her squeal. Then he forced her hands up to the cold wrought iron bars of his headboard and pressed them against the rigid metal until Alex's fingers wrapped around them and squeezed. "Try to get away now, muscle woman. C'mon."

Alex gave him a look of annoyance. "I'm not going to fight you, Justin."

"And why is that? Not in the mood?"

She tried to hide her face in the crook of his neck. "Because things feel different now, okay?"

"How so?"

"You're my, you know...."

"Your what?"

"My boyfriend."

"That's not what you were thinking. Tell me the word you were just thinking in your head."

"Justin...."

"Tell me."

"You're my Dom," she said with a groan.

"What's that? I didn't catch that."

Her head snapped up. "You're my Dom, alright? My Dominant, my lordy-lord master, my all powerful commander, my Domhighness, my—"

"I don't think you're taking this seriously enough."

"I'll show you how serious I can be if you *just let*

go of my hands." She twisted and tugged, trying to wrench her hands away from the wrought iron bars.

"Nope," Justin sighed, "definitely not serious enough. So we're going to play a little game."

Alex became still. She had learned to be wary of his games. "What kind of game?"

"The kind I like."

"*You* like? Will *I* like it?"

"If you play nicely."

Her eyes narrowed. "How do you play this game?"

"It's very simple. You obey. End of game."

Alex began to splutter, and Justin let go of his grip from around her fingers long enough to swat her bottom. She hollered and jerked, but Justin quickly wrapped his fingers back around hers, keeping them pressed around the bars of the headboard.

He said, "Keep your hands on the bars, Alex. Don't let go. That's an order."

Alex, realizing she was already effectively beaten, shoved her face into the crook of his neck again and whined, "Justin...."

"No," he said, his voice full of grit. "Not another word. Don't let go."

He began to disengage himself from under her, pulling his body away slowly as she sank down into the mattress. But she never let go of the bars, and by the time Justin was able to stand up next to the bed, she was gripping the bars so tightly, her knuckles were turning white.

Her breathing was quick. Her face peered toward his, full of fear and rebellion. She was scared, and fighting her inner need to defy him.

Good. The more she resisted in the beginning, the stronger this lesson would be.

Alex had finally managed to make the biggest leap inside her own head: she had accepted to herself that Justin was now her Dom. Justin had come to the same conclusion a long time ago.

The chemistry between them was too obvious to deny. The label fit.

But Justin had given Alex time to get used to the idea on her own, and now that she had, he would give her a lesson in what that meant...a reminder of who was in control.

He came around to the foot of the bed now, climbed on, and planted himself between Alex's straight, splayed legs. Slowly, gliding his warm hands up the back of her muscled calves, he came around her hips, spread his fingers wide, and stretched them across her waist. He paused for a moment, enjoying the feel of her skin under his fingertips, the nervous energy she was sending him.

He hooked his fingers into the waist hem of her panties and began to pull them down over her ass.

Alex's back rose and fell with each labored breath. Her grip around the headboard bars tightened as Justin pulled the panties away from her feet and let them drop to the floor.

"Good girl," Justin whispered, gliding his hands up and down the outside of her legs. Alex's breathing slowed as she calmed down. "Good girl," he repeated.

He ran his hands up her firm thighs, around her

womanly hips, and into the curves of her waist. Alex let out a dreamy sigh, enjoying his soft caresses.

But she didn't like it so much when he slid his hands upward, into the shallow dips of her armpits, and wiggled his fingers.

"Hey!" She shrieked, letting go of the bars to clamp her arms shut.

Justin smacked her on the ass. Alex shrieked again, though not as loud. "Get those hands back on the bars," he growled. "Don't move."

"You're tickling me!"

"I know. Don't move."

Whimpering now, she slowly circled her fingers back around the bars, and squeezed. But when Justin moved his hands up her body to skim his nails against her sides, right over her ribs, Alex let go of the bars again to wiggle. "I can't help it!" She yelled. "It tickles!"

"I know," Justin said with a smile. He slapped her ass cheek, hard enough to leave a bright red palm print, and then slapped the other one for the sake of symmetry. Alex screeched. "Now get those hands back around the bars," he said, "and take it."

"I can't help it if you're tickling me!"

He leaned over her to whisper in her ear, "Am I your Dom, Alex?"

"Yes...."

"And are you my good girl?"

Her answer was a high-pitched whimper: "Yes."

"Then do as you're told. Get your hands back on the bars, and don't let go."

Mewling like a hurt kitten, Alex grabbed the bars.

Justin began to graze his fingers along her sides, joggling them now and then inside the deep recesses under her arms, and Alex shimmied and shivered, howling into the sheet, but did not let go again.

Justin continued his soft, prickling exploration of her body. He pulled the hair away from her neck and ran a single finger down her velvety neck, around her collarbone, over the curve of one shoulder, and down her long, slender back. Then he put two fingers together and grazed them down the bones of her spine until they reached the tip of her ass crack.

But when Justin pulled up one of her feet, Alex howled, "Justin, don't! Please!"

"You said you could take care of yourself, so take this," he said.

"That's not what I meant!"

"Ah, but this is how the game is played. Now hush."

"Justin, please! I'm afraid!"

Justin stopped. "Afraid of what?"

"Afraid I'll kick you!"

He eyed her other leg for a second; she raised a good point. So he shifted over and straddled her other knee. She could still move it up a little, but not much, not enough to do him any damage.

Still, he said to her: "Don't kick me."

Alex's head came up straight. "Justin, please, I can't help my reflexes," she said, her voice near tears.

It pleased Justin to know how important it was to her that she not hurt him. "It scares you, having to fight your own impulses, doesn't it?" He asked.

"Yes," she whispered.

"It turns you on, too."

"Yes." She buried her head in defeat.

Justin said, "You can scream all you want—I'll enjoy that. But if you move, you might hurt me. So don't."

"Justin, please...."

"Shh."

He squeezed her ankle in warning; then, with his other hand, he began to tickle her foot.

Alex screamed. With her head facing the headboard, she howled like a wounded tiger, and Justin kept tickling her.

He alternated between her toes, her heel, and the supple, sensitive underbelly of her foot. Sometimes he would dig his finger pads into the yielding flesh, and sometimes he would wiggle just his fingertips. But whatever he did, Alex kept hollering, letting out great wheezing cries until Justin could hear tears in them.

But she didn't kick him.

By the time he lowered her foot back gently to the sheet and came up to lean over her face, Alex was a sweaty mess.

"Good girl, Alex," Justin said, lifting some hair away from her shiny face.

In a ragged voice she asked him, "Are you done?"

"Not yet," he said. "But you'll like this part more. Get up on your knees, and keep your shoulders down. Spread your legs apart."

Without dissident, Alex did as told, but the agonized look she gave him told him she knew, or at least had an inkling, of what was coming, and she didn't like it at all.

As soon as she was up on her knees, she spread them apart. But it wasn't good enough for Justin; with the shove of his knee, he spread her legs wider.

Her positioning still wasn't to his liking. So he pushed her down in the small of her back, hard, so that her chest was shoved into the mattress, her breasts squished beneath her. Her arms were still stretched over her head, her fingers holding tight to the bars, but now, her ass was raised high to the air.

Justin drew closer between her legs. He rested his hands on both her hips. Gently, he pried her cheeks apart, and got a good look at her most intimate, private parts. Her asshole cringed, and her pussy clenched. Her cunt, shaved to a rosy pink, glistened with her feminine juices. Her satiny pussy lips were wet and inviting.

Justin was not about to refuse their invitation.

He ran his fingers between her velvet cunt lips, separating them, opening them wide, and heard Alex moan.

"Are you going to move, Alex?"

"No," she squeaked.

"Why not?"

"Because you ordered me not to...Sir."

"Good girl," he replied, and promptly buried his face deep in the folds of her cunt.

Alex gasped and cried out. She, like many women, had a problem with letting a man go down on her, especially from behind. It felt intrusive, almost invasive, and far too bold. It made her feel defenseless.

Just how Justin wanted her.

He began to lick her cunt, shoving his tongue deep into her folds, swirling and flicking it around the swollen nub of her clit. Alex's voice rose with her yells, and she shifted her weight from one knee to the other...but she was careful not to close her legs.

Justin didn't let up with his ministrations. He held her legs by her thighs to keep them still, and continued on with his deep, wet, wide exploration.

After a couple minutes, he let his tongue trail up, and up, until it touched the dusky grommet of her asshole.

Alex collapsed on the bed. "Justin, please!"

"Get the fuck up," he said, his voice turned merciless. "Back into position, and don't fucking move until I tell you to."

"Please, Justin, please..."

"You're not comfortable with this. I get that. Time for you to get over it. You know why?"

"Because you're my Dom." Her voice cracked on a sob.

"That's right," he said brutally. "I'm your Dom, and I like doing this to you, so I'm going to do it, and you're going to fucking take it. Now *back into position.*"

She raised herself on her knees, keeping her chest pressed into the mattress, heaving, panting—and Justin grabbed onto her thighs again, biting his fingers into her tender flesh, making her howl once more. He brought his lips down, down, blowing against the trembling folds of her cunt, and Alex's whole body convulsed...but she did not raise her knees again.

This time, when Justin pressed his tongue against her clenching asshole, Alex relaxed. Justin could feel the moment she let go; he could tell when she let herself sink into the sublime pleasure of it. Because it *was* pleasure for her—deep, rumbling, frothing pleasure. The kind of pleasure women are supposed to disdain, and avoid if they can.

If they're allowed to.

Of course, Alex wasn't being allowed to: Justin was forcing her to experience the thrilling ecstasy of a full, lengthy, blissful rimming out, and now that she had accepted that fact, she was enjoying every second of it.

Justin teased her asshole with deft ease, making her whole body quiver and ripple in response. She started to lean back onto his face, only a little, only an inch, but pulled herself away as soon as she realized what she was doing, afraid she had gone too far.

Justin squeezed her by the hips and pulled her onto his face. His tongue swirled against the ring of her asshole, and trailed down to the opening of her cunt, lathering her skin, opening up her peach flesh. He got a full taste of her juices.

By the time he pulled away, Justin's mouth was a mess of Alex's pearly liquid, and Alex was a mess of desperate, ravenous desire. When she no longer felt his lips and tongue against her tingling, nerve-rich flesh, she began to mewl like a starved kitten, begging for a handout.

Justin thrust two stiff fingers into her sopping cunt, and began pistoning them in and out of her deep recesses. After just a few short thrusts, his fingers were wet, dripping from her arousal.

He brought his fingers up to her face.

"Open your mouth," he said.

Dutifully, Alex opened her flushed, full mouth. Justin slid his fingers inside, and Alex began to suck them, hard, using the entire length of her tongue. She gazed at him through half-lidded, spellbinding eyes, and Justin could feel her tongue pulling his fingers further down her throat. She looked so luscious, so fucking beautiful...

Justin almost lost his load right then.

He pulled his fingers out of her mouth with a pop, and watched Alex's pupils dilate in confusion.

He took a breath, paused. Waited for her eyes to focus, waited for his libido to calm down.

Then he grabbed her arm by the wrist and brought it up to her face.

"Suck your own fingers now," he said. "Like you did mine."

Giving him another languid, dreamy smile, Alex hooked two fingers together and began to suck on them, resting her plump lips hard against her knuckles. She stared at him as she sucked, knowing, even now, how sensual she looked.

"Get them good and wet, Alex. It's the only lube you're getting."

She paused when she heard that. Her lips stopped moving, and face filled with fear. When he gave her an evil, malicious grin, she whimpered through her throat.

"Do it," Justin said.

Alex began to jab her fingers in and out of her mouth, coating them with a thick layer of saliva. When Justin pulled her hand away, a string of glistening spit stretched from her finger to her mouth.

He held her arm up by the wrist. "Now...stretch your asshole."

Alex's whimper grew louder as her face betrayed her panic.

"Do it," Justin repeated in a whisper.

He waited, ready for any sign of revolt on her part against this terrifying order, a command he knew Alex would consider the ultimate act of humiliation.

Closing her eyes so she would not have to see herself reflected in his, Alex reached around, dug her hand into the firm flesh of her ass, found her most sensitive, irascible orifice...and pushed her fingers in.

Straining and wailing, Alex plunged both fingers up her throbbing asshole. She started out slow, barely getting the fingertips in at first. But Justin could tell that even now, as she faced her darkest, most shameful degradation, her body was responding to the lasciviousness of it, the wanton, depraved lust that was pumping her blood and taking over her mind.

Her seditious asshole did not clamp shut in an attempt to resist her fingers; no, it relaxed completely under the assault, allowing her wet slender knuckles to ram right through, until they had completely disappeared into her tight hot channel.

Her eyes squeezed shut, and she let out a long, plaintive moan. "Justin," she said in a throaty plea. "Justin."

Her husky appeal was his undoing. Justin pulled off his pants, yanked her fingers out of her ass (getting a short shriek out of the disgraced woman), came up behind her, and jammed his thick straining cock into her tight, soaked cunt. Her pussy pulsed around his cock in a delicious squeeze, making him pause to enjoy the heavenly feel of it. Alex braced herself on her arms and shuddered against him, pressing her butt back to impale herself further on his stiff prick.

After that, Justin didn't go slow, and he didn't take his time; he pounded into her with all his might, stuffing her up with hard cock, grabbing onto her hips and pulling her in to meet every thrust. His hold was unnecessary; Alex was driving herself back against him, smacking her ass against his groin as her pussy clenched all around his long length, trying to suck him into her, all the way to his balls.

After only a few thrusts, she began to come, shivering, trembling, and spasming all around his cock. Justin came soon after, digging his fingers into her flesh as he drummed into her. In the last second, he held himself still, and felt his balls explode up her scorching cunt that seemed to want to milk his cock until every drop of his come had been siphoned off.

Justin collapsed over her back, seeing stars. But quickly, he collected himself, and moved off. He watched as his prick slowly oozed out of her swollen cunt: even now, she was trying to hold him in, squeezing his shrinking cock with each of her convulsive aftershocks.

He slapped her butt, and Alex squealed.

"C'mon, kitten, time to wash up," he said. He pulled her off the bed, led her to the bathroom, turned on the shower, and got them both inside.

A few minutes later, they were back in bed, showered, clean, satisfied, and dressed for bed.

"Still think you can take care of yourself?" Justin asked her, murmuring against her ear. He had already turned off the lights, and was now spooning his body against her back, his arms wrapped around her.

"Yeah," she answered him, half asleep. "But I like it more when you take care of me."

"So do I, Alex. Good night, babe."

"Good night, Justin."

He debated whether to insist she call him Sir, but before he could make up his mind, he realized she was asleep.

CHAPTER ELEVEN

H E AWOKE IN CONFUSION, KNOWING only that something was wrong.

He was in bed, lying on his side, facing the window. The shades were beveled shut, but Justin could see enough light through them to know the sun was only just beginning its steady rise toward day. There was no noise coming from outside.

So what *was* that noise he was hearing now?

He rolled over, and saw empty bed where Alex should have been. She was gone.

The he realized the noise he was hearing was the sound of crying.

Justin bolted out of the bed and ran down the hallway. He found Alex in the kitchen, bent over the counter, weeping, her face in her hands. Her cell phone was sitting on the counter next to her.

He stopped when he saw her, unsure if he should touch her or not. Weeping women were not his forte. "Alex, what happened?"

Alex looked up. When she saw him, she started crying louder.

"Alex, babe, what happened? What's wrong?"

"Everything. Everything's wrong," she sobbed. "Someone tried to hack into my bank accounts."

"What do you mean?"

"I mean, someone tried to get into my bank accounts!" She yelled. "I have a security check on all my accounts, I get notified if someone tries to access my information."

"How?" He glanced at the cell phone. "Did the bank just call you?"

"No, someone else did, someone whose name is on the account."

"Who?"

"Why should I trust you?"

Justin's shoulders stiffened. In a shocked whisper, he asked, "What?"

Alex glared at him through her tear-soaked lashes. "Why should I trust you?" She repeated. "You want me to be honest with you, tell you all these things about me? You've *never* told me the truth about who *you* are!"

"Alex, what are you talking about?"

"You're not Justin Baker!" She screamed. "You're Justin Bentmoore! Jonathan Bentmoore is your brother! Why didn't you tell me?" She brought her hands up to her face as her weeping resumed.

Justin resisted the urge to try to reach for her, knowing it was probably a bad idea at the moment.

"I told you, I don't go by my brother's last name," he said. "I didn't even know you knew about my brother and the hotel until the other night, after we went to the dungeon. I was going to tell you then, but after our scene, you were completely out of it, and I didn't want to bring it up. Then your apartment was broken into, and I didn't think the timing was right."

"Oh, you didn't think the *timing* was right," she sneered. "Is that what you told yourself? You just didn't want to *burden* me with the truth?"

"I didn't realize your reaction would be...this," he said, his voice growing louder. "If I had known, I would have told you sooner."

She started to cry again. Justin tried to touch her arm, and she yanked away from him.

"Alex, why is this so upsetting you?" He asked, helpless. "What was I supposed to do? The Hotel Bentmoore prides itself on providing complete anonymity to its guests. You never told me you'd been there. What was I supposed to say, 'I found out you were a guest at this illicit place called the Hotel Bentmoore, oh and by the way, I'm part owner'?"

"It would have been nice, yes!"

She backed up into the corner of the counter, and all Justin could do was watch her, at a complete loss. "How did you find out?" He finally asked her, his eyes falling once more to her cell phone sitting innocently on the counter. "Who called you?"

"Who do you think called me?" She yelled at him. "Your brother!"

"My...my *brother?*" Justin's eyes widened. "Why would my *brother* call you?"

"To tell me someone tried to hack into my accounts!"

Justin's face was a declaration of confusion. "I don't understand," he said. "Why would my brother know anything about your accounts?"

"You don't know?" She leered at him.

"No." Justin took a single step forward, and stopped. "Alex, I think you think I know more about what's going on than I actually do. Jonathan is the one who runs the Hotel Bentmoore. I have nothing to do with it."

"But you make your stuff for him. All that equipment, all the BDSM stuff in your *secret back room*, you make for him."

"Not all of it, no," he said. "But he is my biggest customer."

"Customer? He *pays* you?"

"Of course he pays me," he said, trying to keep his temper under control. "Like I said, I have nothing to do with running the hotel. Jonathan has that business, and I have mine. Now will you please tell what the fuck is going on?" His voice rose an octave. "Who tried to hack into your accounts? And why is my brother calling you at this hour to discuss it?" His patience was beginning to slip away, and Justin, usually so in control of his emotions, could feel his anger boiling over, fueled on by nervous dread.

Alex's eyes smoldered. "Oh, you want me to spill everything now, don't you?" she hissed. "Well, why don't you just call your brother and ask him?"

"Because I don't want to talk to my brother, I want to talk to *you,*" he said, taking a long stride to put both hands on her shoulders. "Now please, babe, kitten, calm down and tell me *what the fuck is going on.*"

"No." She moved away, out of his hold. "I don't

believe you. I think you knew exactly who I was all along, from the moment I walked into your shop."

"Alex." Justin took a breath, trying to calm down. One of them needed to stay calm, that was for sure. "How could I possibly have known who you were? I wasn't even expecting you that day, remember?"

"I don't know," she said. "But somehow, you goaded me into your shop, you goaded me into your house, and then you goaded me into becoming your submissive, and *I fell for it*." Her words were almost incomprehensible through her tears, but Justin heard them, and they tore at his heart. "I should never have trusted you," she said. "You were lying to me all along, just like everyone always does!"

"Alex, I was not lying to you. I have *never* lied to you." Her tears were wrenching out his insides. "Alex, I love you. Do you understand me? I love you, and all I want to do right now is to help you. Please, babe."

"I'm not your *babe*," she screamed. "You're lying! You're a LIAR!"

"Alex, I swear I'm not."

"You broke into my apartment, didn't you?"

Her words were like a punch to his gut; he took a stumbled step back in surprise. "Alex, how can you even say that?" He whispered. "You're not thinking straight. I was with you at the dungeon the whole night, remember? There's no way I could've gone into your apartment without you—but more importantly, *I would never do that to you*."

"I can't...I can't...."

"You can't what?"

"I can't be here right now," she stated, her voice hoarse and low. "I need to go."

"Alex, wait."

"Don't touch me." He had tried to grab her shoulder again, and she jerked away, her face full of rage. Justin had never seen her look at him like that, and it terrified him. "Don't ever touch me again," she said.

"Alex, would you just please fucking calm down!"

Without saying another word, she grabbed her cell phone from the counter and strode out of the room. A second later, Justin heard the front door swing open, then slam shut.

"FUCK!" He yelled.

His temper finally exploded; he walked over to the punching bag and gave it a few solid blows, until he realized the red smudges appearing on the bag were his own blood.

It did no good anyway.

Alex was gone.

Gone, where?

It took Justin a few minutes to get his impotent rage under control.

He *had* to keep calm. Alex was letting her fear get the better of her, and she was acting recklessly. He needed to rein her in before she did something stupid. If she could not control herself, he would have to do it for her.

That was part of his job as her Dom…even if she didn't see it that way at the moment.

Being a Dom didn't just mean ordering a woman around in the bedroom and making her do sexy kinky things for his pleasure, Justin knew. It meant carrying the weight of the relationship when times got tough, and having the grit to see things through. It was one of the reasons why Justin had never wanted to be anyone's Dom before: he never found a woman worth the heavy responsibility.

But things were different now. Alex was his sub, whether she wanted to remember that fact at the moment or not, and Justin knew he had better get a fucking handle on things, or Alex would end up in some serious trouble.

The first thing to do was to figure out where the hell she'd gone. She'd left the house wearing nothing but a pair of old yoga shorts and one of his oversized t-shirts. Had she slipped on a pair of flip-flops on her way out the door? God damn it, was she even wearing shoes?

Justin grabbed his keys and was about to put on his own shoes to go looking for her on foot when his cell phone rang. It was a blocked number, but he answered it anyway, hoping it was Alex.

It wasn't, but still a welcome voice all the same.

"Hoshi, please tell me you know where Alex is," Justin said as soon as Hoshi had identified himself.

"She just called me," Hoshi answered. "I'm in my car, I'm on my way to pick her up. She sounds worse than I've ever heard her. Justin, what the hell is going on?"

"We had an argument—but that's not what's

important right now. What's important right now is that someone tried to hack into Alex's bank accounts, and she doesn't feel safe."

"Someone tried to hack into her accounts? How does she know?"

"That's a long story," Justin said, wishing he knew the whole thing himself. "The point is, Alex is in flight mode. I need you to stay with her and keep her safe."

"That goes without asking."

"Thank you."

"Justin, why isn't she with you?"

Justin closed his eyes. "She doesn't trust me right now," he said. "She thinks I've been lying to her about a few things."

There was a pause. Then Hoshi asked, "Have you?"

"No," Justin said, "but there are some things I definitely should have told her before about my past."

"You sound like Alex," Hoshi said with a sigh. "You two could take a lesson from each other."

"I fucked up," Justin said. "But I'm not going to let Alex get hurt by my mistake. I need to figure out what to do, but until then, can you keep Alex with you? Don't let her go anywhere alone. She's not thinking clearly right now."

"I can do that for a little while," Hoshi allowed. "But for how long depends. Does she have her bag on her?"

Justin strode into the bedroom, looked in the far corner, and said with relief, "No: it's here. I'm looking at it."

"Good," Hoshi said. "Alex never leaves town

without that bag. As long as you have it, she's not going far. I can keep her with me until she tries to get it back."

"Thanks," Justin said, feeling indebted to the man. "I owe you one, Hoshi."

"No, you owe Alex. Don't fuck this up again, Justin."

"I won't," Justin promised. "Give me your cell phone number." Hoshi gave Justin his number, and Justin wrote it down on a piece of paper. After they'd both hung up, Justin immediately saved the number into his cell phone.

He took a long breath now, trying to get a hold of himself, trying to think. Alex would stay with Hoshi, at least for a little while. With his top priority of Alex's safety out of the way, Justin could relax a little.

Why had she accused him like that? Justin had to admit, that had hurt, a lot. Alex was a brilliant woman, one of the smartest people he knew. He had realized already long ago, Alex belonged at the head of her vast empire, running her company; not working in his little street-front shop, sweeping floors.

She had to realize it would have been impossible for him to break into her apartment. Yet in her tumult, her first reaction had been to accuse him. Why would her mind even go there?

Because she was convinced someone was after her. Why? It wasn't just about the last few days, her broken-in apartment and hacked accounts; it was about the last three years, living a life of secrecy and seclusion. Alex had exiled herself from her former life. Why would she go to such lengths to escape her past?

There was more to this than what she was telling him…and Justin had a feeling there was only one person he could turn to for help.

The one person he vowed he would never, ever, turn to again.

His brother.

"I wondered if you would call."
Jonathan's distinctive voice came through the phone, and Justin swallowed down the bubble of rage boiling up his throat.

"Why Jonathan," Justin said. "Just answer me that."

"Why, what?"

"Why did you have to go and tell Alex who I am?" He squeezed his eyes shut. "Brian called you and told you he saw us together at the club, didn't he."

"He told me, yes. He thought I should know."

"And you couldn't keep your mouth shut to Alex about who I am? You honor all your guests' privacy, but you couldn't honor mine?"

"Honestly, Justin, I was trying to do what's right," Jonathan said. "I thought you would have told her by now who you are, given who *she* is. Brian told me you already knew her real identity when you spoke to him."

"She told me she's Alexandra Wellington," Justin said. "But not the rest. I had to look up that stuff myself. Now she seems to think I should have known all about her from the beginning, because I'm a Bentmoore—and you're implying the same thing. So what am I missing here, Jonathan? Who is she, really?"

Jonathan took a long breath. "I thought you knew about the Wellington Trust."

"The Wellington Trust..." the name stirred his memory again, and this time, it caught on something solid. "The Wellington Trust donates funds to the Hotel Bentmoore," he whispered.

"Yes," Jonathan said. "The Wellington Trust helps fund our programs. It makes it possible for us to offer our services to sexual abuse victims, rape victims, people who really need our help, at basically no cost."

"Why? Why would Alex do this, donate so much money to the Hotel Bentmoore?"

"Out of the kindness of her own heart?" Jonathan suggested wryly. Then he added, "I think it's because her mother was one of the hotel's first benefactors—"

"Benefactors? Don't you mean investors?"

"No. Alexandra's mother considered all her large contributions to be personal donations; when she saw all the good work we were doing with the money, she set up the trust. I think Alexandra wanted to keep up the work her mother started. But I also think it's because she believes in what we do, the same way her mother did."

"Her *mother*...." Justin rolled this fact around his head. "Exactly how connected is Alex's family to our family?"

"Very. Like I said, her mother was the one who set up the original trust, after she saw the good work we were doing." With a sad note, he said, "And she and Emma were very close. Emma loved her like the sister she never had."

"Great," Justin murmured. "So my girlfriend's mother and my brother's wife were BFFs. No wonder Alex thought I would automatically know who her family was."

"We weren't close with Alexandra's whole family," Jonathan told him. "Her mother, yes; but her stepfather didn't know anything about us. Her mother kept us a secret from him all those years. And Alexandra only first learned about us after her mother died, when she inherited all her mother's accounts and assets."

Justin's brows creased. "*She* inherited all her mother's assets? None of it went to her stepfather?"

"No." Jonathan's answer was blunt, with a curious insinuating undertone that made Justin uneasy, but he couldn't put his finger on it, and didn't have time to think about it just now.

"Okay, so I get it now why she thought I'd know all about her as soon as I learned her name," he said. "But *you* knew I wouldn't know. Why did you have to go and tell her who I am, without explaining my side of it?"

"I wasn't trying to make her doubt you, Justin, I was trying to make her *turn* to you, for her own protection. I thought if she knew who are, your ties to me—to the Hotel Bentmoore—she'd trust you more."

"This is about her bank accounts being hacked, right? How do you fit into all this?"

Jonathan said, "I have oversight over three of her accounts. One is the trust, that helps pay for our programs. Another is linked to her investment accounts: it keeps her connected to what's going on at Wellington

Enterprises. The last one is her own private, individual bank account, in her mother's maiden name. She uses that one to draw cash whenever she needs it."

"And you have control—"

"Oversight."

"—*oversight* over these accounts, why?"

"When Alexandra decided to disappear three years ago, she needed someone she could trust, someone with some business savvy, who could hold the reigns on her accounts for her, but leave her a backdoor username and password to access them whenever she wanted to. She asked me if I'd be willing to help her."

"And you couldn't say no, what with her being your biggest benefactor and all," Justin sneered.

"It wasn't like that," Jonathan answered coldly. "I was helping someone I care about, someone who'd just gone through an experience I can only describe as unimaginable, and the child of a dear family friend. Was I supposed to say no?"

"No," Justin conceded. "I would have done the same."

"Good," Jonathan said. "I'm glad to hear that."

His ire up now, Justin said, "I don't give a damn how glad you are, Jonathan. Your plan backfired, you know. Alex left me."

"Where'd she go?"

"She called a friend in town, a guy named Hoshi. He's taking care of her."

"So you at least know where she is."

"Yes, for now," Justin said. "But I don't know for how long. So help me understand this: you have oversight over her bank accounts. Someone tried to gain access to them. You found out, and called her."

"I speak to Alexandra two mornings a week no matter what."

"What? Why?"

"Just to let her know everything is okay on my end with the accounts, and to make sure she's okay, too. She has someone she talks to at Wellington Enterprises, as well. He keeps her apprised of what's going on over there."

So that's why she never wanted to stay the night at my place, Justin thought. *She wanted to take her early morning phone calls in private.* The walls of secrecy insulating Alex were beginning to feel impregnable. "She left her family's business, but she didn't *really* leave it all behind, did she," Justin said softly.

"No, not really," Jonathan replied. "The truth is, she's still very well connected over there. Sometimes, she'll ask my opinion on a business deal, and use me as a soundboard for her own thoughts. A few days will go by, and then I'll find out Wellington Enterprise's board voted exactly how she told me she thought they should. If it were only once or twice, I'd think it was coincidence, but...I think she still wields a lot of influence over there, even from afar."

"Is that why someone tried to get into her accounts?"

"I have no idea. For all I know, it could have been some prince in Nigeria."

"She's also convinced someone broke into her apartment a few days ago. Did she tell you that, too?"

"No," Jonathan said, his voice going hard. "Justin,

if someone tried to break into her apartment, and now her account security is being cracked, she might be in some very real danger. You need to keep her safe."

"Easier said than done when she doesn't trust me anymore. She left me, remember?"

"Find a way," Jonathan said, using the same tone Justin had often heard him use with the hosts of the hotel.

"I'm working on it, Jonathan," Justin said, his own anger rising some more. "So why don't you help me with that? You've known her for years, you must know some way I can get through to her."

"I don't know what I can tell you that would help."

"Then why don't you just start telling me everything you know about her, and maybe something will jump out at me."

"That would take too long."

"Then pick a spot, Jonathan," Justin cried. "Just help me out here."

"Well...I only met Alexandra in person after her mother died. She came visiting the hotel to see what it was all about. I think she was curious why her mother had been involved with us for so long." His voice lowered an octave as he said, "Alexandra was a different person back then."

"How so?"

"She was cocky, impetuous, reckless—"

"Doesn't sound so different from the Alex I know now," Justin said, a small smile playing across his lips.

"No, she was different," Jonathan said. "She was *over*confident. Some of it stemmed from foolish youth, but some of it was a result of having no supportive father figure in her life."

"What do you mean? I thought Alex and her stepfather were close."

"That is what she wanted you to believe," Jonathan said, using that curious insinuating tone again. Justin put his fingertips to the bridge of his nose and squeezed. Getting information out of his brother was an arduous task.

"So you met her after her mother died," Justin said, "and she was just another smug rich girl, in need of some guidance. You helped her out, cause that's what you do."

"I wouldn't put it that way—"

"I know," Justin cut in. "Fast forward. There's the abduction, the fire. She comes to you for help, to heal. How do you do that?"

"It took a long time, and...a lot of people. Even I tried to work with her."

Justin's eyes went wide. "You? I thought you and Emma had an agreement you would never work as a host again."

"We did; we do. But this case was different. Like I said, Alexandra was the daughter of an old friend. She was like family. I thought what she needed was a strong, loyal, father figure in her life. Boy, was I wrong."

"So what *did* she need?"

Jonathan went quiet. "I don't know if I can tell you that, Justin."

"Why not?"

"It's a breach of confidentiality."

"What about everything else you just told me?"

"That was all family business stuff. You would have known it already if you'd kept yourself more involved over the years."

"Fine," Justin roared. "Then don't tell me anything I can use to get through to Alex, don't help me, and watch her suffer all over again. Because I'm doing my damndest to help her, Jonathan, but I don't know if I can save her from whoever, or whatever, is coming after her this time, if I don't have some help." When Jonathan didn't say anything, Justin added, "If you're not willing to help me, at least do it to help Alex. She needs you now."

Justin let his voice drop. There was a moment of silence on the line.

At last, his brother said, "I am not the right person to answer your questions. The person you need to talk to is Mr. Cox."

Justin could feel the blood drain from his face. "Cox?"

"He was Alex's host at the end. He was the one who finally got through to her."

Justin took a long breath. "Cox," he repeated, and squeezed his eyes shut once more.

Mr. Cox had a reputation at the Hotel Bentmoore for being the biggest, meanest, most sadistic asshole there ever was. He was also an expert Shibari artist.

Two things Justin was not.

How could Alex have found solace with a man like Cox? And if she did find comfort with him…what did that say about her feelings toward Justin?

Steeling his heart and mustering all his courage, Justin said: "Give me Cox's number."

It was answered on the second ring...by a woman.

"...Hello?"

"I'm looking for Cox?" Justin said.

"Hold on." The line went quiet.

Justin realized this must be Ella, Cox's slave. It filled Justin with amazement, the fact that such a man like Cox could find a woman out there willing to be his devoted slave.

From far away, Justin heard, "Cox. Cox! Phone for you!" He heard some grumbling, and then the woman say, "I don't know. Someone who has your private number. Should I take a message?"

There was more grumbling. Justin heard static noise as the phone was moved.

Cox's voice, loud and clear, came through the phone: "Whoever this is, it'd better be important. You woke up my slave."

"Even your *slave* calls your Cox?" Justin blurted out, amazed.

"Two seconds," Cox grunted. "One...."

"It's Justin," he said. "I need your help."

"Justin," Cox said, turning the name over in his mouth. "What's wrong? Is your brother okay?"

"My brother is fine," Justin stated, gritting his teeth. "I need your help."

"With?"

"Alexandra Wellington."

"Alexandra...hold on." There was some whispering in the background, more white noise, and then Cox came back on the line, clear as a bell, with "I'm here. I had to switch rooms so Ella could go back to sleep. What's going on?"

Justin gave him the rundown, emphasizing his own take on events, and leaving out some of the business details his brother had given him.

"Jonathan told me to call you, so I am. What can you give me?" When Cox was quiet for a long moment, Justin said, "C'mon, Cox, talk to me. Alex needs help. Even Jonathan knows it. That's why he gave me your number."

"It's not that I don't want to help you," Cox said. "It's that I don't know what to tell you. I can't give you anything certain; I can only tell you what I think. But it's all speculation."

"Then give me that," Justin said. "I'll take anything."

There was a pause. "Alexandra was handed over to me after a long line of hosts. Did your brother tell you that?"

"He told me you were the only one who could get through to her; his words."

"She and I had never even met before that," Cox said. "I have no idea what she was like before. But when I saw her for the first time in my activity room, my first reaction was that she needed a hospital, not the Hotel Bentmoore."

"She was that bad?"

"She was that bad. She was thin; she was dirty. She

looked like she hadn't had a decent meal or shower in a week. She wouldn't look me in the eye, and wouldn't say more than two words to me. It was like…it was like she was in shellshock."

"Wow," Justin said. "It's hard for me to picture her that bad."

"And keep in mind, this was after she'd already been at the hotel for a while, going through a whole slew of hosts trying to help her. I was the last resort." Cox let out a snort. "Your brother always seems to leave me as a last resort."

"That's cause you're an asshole."

"Not denying that. But even I wasn't prepared for what I saw when she walked in the room. I really didn't know if I could help her. A big part of me thought not."

Justin knew how much it cost Cox to admit that. "But you did help her," he said. "How?"

"By accident, that's how."

"What?"

"The scene I planned with her went wrong." Cox stopped, and Justin remained quiet, knowing the veteran host must have been remembering that long-ago scene. It was probably a bizarre feeling for a man like Cox to know one of his scenes had gone wrong, given how careful he usually was. Cox had a mind of a professional chess player: he was always three steps ahead.

But when Cox was quiet for too long, Justin prompted him with, "Tell me."

"My first mistake was using MFP rope," he said.

"MFP rope?"

"Multi-filament polypropylene," Cox said. "It's a synthetic rope. Synthetic fiber rope is typically stronger than natural fiber rope, but it burns faster."

"Ah," Justin said, feeling an unmistakable prickle of foreboding.

"My second mistake was combining my kinks," Cox said. "You know what that means?"

"Yeah. I do that all that time."

"Most Tops do, without even thinking about it. They'll tie a woman up and then flog her, they'll do some tickle torture in the middle of needle play... they'll use different techniques, different tools, in the same scene, and that's usually fine. But rope is different. A woman who's never been in rope before needs time to get a feel for it, experience the rope on its own, before any other kink is thrown in there. Otherwise, she has too much to process."

"But you didn't follow that rule."

"No, I didn't," Cox said. "But the truth is, Alex was in such bad shape, I *wanted* to give her more than she could handle. I thought maybe it would help break her through to the other side. I believed back then having a hysterical woman on my hands would be better than having a numb shell of a person at my feet. But it didn't work out that way."

"So what happened?"

"I got her suspended about two feet off the ground, horizontal, in a Ryouashi Gattai Ichimonji—"

"A what now?"

Cox sighed and said, "Imagine she's lying down in the air, her legs and feet tied together, okay? The rope is going under her, keeping her suspended. But—and this was my next mistake—instead of tying her arms to her sides, I left her elbows and upper arms free. Her wrists were tied together, but her elbows were not secured. She was just resting her hands on her stomach." He paused. "Then I made my biggest mistake of all. I got out the candle."

"Cox...."

"The plan was to do some wax play on her stomach and arms. Shern had told me Alex had enjoyed wax play with him; I thought I was being smart, sticking with what she already knew. Of course, what I hadn't considered was that Shern had done wax play on her *before*. Alex heard me light that match, saw the flame, and freaked the fuck out."

"It was a trigger," Justin whispered.

"A big, fat, ferocious trigger," Cox affirmed. "She started screaming...I ran over to try to calm her down, *still holding the candle*, and she reached up with both hands tied together and tried to knock the candle out of my grip. She ended up punching my arm. It didn't knock the candle out of my hands, but the flame brushed the main line."

"Oh no."

"Oh yeah, and if you've ever seen MFP rope burn, you'll know: that stuff doesn't char, it *melts*. It dissolves, fast."

"What did you do?"

"The only thing I could do. I grabbed the main line with my hand to catch it before she fell on the floor."

"But it was burning at that point."

"Yeah, inside my hand. But I couldn't let her drop. Even two feet off the ground, she could still end up with a broken neck."

"So how'd you get her down?"

"I lowered her as slowly as I could while the rope melted away in my hands. The rope was burning up, but it was burning down, too. All Alex could do was flail around and scream."

"Oh, God."

"I got her down, and then I started cutting the rope away from her as fast as I could."

"You use those, what do you call them, EMT scissors—"

"Shears, yes. They're designed to get under clothes; they're perfect for rope. Never had I cut myself with them—until that scene. I needed to get her out fast, and she was completely panicking…by the time I was done cutting the rope a way, my hands were a bloody mess. This was on top of the burns I'd already gotten from the rope."

"Jesus," Justin said, appalled. "It sounds insane."

"It was. In the end, Alex wasn't hurt physically, I got her out of the rope in time, the fire never touched her…but mentally…she was supposed to be in my care after having just gone through one of the worst traumatic experiences a person can go through, and here I'd just put her through another one. I really thought I'd just flat-out wrecked her, no going back. But…that's not what happened. That scene ending up being a turning point for her."

"How?"

"Well, this is the speculation part," Cox said. "I think...I think it was seeing my burned up bleeding hands that brought her back."

"What?"

"She saw what I'd done to myself to save her," Cox explained. "I could have let her drop, and she knew that. It took all my strength to hold onto that burning rope and not let go so she wouldn't get hurt. Then I cut my fingers up to get her loose as fast as possible. She realized that, too."

"She saw you were willing to hurt yourself to keep her safe," Justin said, feeling all the puzzle pieces clicking together in his head.

"Exactly," Cox said. "I think she needed someone to show her how far they'd be willing to go to help her. She'd never had that before."

She has that from me, Justin thought. Then a smaller voice inside his head said: *Does she know that?*

"So she trusted you after that? She worked with you, and got better?"

"Well, it wasn't that easy," Cox said. "But she opened up to me about the abduction. She really just needed someone to talk to at that point, someone to tell her she didn't have to feel ashamed of what she did to survive."

"Why would she feel ashamed?" Justin asked. "Cox, what really happened to her?"

For a moment, Cox was quiet. "Justin, I can't tell you that," he finally said. "That part is for her to tell you."

Justin's voice hardened as he said, "Cox, if I don't

find a way to help her, she'll be running for the rest of her life—or worse."

"If she finds out I told you, she won't trust either one of us ever again," Cox replied. "That's not helping her. If you really care about her as much as you say you do, you'll find a way to get her to tell you herself."

Justin clenched his teeth together, realizing he would get no more information from the other man. "Cox, just tell me this," he said. "Was Alex raped?"

"No," Cox said. "She wasn't raped." His voice turned sad as he said, "We have rape victims come to the hotel all the time; we would have known how to help her if that had been it. No."

Justin now understood: whatever Alex had gone through, it had been, in some way, worse.

"Look, that's all I can tell you," Cox finished. "Figure out how to get through to her. Make her understand how far you're willing to go to help her. Or maybe you're not, I don't know."

"I love her, Cox. I'm willing to go all the way if I need to."

"Then do it. Show her what you've got. Love is worth breaking the rules now and then."

"Advice on love from a self-proclaimed asshole?"

"So maybe I'm reformed, a little," Cox said. "I'm not complaining."

"Is your slave?"

"Only when warranted."

"You mean when you beat her ass bloody?"

"Is there anything else I can do for you, Justin?"

"No," Justin said, grinning into the phone. "Thanks

for your help, Cox."

"You're welcome. Let me know what happens."

"I will. And tell Ella I say hi...and I'm here for her if she ever needs to run away."

"Ha ha."

The line went dead. Cox had hung up.

Justin stared at the phone for a moment, smiling. Then he carefully rested it back on the counter. His smile faded.

He needed to get through to Alex. That much was certain.

A plan was forming in his head...a dangerous, foolhardy, and basically *insane* plan. One that might end up with him in the hospital. But it was the only plan he could think of, it had a chance to work, and Justin had no other options.

He picked up the phone again and started dialing.

Before the other person had a chance to say hello, Justin started to talk. "Brian, it's Justin," he said. "I'm about to ask you for a big favor. I need your help—"

"I know."

"You know what?"

"You need my help. Cox just texted me."

"*What?*" Justin said, shocked. "He just texted you right now? How did he know I'd be calling you?"

"How does Cox ever know what he knows?" Brian replied. "So what do you need from me, Justin?"

"I need you to meet me at The South Bay Spot with all your fire flogging gear."

"Excuse me?"

"Your fire flogging gear. Bring it."

"Justin, tell me the plan here."

"I will when we get there."

"I'm not fire flogging someone I don't know, Justin. The person needs to give me consent."

"You know the person, and you have his consent," Justin said. "The person you're going to be fire flogging is me."

CHAPTER TWELVE

LATER.

Justin slipped his phone in his back pocket and said, "Hoshi just texted. They're on their way. You ready?"

"I'm ready," came Brian's reply. "The question is, are you?"

"As ready as I'll ever be."

Brian stopped checking the St. Andrew's Cross to turn around and look at him. "This is a new experience for me, too, you know," he said. "I've never topped a Dom before."

"Enjoy it while it lasts," Justin said. "I'm really hoping this scene doesn't go on for too long."

"And if it does?" Brian asked him. "I don't think you realize how much stamina this is going to take, Justin. Fire *hurts*. This isn't just show; this is the real deal. If you can't process the pain, you won't be able to handle it."

"I'll handle it. However long it takes," he said. "Losing Alex would hurt a lot more."

"You really love her, don't you."

"Wouldn't you do the same for Samantha?" Justin

asked, defensive.

"Yes," Brian said quietly. "But you know my story. When the time came, when I thought my only choice was to let Samantha go, I let her go. She was the one who had to come back to me."

"You let her go because you thought it was what was best for her," Justin said. "Letting Alex go, letting her keep running, is *not* what's best for her. She needs to face whatever's haunting her."

"I hope you're right, Justin. If you're not, you're going to end up burned, metaphorically *and* literally."

"Thanks," Justin said, frowning. "You make—"

"Shh," Brian quieted him. "I think they're here."

The noise Brian had heard were the voices of Hoshi and Alex coming through the front foyer.

Inside the dark quiet foyer, Alex was looking around. "Why would Justin ask me to meet him here?" She asked. "There's no one here."

"I think that was the point, Alex," Hoshi told her. "He wanted you to come here so you two could talk alone."

"He could have told me to come to his house."

"This is a neutral space for both of you."

"This is Justin's arena," Alex said quietly. "It's still his space."

"At least you're here," Hoshi said. "I don't think you'd have agreed to go back to his house."

"Maybe not," Alex was forced to agree. She looked around. "Where is he, anyway?" She made her way to the main dungeon room, and Hoshi followed behind. "And what is that smell?"

Inside the spacious back room, Justin and Brian were waiting for her. As Alex's eyes came to rest on Justin, she stopped. Hoshi moved over to stand next to her, and then he, too, stopped.

The room had been emptied of every single piece of equipment, all of it, save for the eye-catching St. Andrew's Cross sitting at the head of the room, and a simple, metal chair placed before it.

"What's going on, Justin?" Alex asked. "And why is he here?" Her eyes shifted to Brian and went wide. "I know who you are. You're Mr. Sinclaire. You're a host at the Hotel Bentmoore."

"Former host," Brian said. "I don't work there anymore. I'm here as Justin's friend."

"Isn't that sweet," Alex jeered. "What happened, Justin, you decided you needed to call in the reinforcements? Couldn't handle me on your own?"

"I don't need to *handle* you, Alex," Justin said softly. "I need to help you. But I can't if you won't let me. So I need to make you understand."

"Understand what?"

"How much you mean to me. How far I'm willing to go for you." He jerked his thumb toward Brian. "Brian here is going to help me. If, by the end, you want to walk away...I'll let you go."

"End of *what*, Justin?"

"Our scene."

"I don't want a scene with you," she said. "I just came here to get my bag. Give it to me, and I'll go."

"No," Justin shook his head. "I'll give you your bag after the scene is over. But the scene I have planned is not between you and me. It's between me and Brian."

"Justin, what are you talking about?" Alex asked, exasperated.

"Brian is going to do a flogging scene on me," Justin said slowly.

Taking this as his cue, Brian moved to the St. Andrew's Cross, and picked up a pair of long yellow floggers dangling from a hook on one of the back bars. Holding the floggers to his sides, he turned, waiting.

"You're going to sit down and watch," Justin continued. "That's all. If you can sit there and watch me get flogged, then when the scene is over, I'll give you your bag, and you can leave. If you can't...if you can't take it, if you can't watch the scene to the end, then you have to tell me the truth."

"What truth?"

"The truth about what happened that day of the fire. About the abduction, about how you got out, and about how your stepfather died. You have to tell me what you went through that was so awful, you've been running away from it ever since."

For a moment, Alex stared at him in surprise. Then she said, "What makes you think I can't sit here and watch you get flogged?" She sniggered as her eyes filled with righteous anger. "I think it would be a fitting punishment for the way you lied to me!"

"I wasn't lying to you, Alex," Justin said. "But I

did keep the truth away from you. I'm never doing that again. The question is, can you make the same promise to me?"

Alex turned to Brian. "Go ahead," she said to him. "Flog him. I'll watch." She moved over to the metal chair, sat down, and shifted her hips like a person getting comfortable. "Go on, get to it," she said.

Brian gave Justin a wide-eyed look. Justin nodded back. Then he peeled off his shirt, flung it to the side, and stepped up to the St. Andrew's Cross.

Brian, still standing to the side holding the floggers, jerked his chin toward Hoshi. "You understand what's about to happen?"

"Justin gave me an idea, yes."

"Oh, you're in on this, too?" Alex said, looking up at Hoshi, the betrayal clear across her face. Hoshi didn't look at her and didn't respond.

"I'll need your help," Brian said.

"What do you need?"

"Just one thing: I'll need you to make sure she—" he jerked his chin toward Alex now—"stays put in her chair so she doesn't get hurt."

"I can do that."

"Thank you."

Brian knelt down to Alex, surprising her. "Don't try to come into the scene," he said. "Don't even get out of this chair. Understand?"

"Oh, I'm not going to stop him from getting flogged, believe me," she answered him. "I *want* to see this."

Brian stood back up, frowning, and nodded at Hoshi.

Then he walked back to the front of the room where Brian stood leaning against the St. Andrew's Cross.

But to Alex's confusion, Brian walked past Justin's straining body, over to a small bucket sitting in the corner of the floor, right next to a small decorative globe that looked very much like an expensive flowerpot.

To Alex's further confusion, Brian took hold of both floggers in one hand, and with his other, he reached out to grab a lighter from behind the shiny marble pot. He clicked the lighter on, and dipped the lit end of it into the hole.

A flame shot out.

It wasn't a plant pot, Alex realized; it was a fire pot.

"What are you doing?" She shrieked.

"This isn't going to be just a flogging," Brian told her. "This is a fire flogging scene. I'm going to fire flog Justin."

"But he'll get burned!"

"He might, yes."

"Don't!"

"You know how to stop this, Alexandra," Brian said. Alex said nothing.

Brian passed one of the floggers back into his other hand, so that he now held one in each palm.

Then he dipped both floggers into the bucket at once. When he raised them up, they were dripping. Alex got another whiff of the same scent she had smelled before, and realized what it was: alcohol.

Brian held the floggers over the fire pot.

They blazed to life.

He looked over to Alex. She was sitting stiff and

tense in her chair, the fire reflected in her eyes.

Holding the floggers out in front of him, Brian took position behind Justin's prone body.

He didn't ask if Justin was ready. He didn't give the man any warning at all. He just lifted the floggers, took aim, and let fly.

The floggers didn't just sail through the air; they *roared*. The noise was incredible, like heavy bladed fans rushing past. Every time the floggers whirled past in a blaze of light, even from her distance away, Alex could feel the heat rush at her face.

Brian began to flog Justin's back using a Florentine technique, using both floggers with smooth and rapid flourish. They came down and around in perfect figure eights, and each time they swooped through the air, they would blow Justin's back with fiery kisses.

Justin's back muscles began to tense and ripple under the skin; he grabbed onto the cross with both hands and held on tight. But he did not utter a single sound. The only noises in the room were the seething gusts and crackles from the fire.

Brian began to move his arms faster in tight, level circles across Justin's back. He took a tiny step forward. The flaming tips began to brush against Justin's shoulders, leaving trails of dancing fire on his skin before they quickly went out.

The flogging only lasted a little over two minutes before the flames died, but to the four people in the room, it felt like a lot longer.

By the time Brian turned around to look at Alex again, she was sitting in her chair with her knees up against her chest, her arms hugging her legs, looking like she was on the edge of panic. Hoshi was now standing over her, a protective hand on her shoulder.

"I watched," she said, her voice high and strained. "Can I go now?"

"We're not done yet," Brian said. He walked the floggers back to the bucket and dipped them into the alcohol once more.

As he held them in the alcohol, he heard Alex call, "You're doing that to Justin *again?*"

"I've only done one pass," Brian called back.

"How many *passes* are you going to do?" She yelled.

"Until I run out of alcohol...or until Justin passes out. Whichever comes first."

"Oh God."

Brian didn't look back at Alex; he didn't need to. He could tell from her voice, she was starting to lose control. Her rising hysteria was radiating off her like the heat from the flames.

Brian pulled the floggers out of the bucket, held them over the fire pot, and the floggers roared anew.

We use Kevlar floggers for fire flogging, and a mix of isopropyl alcohol, he had told Justin during the setup. *Some people can take as much as 95% alcohol... but I won't use that much with you.*

Why not?

Because you've never been fire flogged before. You don't know how much it'll burn you, or how long a pass you can take.

If you use more alcohol, it'll burn harder and longer?

Yes.

Then use more alcohol, Justin had said. *Use as much as you can without lighting me on fire.*

And what if I do light you on fire, Justin? Brian had asked him. *I'll have no spotter, nobody to put you out if the flames sit on your skin too long. You could end up burned.*

Hopefully it won't get that far.

And if it does?

———•⟪⟫•———

That question now glowed in Justin's mind, just as hot and scalding as the flames licking at his flesh.

What if the scene went too long, too far?

Who would last longer, him, or Alexandra?

The stench of alcohol filled the air. Justin could feel the heat drawing close. He pressed himself into the Cross, bracing himself for another onslaught.

Brian stepped forward and, once more, renewed his rhythm of dancing fire across Justin's shoulders and back. The floggers cut through the air like fanning blades, and the flames soared with them, forming glowing, scorching, searing circles of light.

A few feet away, Alex let out a short, high-pitched cry. It was the cry of a creature in terror, the cry of a trapped, cornered beast…it was the cry Justin could not release, resonating from Alex's throat, echoing inside his own ears like a siren of alarm.

Brian didn't stop.

He flogged Justin's back with lightening speed and stinging accuracy. When he began to move down Justin's sides, Justin's back muscles twitched and rippled, as if trying to recoil away from the sizzling heat that threatened to turn him into a human barbecue.

By the time the floggers went out again, Brian was sweating, and Justin was moaning with each breath.

As Brian went to relight the floggers, he glanced at Alexandra. She was pale as a sheet, her eyes filled with dread. Hoshi was standing behind her, holding both her shoulders down so she wouldn't get up.

She caught Brian's furtive glance and said, "Please, please don't do that to him again."

"You know what Justin needs for me to stop," Brian reminded her.

"I can't," she cried. "I can't."

"Then that's your choice."

Brian dunked the floggers back into the bucket, brushed them over the fire pot, watched them spring to life, and walked back to the Cross, holding the flaring floggers out before him.

"Please!" Alex cried. "Please, I can't watch this any more!"

"You won't have to for much longer," Brian said, lifting up the burning floggers. "Justin can't take much more of this."

"You'll burn him!"

"Probably," Brian said. "Does that matter to you?"

Alex's face was a mask of anguish.

Brian gave her another second to answer. When she did not, he let fly the floggers.

This time, Alex could not stay quiet in her seat. She began to shriek and wail each time the floggers pressed into Justin's back. Sometimes the fire would remain a moment too long on Justin's skin, and each time, Alex would let out a desperate yell.

"Stop it! Stop it!"

Over the roar of the flames, Brian answered, "You know what he's waiting for."

"I can't...I can't...just stop it..." The chair scraped against the floor.

"Don't let her up, Hoshi!"

"STOP IT!"

"Give Justin what he wants!"

"I CAN'T!"

The flames ruffled through the air, cutting into Justin's back...and at last, just as one tiny spark flashed bright against his skin before getting blown out by the next pass of the flogger, he let out a whine of agony.

"STOP IT!" Alex screamed. "YOU'RE HURTING HIM!"

Brian didn't stop. He could hear the sounds of a scuffle going on behind him as Alex was trying to get out of her chair, but he still didn't stop.

"STOP IT!" Alex kept hollering. "STOP IT!"

"You're the only one who can stop this, Alexandra!"

Brian began to go faster with the floggers. Justin let out another wail.

To Alex, it sounded like the sound of death. "OKAY! I'LL TELL HIM! I'll tell him," She screamed. "Just please stop. Please stop."

Brian stopped swinging the floggers and let them

drop to his sides. Within a second, they were out.

They all watched as slowly, painfully, Justin peeled himself away from the Cross. He turned around.

Alex was staring at him through eyes filled with tears and torment.

Finally, through trembling lips and choked throat, Alex said, "It was Joshua. Joshua had me kidnapped. *My father tried to kill me.*"

It was all she could get out before she was overcome by wracked sobs. Alex fell to the floor and lay there, shaking and howling, a vision of grief and misery too terrible to be borne.

They got her a blanket and wrapped her up. Then Brian and Hoshi quietly exited the room, leaving Alexandra and Justin alone.

Justin cradled her in his arms, right there on the floor, caressing her face and back, trying to soothe her as best he could. Her crying had subsided somewhat, but now she was staring off into space, her face a blank mask of emptiness.

Her vacant look alarmed Justin more than her hysterical crying had done. He squeezed her fingers underneath the blanket; Alex did not react. Her hands were ice cold.

But after a few moments of his gentle soothing, she began to warm up, and her eyes came back into focus.

"Justin," she whispered, looking up into his face. "Are you okay?"

"Oh my god, *you're* asking *me* if *I'm* okay?"

Justin couldn't hold back his laugh. "I love you, you know that?"

"You're the one who just got fire flogged, not me," she told him. Then her eyes went wide. "You love me?"

Justin smiled as he stared down into her face. "Yeah, I love you. Why else would I be willing to let Brian fire flog me? You think I'd do this for any woman?"

Alex stared at him, amazed; then a dreamy smile spread over her lips. She closed her eyes, drew the blanket tighter around herself, and snuggled against his chest.

"I'm sorry I did this to you, Alex," Justin murmured against her hair.

She pulled away enough to look up at him. "Are you, really?"

"A little, yes," he said. "But I didn't see any other way to get through to you. Do you forgive me?"

"Yeah." She drew a ragged breath, and another shudder ran through her.

"So talk to me." Justin hugged her tighter, letting her feel his heat and solid security around her limbs.

Alex took another long breath and said, "What I told you before about my stepdad and I being close, about him being such a great father?"

"Yeah?"

"It was all a lie. The truth is, Joshua never cared about me at all. He barely even knew me. He never came home, even to see my mother. He was always away taking care of the business and doing other stuff. It was always just my mom and me."

Then why did your mom stay married to him? Justin

wanted to ask, but he kept the question to himself; he thought he knew the answer, anyway.

Theirs had probably been a marriage of convenience. After the love died—if it had ever been there at all—Alexandra's mother had no reason to divorce her husband. She didn't want to go through the scandal and ordeal of a divorce, so she had left things the way they were, allowing Joshua to live his life, while she lived hers. It was a marriage of mutual apathy, not hate.

Of course, she couldn't have known the evil Joshua was capable of.

"After my mother died," Alex went on, "I went a little crazy with my grief, but Joshua didn't care. Looking back, I think he actually liked me better when I was getting into trouble. It brought him sympathy. But then...then I discovered the Hotel Bentmoore." She let out a tiny, sad laugh. "Can you imagine how things would've been different between us if I'd met you then?"

"We wouldn't be where we are now, that's for sure."

"No, we definitely would not." She paused, and the smile left her face. "Your brother really helped me to calm down and find myself. By the time I returned to Wellington Enterprises, I was ready to take more control of the company, make bigger decisions...and Joshua didn't like that one bit." Her voice lowered. "He wanted to acquire a company in the Ukraine, some manufacturing plant, and I convinced the board to vote against it. I think that's when things really changed between us."

She took a long pause. Justin waited.

"Joshua started acting all nice to me, like he wanted to be the father he never was. He said he was sorry for all the years we weren't close when my mom was alive. He *wanted* me to have more control over Wellington Enterprises, he said, so that some day, I could take the reigns over from him completely, and he could retire." Her lips turned down. "It was all a lie. But he put on a good show, I have to admit. He fooled everyone...including me."

"Alex, I don't understand," Justin interrupted. "Why would he need to put on this charade? Why didn't he just try to kick you out of the company?"

"Because technically, Wellington Enterprises was always mine," Alex said. "I was a kid when Joshua married my mother, but he never legally adopted me. Wellington Enterprises belonged to my mom, not him, and after my mom died, she left everything, her entire fortune, to me, and she made sure with the lawyers there was no way he could fight it. Joshua acted like he owned the place, but really, he didn't have a claim to any of it. If I had wanted to, I could've fired his ass any day of the week."

"Did *you* know that?"

"No, not really; but Joshua did. God, it must have driven that megalomaniac crazy, knowing I owned the business he had been running for most of his adult life." She paused, and Justin could tell she was remembering, and probably for the millionth time, wondering what she could have done differently. "When he started acting so nice to me, like a friend...like a father...I

245

was so happy, Justin. I thought I would have a family again. I thought that my mom was gone, but at least I'd still have *someone.*" Fresh tears started to run down her cheeks. "But the whole time, he was just trying to fool me, so he could...so he could...."

"Shh, sweetheart." Justin began to rock her in his arms. "I'm here now. You're safe."

She drew her legs up, and Justin could tell she was trying desperately to collect herself, to ease down her emotions enough to finish her story. Now that she had started to tell him, she wanted it all out.

"He wanted us to sign legal papers making me his legal heir, and he, mine," she continued. "But I put off signing the papers." She stopped. "Did I know, back then, he was just pretending? I think...I think a part of me did," she whispered. "Deep down, I knew it was too good to be true. Nobody could change that much, that fast. But I wanted to believe it, Justin. I wanted to have a father." Her face crumpled, but she recovered quickly. "I think he must have thought up his grand plan soon after that. My final demise." She couldn't bring herself to use the word *kill* again.

Justin helped her along with, "So he had you kidnapped, and pretended he didn't know anything about it...."

"Some goons were hired to grab me right off the street. Joshua knew where I'd be and when; it was easy for him to tell them where to find me. They holed me up in that cabin for three days. The whole time, I wondered why I hadn't been released yet. I thought they were just waiting for a ransom. It never occurred to me there was no ransom, that my dear loving stepfather had planned my ultimate solution."

"They never let on he was behind it all?"

"No, they didn't. Finally, on the third day, I heard them call Joshua, asking for the ransom money. I thought…at the time…it was weird they hadn't asked for it before…"

You and me both, babe. Justin squeezed her body, helping her to go on.

She continued, "I was shocked when he showed up at the cabin. I had no idea he knew where I was, where they were hiding me, but I was so *fucking happy* to see him…I thought he was there to rescue me…"

She needed a minute after that to cry some more. It was a wonder to Justin she had any tears left, but then, she had been storing them up a long time.

"As soon as Joshua saw me there, tied up in the corner, he asked them why I was still alive." Her voice steeled. "He told them they were supposed to have gotten rid of me immediately. That's how he put it: 'gotten rid of me.' Only one of the men spoke very good English; he seemed to be the ringleader. He told Joshua they had been ordered to keep me alive, and they only called him because they had decided they deserved more money to make up for their troubles. They didn't know my abduction would make the news."

"Wait a minute—they'd been ordered to keep you alive? By whom?"

"I don't know, Justin. That's just the thing: I don't know." Her hysteria rose and she swallowed, hard. "But that's when I realized Joshua was in on the whole plan.

He had wanted me out of the way. That was also when I realized unless I did something to save myself, I was not getting out of that cabin alive." There was another moment of retrospection, another flashback. "I can't describe to you what that felt like. The fear…the rage."

"God, Alex," Justin whispered, instinctively hugging her tight.

Alex ignored him now. "I thought to myself: *if I can't get out of this alive, I want him to go with me.* I wanted him to die for what he'd done to me. I started telling the ringleader I would pay them double whatever they had been promised if they'd let me go, and kill Joshua instead."

"Jesus."

"I told them I would never tell anyone who they were. That I couldn't, since then *I'd* be an accessory to murder. And…they started to listen to me, Justin. They started to think about what I was saying. Then the FBI showed up." She started to laugh, a bitter, overwrought snicker. "You should have seen Joshua's face," she said. "He looked like a trapped animal; like a rabbit in a jaw trap. But he would never have chewed his own leg off to get away. He was too cowardly for that." Her voice lowered to a murmur. "He just thought he could use me, instead."

"What happened?"

"The kidnappers thought Joshua had brought the FBI to them. They didn't believe he didn't know he'd been followed. Joshua tried to convince them he really wanted me dead, that he had never wanted the FBI getting involved—that's the only time I ever heard the real truth from him. But the ringleader, he was a smart guy. He knew the game was up. There was no way they would be getting out of that cabin alive without spending the rest of their lives in jail. But Joshua...."

"Go on...."

"Joshua still wanted them to kill me, right then, even with the FBI surrounding us. He told them if they'd just give him a gun, he'd kill me himself. He was obsessed at that point...and I think he thought there was still a way for him to get out of there looking innocent."

"How could he possibly think that?"

"My stepfather was not a stupid man, Justin. He always had a contingency plan up his sleeve...but he didn't count on the ringleader not being a stupid man, either. The guy knew he had two hostages at that point; if he killed me, he would only have one, and the FBI would not negotiate with a killer. Joshua was used to giving orders, but he wasn't used to dealing with *these* kinds of men." She tittered again. "His powers in the conference room were not going to help him this time," she said. "I told them if they would let me go, I could help them escape, and convince the Feds outside to back off. I could help them leave the country, if that's what they wanted. And they listened."

"So you were getting through to them?"

"Oh, yeah. They were desperate, and they knew my plan made more sense than Joshua's. One of them untied me, and that's when Joshua went crazy. He saw I was going to go free, his plan was ruined, and he...snapped."

When the vacant emptiness began to enter her eyes again, Justin asked softly, "What did he do, Alex?"

"Before I could even stand up, Joshua had wrestled the gun out of one of their hands," Alex said. "But he didn't point it at them, Justin. He pointed it at me. He almost shot me. My own stepfather almost shot me. I...I...."

"You didn't get shot, Alex. He didn't do it."

"He didn't do it because he didn't get the chance," she said. "One of the other guys shot him before he could. Ironic, don't you think? One of my abductors saved my life." She started to laugh again, and there was far too much madness in her voice for Justin's liking. It was time to finish this up.

"What happened after that?"

"Everyone was just kind of shocked for a minute by what'd happened. I knelt by Joshua, just to see if he was still alive, but he was already dead. The ringleader started yelling. The one who had just shot Joshua started moving towards me. I didn't think about it: I just grabbed the gun out of Joshua's hand, stood up, and started shooting...everything."

Justin tried to picture it in his mind's eye, but could not; the scene was too harrowing. It hit him then what a miracle it was Alex had gotten out of there alive, in one piece, unhurt...at least physically.

She continued, "I knew there were containers of kerosene stacked up all over the place, but I'd never shot a gun in my life, and all of a sudden, there's a fire coming from the back room. I mean, it was just an inferno before I could even tell what was going on.

Does that make any sense?"

"Yes. Go on."

"The guys saw the fire, too, and they started screaming. The ringleader started yelling orders—I think he wanted them to try to put the fire out. But I just wanted to get out of there. They were distracted, I saw my chance—so I made a run for it. I was out the door before anyone could stop me."

"You escaped."

"Yes," she said. "I never looked back. I just ran. A second later, I heard this—this—*explosion* behind me, and a huge shockwave knocked me on my face. The heat…the smell…oh god, the smell…."

"It's all over now, Alex. You're okay."

"That's just it, Justin. I don't know that it *is* over." She pulled away from him, her round, tear-rimmed eyes not two inches from his face. "I've had a lot of time to go over things in my head, think about what happened, and what Joshua said to those people, and—*he was not acting alone.* He had someone else working with him, someone on the inside of Wellington Enterprises."

"I understand why you think he had someone else helping him, but how do you know it was someone at Wellington Enterprises?"

"Just by the way it was done, the things he said, and what he would've had to do after he got me out of the way. Joshua's whole world was the company. He wouldn't have known how to hire three foreign guns-for-hire to set up an abduction. It's not the kind of thing you request resumes for. He must have had an associate, a trusted friend, someone who knew how to get it done, and give the orders in Joshua's place. And then this friend must've also been in a position to help Joshua keep control of the company after I was gone. There was bound to be a shake-up on the board, people clamoring for more control at the top."

"There couldn't have been that many people who fit that description," Justin said. "People who were that close to Joshua, already in a position to help him keep his seat on the throne, and evil enough to help him commit a kidnapping." He left off the word murder; he didn't want her falling apart again.

"The problem was, there were far too *many* people who fit that description," she said. "Or at least, could have, in my opinion. I didn't know Joshua's trusted people that well. After he was gone, I didn't know who I could trust anymore. Everyone was offering me their help, and all I could think about was whether they were in on the plan to get me out of the way."

"So you left."

"I ran. I couldn't live with that fear."

"Alex, why didn't you ask Hoshi for help? Or my brother? Why did you insist on living this lie for so long?"

"Because," she said slowly, "it was easier." She sighed and looked down. "Once I decided to leave, I didn't see a reason to pursue the truth anymore. Joshua was dead, I was gone from the company, nobody had a reason to come after me anymore...."

"But you aren't really gone from the company, are you? Not completely. Jonathan told me you still hold a lot of sway over there."

"He did?" Her eyes narrowed. "What else did he tell you?"

"That your mother was one of the original supporters of the Hotel Bentmoore. That our families have been close for years. That, basically, I'm an ignoramus."

"He did not say that," Alex said, putting a hand over her mouth to cover her smile.

"Not exactly, but this time, he would've been right," Justin said. "He told me you still have contact with someone inside Wellington Enterprises."

"Yes, that's true. Peter Ames, the president I appointed before I left. He's chairman of the board."

"How much do you trust this guy?"

"You think Peter is trying to come after me?" She frowned. "Peter wouldn't do that. I trust him as much as I do your brother."

"Well, if someone is trying to come after you again, Alex, then we need to find out who. And until then, we need to get you to a safe place." His brows creased, then relaxed. "C'mon. We're leaving."

Justin pulled her to her feet. Alex asked, "Where are we going?"

"We're going to go back to my house so I can pack a few things," he said, "and then we're going to the Hotel Bentmoore. You'll be safe there until my brother and I can figure this all out."

She stopped her feet, and Justin turned around to look at her: she was smiling at him in rapt wonder. "I love you," she whispered.

"I love you too," he said, squeezing her hand. "Now let's get the hell out of here."

CHAPTER THIRTEEN

I
N THE END, ALL FOUR of them, Justin, Alex, Brian, and Hoshi, returned to Justin's house. Hoshi argued that he should be able to accompany Alex to this mysterious Hotel Bentmoore, too; after all, two people protecting her were better than one. Justin had to agree.

As soon as they were inside the house, Justin called his brother, gave him a rundown of their plan, and for the first time ever, felt no tension on the line as they spoke. Justin didn't have time for it; all his concern now was on Alex, and getting her somewhere she would feel safe.

Once he was off the phone, Justin asked Brian to start searching for airline tickets. "Book us on whatever gets us there fastest," Justin instructed. "I don't care how much it costs."

"No problem, boss." Brian gave him a wry smile.

Justin, caught off guard by the look, said, "What?"

"Nothing," Brian answered. "It's just, you sounded amazingly like your brother just now." He started walking away before Justin could conjure up a reply.

Justin found Alex in his room, lying down on his

bed. Her eyes were closed, her face relaxed, her cheek resting in the curve of his pillow. She looked luscious, and exactly where she was meant to be.

He thought she was dozing, and didn't want to disturb her. But as he began to strip off his clothes for a shower, he heard her ask, "How's your back?"

Justin turned around and said, "I didn't mean to wake you."

"I wasn't asleep," she said. "Just closing my eyes a bit. Turn around, let me see."

Justin turned around and let her have her first look.

"There's not a mark on you!" She exclaimed. Justin turned back around to see her look of shock and annoyance. "I thought you'd be all burned!"

"Nope," he said. "It itches some, though." He scratched his back. "Brian warned me about that. But he knows what he's doing. You know, fire flogging's not that bad."

"*Not that bad?* You mean it didn't hurt at *all?*"

"Some," he admitted, "but not as much as I thought it would. It's more fear play than pain play. I could hear Brian trying to build up *your* fear though. I decided not to interrupt."

"So all that time, Brian made me think you were going through agony, and could end up disfigured, when really it *wasn't that bad?*" She yelled. "I aught to hit you!" And she bounded off the bed, looking as if she'd do just that.

"Ah ah ah," Justin waved his finger at her. "Not allowed. At least, not yet. You want another tackle scene with me later, we can arrange that."

"You!"

"I'm going to take a shower," he said. "I smell weird. Care to join me?"

She couldn't help smiling at his devilish look. "No," she said. "I'm going to go get something to eat from the kitchen. I'm starving. I'll shower after you."

"Okay."

He pulled her in for a kiss, but she resisted. "Go shower," she said. "You *do* smell weird." Justin grinned, pulled her in harder, and managed to kiss her on the mouth as she struggled. She pretended to balk, but Justin could see the amusement, and surrender, in her eyes.

He got into the shower. *So this is what I've been avoiding all this time,* he thought. *Being a Dom is not what I thought it would be...it feels pretty fucking great.* Then he thought, *being* Alex's *Dom is pretty fucking great.*

He felt happy—elated, actually—and freer than he'd ever felt before. He had the woman he loved at his side, and she loved him in return.

Everything else could be figured out.

When he got out of the shower, Alex wasn't in the room anymore. Justin got dressed and walked down the hall to the living room, where he found Brian sitting on the sofa with the laptop on his knees, his eyes focused squarely on the screen.

"I can get you to the hotel by four o'clock," he said. "But you'll have to leave for the airport in half an hour."

"Works for me," Justin said. "I need two minutes to pack a bag. Where's Hoshi?"

"In the kitchen."

Justin walked into the kitchen and found Hoshi leering over a bowl of Frosted Flakes, looking frustrated.

"You don't like Frosted Flakes?" Justin asked him.

"They were the only thing I found in your cabinet," Hoshi said. "I've never had them before. They're sweeter than I expected. What time are we leaving?"

"Alex and I are leaving in half an hour. Are you still coming?"

"Yes," he said. "Whatever toiletries I need I can buy at the airport. I'm assuming, once we're at this hotel of yours, she'll be able to relax her guard a bit."

"The Hotel Bentmoore is like Fort Knox," Justin said. "It has an underground floor that nobody can get into without the right access. She'll be safe there."

"Good." Hoshi went back to his cereal.

Justin looked around. "Where is Alex, anyway?"

Hoshi's spoon stopped mid-air. "I thought she was with you," he said. "She's not in your room?"

"No...." Justin went back to the living room and asked Brian, "Have you seen Alex?"

"No," Brian replied, frowning. "She's not in your room?"

"Alex? Alex!" Justin called. There was no answer. He began hunting the house, calling out with every breath: "Alex!"

Brian and Hoshi joined him in the search. She was

nowhere to be found.

At last, just as Justin was looking around his bedroom a third time for any sign of her, he found the note on his drawers, fluttering from the breeze coming from the open window.

I can't be with you, it said. *I'm sorry. Please forget me.*

Justin read it three times. Then he crumpled up the note and threw it across the room.

CHAPTER FOURTEEN

B*RRRING. BRRRIIIINNNG. BRRRRRRRIIIIING.*

The annoying *brrrinnging* kept getting angrier in his ears until Justin realized he would have to get up and investigate what it was.

It seemed to be coming from the living room.

Then he realized it was the doorbell.

He opened the door; Adam stood there. Justin was surprised to see him...or maybe he wasn't surprised at all. It was hard to tell.

"Can I come in?" Adam asked.

"Sure, why not," Justin answered. "Me casa es su casa and all that." He waved his arm wide into the room behind him, and the liquid inside the glass he was holding sloshed onto the floor.

He had forgotten he was holding it.

"You're in a good mood," Adam said, walking into the room and narrowing his eyes at Justin's glass.

"This good mood is being brought to you by Crown Royal," Justin said, holding up the glass in a toast, then swallowing a good chunk of it down.

Adam's eyes narrowed even more, but his voice was cordial as he said, "You're drinking the hard core stuff? You're usually a beer kind of guy."

"I've decided beer and I should have an open relationship," Justin said. He took another swallow from his glass, smacked his lips, and started walking back toward the kitchen.

Adam followed behind. "Khloe and I are worried about you," he said. "You haven't been in the store for four days."

"I'm taking an extended vacation. You always told me I should."

"Yeah, but not like this—Justin, when was the last time you showered?" Adam had walked a little too close behind Justin's back, and was now grimacing. "Or got some real food into you?" They reached the kitchen, and Adam took a good look around. "Let me guess. Four days ago."

"I've decided," Justin said, "I need to stop sweating the small stuff. Let myself *be,* you know? Enjoy life on my own terms for a change."

"Is that what you've decided," Adam murmured. "And this—" he waved his hand around the filthy kitchen—"is enjoying life on your own terms?"

"Don't judge me, my friend. I'm a free bachelor, I should be able to act like one."

"I see." Adam looked around the room again. "Right. You're staying at my place."

"No, I am not," Justin replied, still smiling. "I am staying right here. I'm waiting."

"For what?"

"For Alex to come to her senses." His grin disappeared. "Or for the pain to go away. Whichever first. But hey, my plan is working. I already feel better." He tipped the glass into his mouth, emptying it completely.

Adam grabbed it away from him. "Justin, this needs to stop," he said. "Alex left. She is not coming back."

"I'm not going to believe it until she tells herself," Justin said. "She needs to come back here and *tell me herself*. Then I'll believe it."

"She's not coming back, Justin. Your brother told you, Alex *never* returns to a place she's already been. She's back to running. I'm sorry, but that's the way it is. You have to accept it."

"No," Justin said, "she'll come back, and explain why she thinks it won't work between us. She owes me an explanation. She's not going to just leave me without saying goodbye. She wouldn't do that to me." His face fell. "She wouldn't do that to me."

"Christ, Justin...let's get you to bed. You need to sleep this off."

"Dude, I'm fine."

"That's the alcohol talking."

"Alcohol is a wise individual," Justin declared, right before tripping into the wall, crashing to the floor, and blacking out.

When he woke up, he was in his own bed, the clock said two p.m., and his skull felt like it had a troll inside, hammering itself out a nice-sized home.

Justin walked into his kitchen holding his head on, and found Adam sitting at his kitchen table, looking down at his phone.

"You're still here?" Justin asked.

"Khloe is bringing you some real food," Adam replied. "Meanwhile, here." He pushed over a glass of water and two pills. "For the headache."

"Thanks." Justin swallowed down the pills and half the water. Then he took a better look around the room: his kitchen was clean. "What happened?"

"You passed out," Adam said. "I got you into bed. I cleaned your kitchen. You woke up. The end."

"Thanks, man," Justin said. "For everything."

"No problem."

"God, my head," Justin murmured, rubbing his fingers through his hair. Then he asked, "Who's minding the store?"

"No one," Adam said. "I put the CLOSED sign up and locked the place down on my way over here. I was supposed to meet Khloe back there for lunch, but obviously that's not going to happen."

"I'm sorry, Adam. I guess I'm in bad shape."

"No, really?" Adam rolled his eyes. "You need to get out of this house, Justin. Look, why don't you come back to the store with me for a couple hours? Get some sun, rejoin society for a while? Then you can stay at my place tonight, and I won't have to worry about you crashing into any more walls."

"I won't stay with you," Justin said, "but thanks for the offer. And I will come back with you to the store." He rubbed his cheek. "I should shower and shave first."

"Yes, you definitely should do that," Adam agreed.

"With bleach."

"Ha ha. I'll be back in a few."

"Take your time. Really; take your time."

"Thanks again," Justin said dryly, and walked back down the hall.

The shower made him feel marginally better. By the time he was shaved and dressed, he felt almost human.

Then he found a piece of tissue on the floor with red lipstick blotted on it, and the feeling went away.

He walked back to the kitchen wearing a clean shirt and jeans. Adam was still sitting at the table, looking at his phone again.

"I'm a little bit fuzzy on what day it is," Justin said, "and—was Brian here at some point?"

"It's Thursday, Brian was here, and he stayed with you last night."

"He did? Jesus, I don't remember."

"He had to go into work this morning, so he asked me to check up on you. It's a good thing I did, too. By the look of it, you were trying to drink yourself into a coma." He gave Justin an accusatory look.

"I'm sorry, man," Justin said. "I've just...I've never gone through this, you know?"

"A breakup?"

"This isn't just a breakup," Justin said. "Not for me. I keep thinking Alex is going to just walk through that door, tell me it was all a misunderstanding...that she'd never leave me."

"I understand, Justin," Adam said gently, "I do. But you have to accept the fact that Alex made her choice. She's gone. She's not coming back."

"I can't accept that. I can't." Justin's eyes darkened. Then, to change the subject, he asked, "Where's Hoshi gone?"

"He came by the store today," Justin said. "He told me to tell you he'll be in town for another couple days, but then he's taking off, too."

"He's sticking around another couple days, huh? Maybe he thinks Alex is coming back, too."

"Or maybe he wanted to give you a few days to recover a little before he says goodbye."

"Yeah, well, a few days isn't going to cover it."

"You need time. We get that."

"What I need are *answers*."

"You're not going to get them, Justin. *Alex is gone.*"

Justin had no response to that. The fact was, Adam was right: Alex *was* gone.

If only his heart would believe it....

"When is Khloe supposed to get here with the food?" He asked, seeing Adam glance down at his phone again.

"Any moment, I'm thinking. I tried calling her for an ETA, but she's not answering."

"Listen, let me pay for it."

"No, Justin, it's not a big deal—"

"—I'm going to pay—"

"—I got it, it's really not that much—"

Justin slapped his hand on the counter. "I'm paying," he said, "and that's it. It's the least I can do. Now...where'd my wallet go?" He looked around the kitchen, stopped, looked vaguely straight ahead, and slapped his forehead with his palm. "I left it in my car," he said. "I'll be right back."

"You left your wallet in your car for four days? It's a good thing you live in a good neighborhood."

"Yeah, well, when I left it there I thought I was going to be turning around and heading right to the airport, remember?"

Adam, looking contrite, said, "Sorry, man."

"Yeah," Justin said, looking down at the floor. "Let me go get my wallet, and I'll give you your money."

"Justin, you really don't have to—"

"Don't," Justin said. He strode to the front door. "I'll be back in a sec."

Outside, his car was sitting in the driveway, exactly as he'd left it four days ago...back when he had Alex, and the world seemed sane. He could see his wallet sitting inside the storage bucket, right underneath the radio.

He pressed the button on his keychain to unlock the driver's side door. The car let out a shrill little *cheep cheep.*

He pulled on the door handle, opened up the door, reached his arm inside to grab his wallet...and out of the corner of his eye, caught sight of something in the back seat.

It was a big, fat, crème colored messenger bag.

Alex's bag. The one she took everywhere. The one she never left behind.

It was still in his car.

Justin ran back inside the house, his wallet forgotten.

"Adam," he called, heading straight to the kitchen. "Adam, I—"

"I've got trouble, man," Adam said, his expression stopping Justin in his tracks.

Justin saw Adam's hand squeezed around his cell phone. "What's wrong?"

"It's Khloe," Adam said. "She's terrified. She thinks someone's following her."

CHAPTER FIFTEEN

IT TOOK JUSTIN TWO SECONDS to create the plan in his mind. It was foolish and reckless, impractical at best—but it was the best plan they had as far as he could see.

"Where is Khloe now?" He asked Adam.

"She's still walking down Main Street," Adam said, "on her way back to the shop. She's texting me. She think's someone's following her down the street."

"Text her back: tell her to pretend like she doesn't suspect anything," Justin said. "Tell her to stay in public, and act normal. We'll be there in a few. C'mon." He motioned for Adam to follow him.

"What are you talking about? I should tell her to get somewhere safe and call the police," Adam said, standing up.

"No! Don't do that," Justin said, turning around. "She should act cool. Pretend like she's doing some window shopping. We can be there in fifteen if we hurry." This time, he didn't wait to see if Adam followed him, but strode out of the house and out to his car.

Adam slid into the passenger side door just as

Justin started the engine.

"Why am I telling her to do this?" He asked, still punching the text message into his phone.

"Because if she calls the police, this guy will see them coming from a mile away, and disappear," Justin said. "If we work together, we may have a chance of trapping him."

"And why would we want to do that?"

"To find out where Alex is."

"Justin, what are you talking about? Why would this guy following Khloe know anything about Alex?"

"Look behind you, man."

Adam turned around and looked into the back seat. "Her bag," he breathed.

"Exactly," Justin said. "Alex would never have left that bag behind, not unless *something else is going on*. Adam, I think she might've been kidnapped again. This guy following Khloe might have the answer."

"Why would you think *that?*"

"Cause it's all I've got to go on," Justin said through gritted teeth.

"Justin, if this guy *does* have something to do with Alex's disappearance, then right now, Khloe might be in some really serious danger," Adam said, his voice tight.

"As long as Khloe stays in public, nothing will happen to her," Justin said, hoping to God it was true. "Just keep texting her to keep her calm. Tell her we're almost there. She'll look like she's preoccupied with her phone, that's all. Nothing unusual there."

"She's standing in the middle of the sidewalk by

the coffee shop. She says she thinks the guy is two stores down."

"Good. Tell her I'm pulling onto Main Street now," Justin said, making a sharp turn that made both of them lean right. "I'm almost behind the store."

He pealed into the back private parking lot, stopped the car across two parking spots, and killed the engine. "Tell her to start *slowly* making her way to the store. It'll look dark, but we'll be inside, waiting."

"Justin, what do you have planned?"

"C'mon."

They entered the store through the backroom. As they made their way to the front, they crouched down and kept low behind the counter, so that anyone looking inside the place through the wide front windows would think there's nobody home. The lights were off, and the CLOSED sign still hung.

Adam texted madly into his phone. A second later, he murmured, "She's coming."

"I see her," Justin whispered back. "Tell her to come inside, but don't turn the lights on, and don't touch the sign. Make it look like she's keeping the place closed."

From behind the counter, Justin watched Khloe slowly meander her way toward them, looking down at her phone as she walked. She was doing a fantastic job: as far as any onlookers were concerned, she was just another naïve young woman who would someday learn the hard way it was not a good idea to be texting while walking. She may have looked a little upset, but that was probably due to the heated conversation she was having with her phone.

Adam punched in a few more buttons and slipped his phone into his back pocket. "I told her," he said.

"She's here," Justin whispered, jerking his chin toward the door. "Get low."

Khloe, keeping up the grand performance, looked very nonchalant as she stopped in front of the door. She took her own sweet time finding the right key to open it. Justin thought she deserved an award for the show she was putting on; she didn't look scared at all.

She got the door unlocked and came inside, but as instructed, didn't turn on the lights, and didn't take down the CLOSED sign. Instead, she walked right past the counter to the back of the store, and disappeared through the dark curtains.

Adam's feet shifted; Justin motioned him to wait. They watched through the front window.

A second later, a man came into view. He walked slowly past the window, looking like he was strolling down the street; but he kept gazing through the glass, into the shop.

When he was a little bit past the window, he stopped, looked left and right, seemed to think about it for a second...and then he came back, gave the door handle a little test jiggle, and slowly opened the door, just enough for him to slip through.

Again, Adam shifted, and again, Justin motioned him down.

Once the man was inside, he held onto the door as it closed shut; it slid closed with a *snick*. He looked around the shop, saw the curtains in the back, and began to make his way over.

Adam and Justin hunched down lower behind the counter, hearing the man walk by the other side. Justin got ready to spring. He could feel the adrenaline goading him to move, *move already,* but he kept firm in his spot, waiting for just the right moment....

Only when the man was in his center view, about to move aside the curtain, did Justin spring. Adam moved a millisecond behind. Together, they pounced on the guy, and had him immobilized before he even knew what was going on.

"Get the fuck off me!" He yelled as Adam held him in an arm lock. He and Adam struggled; Justin reached behind the counter, got out a wicked-looking knife, and held it to the man's throat.

"You picked the wrong shop," he said in a icy whisper, "and the wrong people."

Khloe came out from behind the curtain, saw what was going on, and said, "Jesus, Justin."

"Get him in the back room," he ordered Adam. "In the chair."

Adam half pulled, half dragged the man through the curtains and into the back room, where he dumped him into "the chair," Justin's latest project: a kinky, multifaceted chair designed for long, sexually charged, interrogation scenes.

It was about to be tested in an interrogation scene that was going to be all too real.

Adam slammed the man into the chair, and Justin cuffed him in. The straps and cuffs were fastened to the chair at the wrists, ankles, and shoulders; they closed with slick metal buckles, but Justin had some small padlocks handy, too.

Within moments, the man was trapped, and he knew it.

"Let me go," he ordered, struggling against his bonds. "This is crazy."

"You were following my girlfriend," Adam said, fists clenched at his sides. He looked over at Khloe and asked, "Are you okay?"

"I'm fine," she said, sounding slightly amazed at everything that had just happened. "Much better than this guy will be soon."

"Let me go," the man repeated, looking at each of them in turn.

"Why were you following my girlfriend?" Adam asked him, looking down at the pale, nervous man.

"I wasn't following your girlfriend!" He yelled, his lips white.

Justin pushed in front of Adam, put both hands on the armrests of the chair, leaned into the man's face, and asked in a cold whisper, "Where's Alex?"

"I don't know where she is," he said, his head moving from side to side.

"But you know *who* she is," Justin pounced, leaning further in. "You know she's missing. You know she's in danger."

"No, I don't, I didn't, I swear it."

"I don't believe you." Justin reached out with the knife and held the point of the blade up to the man's face, right against his cheekbone. "I think you know exactly where she is," he said, his voice low and menacing. "And I want you tell me."

"I don't, I swear, I have no idea where she is," the man blubbered, trying to move his face away from the sharp edge.

Justin put the blade against the man's arm, right over the sleeve, and with calm, expert precision, began to slice a long, even cut, right through the man's clothes. Justin did not go deep enough to cut skin…but the fact that he could cut through the clothes without disturbing a single hair on the man's arm spoke volumes about his skill.

The man's eyes grew wider and wider as Justin sliced through fabric all the way up the arm. "Stop," he begged, trying vainly to pull away, "stop—"

"Justin." Khloe said his name like an answer to a horrible question. Justin held the knife inside the man's sleeve; he didn't move it, but didn't pull it away, either.

"Tell me," Justin repeated, "where Alex is."

"I don't know, I don't know, I swear—"

"Justin." This time Adam stepped forward, and put his hand on Justin's arm.

Justin removed the knife and stepped away. Adam stepped between him and the chair. "My friend here thinks you know where his girlfriend is," Adam said. "And considering the fact that you just scared my own girlfriend half to death, personally? I'm not inclined to help you. But since I don't want to see this chair ruined with blood, why don't you tell us what you know, before things start to get ugly."

"Dude, I'm telling you, I have no idea where

Alexandra is!"

"Then how do you know her name?"

"I was trying to warn her!" The man said in a high-pitched yell. "Look, if you'll just reach into my pocket, you'll find my ID. My name is Sean Davis. I'm a private PI." When neither Adam nor Justin moved, he said, "Please, just look at the damn ID! I'm a PI, not some hit man!"

Adam sighed and shoved his hand into the guy's front pocket. He pulled out a wallet, opened it up, and said, "There's an ID here. Says Sean Davis, PI."

"See?" The man said. "I wasn't trying to hurt anybody. You've even seen me in here before. I came in a few weeks ago. You got nasty with me."

"He's right," Justin said. "He *was* in here. Alex helped him. I didn't like the vibes I was getting off him back then, either."

"But I didn't try to hurt Alexandra back then, did I? And I wouldn't have now, either. I would have offered her my *help.*" He looked at Adam and said, "It's why I was following your girlfriend here."

"Start talking," Adam said.

"I was following *her* because I thought she was *Alexandra.* She's wearing the same damn hat. Don't you see?"

Adam and Justin looked at Khloe.

She had dressed down today, and was wearing a simple pair of skinny jeans, one of Adam's old t-shirts, and her red beret...the same beret she had taken Alex to buy the day Hoshi had come into town. With her hair stuffed under her cap, and her face averted, Justin had to concede it was possible she could pass as Alex.

"I was going to warn her about what's going on," the man continued. When he saw he wasn't making any headway, he yelled, "Look, if I knew where Alexandra was, why would I be following another girl? It makes no sense! If I had Alexandra, I wouldn't be showing my face around here, would I?"

Adam looked at Justin. "He's right, man," Adam said.

"He might not know where Alex is, but he knows *something*," Justin said. He crossed his arms with the knife in his hand and said to Davis, "So talk. Why were you trying to trail Alex? What were going to warn he about? And who hired you?"

"If you let me out of this chair, I'll talk," Davis said. "But not with a knife to my neck." When Justin hesitated, Davis said to Adam, "I'm trying to help here, but it's hard to think when someone's holding a knife to your throat. Let me up, and I'll talk, I swear."

Adam answered him, "You do realize if you try to run, my friend here will slice you up, yeah?"

"Yeah," Davis said, his voice jittering, "he's made that pretty clear."

A moment of silent deliberation passed between Adam and Justin. Then Adam sighed. "Let him out," he said, beginning the work himself on one set of buckles. Khloe and Justin started in on the others, and they soon had Davis free of the chair.

"Thank you," he said, rubbing his wrists. "Jesus. What kind of chair is this?" He looked around the room. "Oh my god," he whispered. "What do you people *make* in here?"

"Tell me about Alex," Justin said. "What do you know?"

"Your girlfriend's in a heap of trouble, that's what I know," Davis said, looking down at his ripped sleeve and scowling. "This was a new shirt...."

"I'll buy you a new one. Talk."

Davis began to peel off his coat and roll up his torn shirt sleeve. "You know who your girlfriend is, right? Alexandra Wellington, of Wellington Enterprises?"

"Yeah, we all know all that," Justin said, brushing it off. "How do you fit in?"

"About two months ago, I was hired to look for her. Some guy was willing to pay me big bucks to fly all over the country to find her. It wasn't easy, but I finally did—working in your shop...which is not quite the shop I thought it was," he said, looking around again. "If this is the kind of stuff you really sell, I am *seriously* off my game."

"Why did someone hire you to find her? What did they want with her?"

"It's not part of my job description to ask," Davis said. "Especially not when the pay's so good. My job was to confirm I found her and report back. At least it was, until...."

"Until?"

"Until things got out of my comfort zone, okay? I don't mind tracking people down, I don't even mind breaking into their apartment for a quick looksee—"

"That was you?" Justin yelled, taking a step toward Davis, who put his hands up to ward him off. "You scared Alex shitless—"

"I was told to go in and confirm it was her, okay? It didn't do me any good. That woman knows how to travel incognito. And then that feeb showed up two days later—"

"Feeb—you mean FBI? Hoshi? How did you know Hoshi was FBI?"

Davis gave him a look. "Oh, please. It was obvious. If that guy isn't FBI, I'll eat my torn-up coat. I got some good photos of all three of you at the coffee shop down the street, sent them over to my client, and he told me to keep trailing the target, but keep my distance. I was still getting paid, so I was fine with that."

"What changed?"

"The client," Davis said. "He started asking me all these questions about what my job included, and how far I was willing to go if the payoff was right. Started talking about how much money this girl had, and telling me if I were willing, there'd be a big payoff."

"Willing to what?" Adam asked.

"That's just it, I don't know," Davis said. "I didn't want to ask. The guy was starting to creep me out. At the end of our last conversation, he started talking about how Alexandra wouldn't be a problem for much longer, that soon she'd be out of the way. I didn't like the sound of that. Like I said, I'm a PI, not a hit man. I thought I should tell her something's up." He looked at the others. "You say Alexandra's missing? That's bad. That's real bad. She could be in some serious danger."

"I know," Justin said. "I need to find her."

"I thought Alex took off," Khloe said. "Maybe

that's a good thing. Maybe now *nobody* will be able to find her."

"If I can find her, so can someone else," Davis said.

"And she didn't take off willingly, Khloe," Justin replied. "Her bag is still in my car. She never goes anywhere without that thing."

"You think she's been taken?" Davis asked, his face grave.

"It wouldn't be the first time," Justin answered. "We need to find her. Davis, you never answered my first question: Who hired you?"

"Some guy," Davis said, "named Peter Ames."

CHAPTER SIXTEEN

TWELVE HOURS AND A LIFETIME'S worth of high blood pressure later, Justin found himself where it had all began: back at the Hotel Bentmoore, in his brother's office, standing next to the enormous antique desk that used to belong to his father. His arms were crossed, his body tense, his every thought on the ticking clock on the wall. He gazed out the clear glass window into the tended landscape beyond, silent and still.

This was not the homecoming he could have ever imagined.

"Tell me again why we're waiting," he said.

"Peter's a little delayed, but he should be here soon," Jonathan said from somewhere behind him. "As soon as he arrives, I'll have him escorted straight here. He'll have the answers we need."

"If he doesn't lie," Justin said, his tone full of grit. "I don't know why you'd even believe this guy after you heard what Davis said."

"I heard what Davis said, but it doesn't make sense. Peter would never lay a finger on Alexandra."

"How can you be so sure?" Justin looked over his

shoulder to stare at his brother. *"How can you be so sure?* He might have her stuck somewhere right now, and we're wasting time talking to him, instead of trying to find her."

"I've known Peter for years, Justin. He's just not capable of doing what you're suggesting. And let's say he does have her," he said, putting a palm up to cut off Justin's retort, "let's say he does. Why would Peter give Davis his real name? And then why would he call me, and ask me to meet him *here?* If he had Alexandra, he would know it would be foolish for him to come here. But *he* called *me,* and asked me for this meeting. I think he does know something, yes—but I think he wants to help."

"I hope you're right," Justin said.

Jonathan put his hand on Justin's shoulder. "We'll figure it out," he said, "I promise."

Justin went back to looking out the window, his dark thoughts turning inwards.

How long had it been already? How long had Alex been missing?

Four days he'd spent in a drunken stupor, thinking she had up and left him without so much as a goodbye. Then the time it had taken to talk to Davis, contact his brother, learn of Peter's surprising phone call, and finally formulate some kind of a plan. Then the time it had taken them to get here.

Too much time. Too much time....His heart felt like a fifty-pound weight in his chest; it was hard to breathe without pain.

His Alex was somewhere out there, needing his

help, needing *him*, and he couldn't reach her. He didn't even know how to find her.

He didn't know how much more of this he could take.

And the one person he'd thought to call, the only person he thought might understand, stood calmly behind him, looking as confident and unflappable as always.

Justin made a noise in his throat.

"What?" Jonathan asked.

"Nothing," Justin said. "It's just...here I am, asking for your help, *begging* for your help, something I promised myself I'd never do, and I'm not even sure you can help me."

"I don't know why you would have hesitated to call," Jonathan said. "You know I'll help as much as I can."

"Yes," Justin said. "But you're not doing it for me, are you? You're doing it for Alex...which is probably why you're helping at all."

"What?"

"It's okay, Jonathan. I get it."

"What the hell is that supposed to mean?"

"Oh c'mon," Justin exclaimed, fed up. "If I had called and asked for help with my girlfriend, some nobody, you wouldn't be working so hard right now to help me, would you?" Justin turned back toward the window. "You'd send Trowlege, or one of the other worker bees around here to help me. You'd never have tried to help me yourself."

Jonathan grabbed Justin by the arm and swung him

around. "That's a god-awful thing to say," he said. "Why would even you say that?"

"Because it's true," Justin said. "You haven't given a damn about my life since Dad died and you sent me away. You always made sure I was getting by, that I wasn't getting into trouble, but that was it. You don't care what I'm doing with my life, as long as I'm not interfering with yours."

"Justin, I don't know where you got this idea from, but it's a flat-out lie," Jonathan said, stricken. "I have *always* cared about your wellbeing; I have *always* wanted you to be a part of this family. You're the one who created this distance between us, not me."

"Oh, is that what you told yourself years ago when you sent me away?" Justin said, the thickness in his throat betraying him. "Did I do that to myself? Both my parents were gone, Jonathan, and you couldn't wait to get rid of me. Did I ask for that, too? You speak to Alex twice a week, every week, *for years,* and you never bother trying to talk to me all. Did I ask for that?"

"I did try to call you! When you were at school, every damn week when they'd let me I'd try to call you! You never accepted my phone calls! I had to ask Trowlege to call you just so you'd pick up the phone!"

"That was years ago, Jonathan! And that's not even the point!" Justin's eyes squeezed shut and he took a long, labored breath. "Forget it. Forget I said anything. Now is not the time."

"No, it's not, but you're finally talking about it, so it's on," Jonathan replied. "You think I sent you away because I couldn't wait to get rid of you? Is that what you thought?"

"What else was I supposed to think? You never knew me growing up. You were so much older. You already had your own life. Maybe you were jealous when I came along—you didn't have Dad all to yourself anymore. I don't know. But you didn't have to send me away to boarding school so soon after my Mom and Dad died. You could've kept me around... but you didn't."

"You think you understand what I was going through, Justin? Well let me explain it to you a little better: I was a stupid young man, just out of business school, trying to figure out what the hell to do with my life—and then my father goes and kills himself and my stepmom in a car accident."

"It wasn't his fault!" Justin shouted.

"I know!" Jonathan yelled back. Lowering his voice, he said, "But it happened. The family I knew was gone. I loved you, Justin. You were the only family I had left in the world. But you blamed me for Dad's death."

"I never blamed you."

"Yes, you did. You were blaming everyone; you were blaming the world. But you were out of control with your rage. You were hell-bent on killing yourself or winding up in jail."

"I wasn't that bad," Justin said...but his voice now held uncertainty.

"Oh?" Jonathan said. "Do you remember two months after the funeral, when you knocked out all the windows at the high school's gym building? Or when you got drunk one night and stole a car? All the fights you got into? The friends you were hanging around with? Do you remember all the times I had to come get you out of jail?"

Justin looked at him, unable to think up a reply.

"Case workers from Child Protective Services were knocking on the door," Jonathan continued. "They told me if I couldn't get you under control, I could forget about getting custody: they'd take you away from me forever."

There was a long pause. "I guess I didn't realize how bad I was," Justin said. "I remember going a little wild, but that's all."

"You were sneaking out every damn night, and there wasn't a fucking thing I could do to stop you," Jonathan said. "The social workers told me if I didn't get you help, you'd end up an addict, in jail, or dead. And there I was, a young guy with no experience with kids, no help, and no options. And remember, Dad left the business in ruins when he died. I had to take over that, too, so we wouldn't end up in bankruptcy."

"I guess I never thought about how hard you must've had it," Justin whispered. "Taking over the business, and your baby brother. I guess it makes sense, you wanting to send me away."

"No, Justin, no," Jonathan said. "I never *wanted* to send you away. But I didn't see any other choice. I needed to get you help for your anger. The boarding school was top notch, it had a great reputation, and it offered me to give you the counseling you needed. I thought if I sent you there, you'd have a chance...

but more importantly, I'd still be able to hold onto custody. I wouldn't lose you completely. I didn't even care about the business anymore, Justin. I just didn't want to lose my brother."

He shook his head and looked away. "But I lost you anyway. By the time you came home that summer, you were a different person: calm, polite...but you hated me." He looked back. "You're my brother, Justin, and I love you. But I don't want to impose myself into your life. Whatever relationship you want us to have, it's up to you. I'm here, whenever you're ready."

This time, it was Justin's turn to look away. He leaned his head against the shining glass window and closed his eyes.

For the first time, it occurred to him just how bad it must have been for his older brother after their father had died. It had been easier for Justin to hate him than think the all-controlling Jonathan Bentmoore had gone through his own personal hell, too.

All these years, was it possible Justin had been so wrong—about his brother, about everything? Yes, he supposed, it was. It was something for him to think long and hard about...after he found Alex.

The phone rang on the desk. Jonathan picked it up. "Yes?" He said. "Yes, thank you." He put the receiver down and said, "Peter's car just pulled into the garage. Dalia will show him in. Trowlege is bringing up Davis."

"Good," Justin said. "Let's do this."

A second later, the door to Jonathan's private elevator binged and slid open. Out came a stoic-looking Trowlege, followed by an astonished Davis, who stopped just outside the elevator door to peer around the room in fascination.

"Where are we now?" He asked. He saw Justin and exclaimed, "Justin! Do you have *any idea* what kind of place this is? This man, Mister...."

"Mr. Trowlege, Sir," Trowlege offered.

"Trowlege," Davis continued, "took me downstairs, and there's this whole—this *whole floor* of rooms, with all kinds of stuff! And this woman...." He suddenly became flustered, and his voice faded away. "Well, it's just, it's amazing is all it is."

"I know," Justin said. "Listen, the man we think was your client is almost here. I want you to sit down, listen to him talk, and tell me if you think it was him you spoke to."

"And if it's not?"

"If it's not, we'll figure something out," Justin said, glancing at his brother, who looked back at him with a worried frown. "Just have a seat."

Davis hesitated. "You know, I know I said I'd help, and you've all been amazing, especially the service," he said, glancing back at the elevator door. "But I don't know if I can do this. If word gets out I'm snitching on my clients...."

"You don't want to help us anymore?" Justin asked.

"I want to help, man, really. I just don't want anyone knowing it was me."

"I understand. You can go."

Davis's eyes went round as he asked, "I can?"

"Sure," Justin said. "The front lobby is that way. If you go out and turn left, there'll be a gas station about six miles down." He smiled coldly. "I'm sure if you walk real fast, you'll reach it before it gets *too* dark. There's spotty cell phone service on that stretch of road, but I'm sure they'll have a landline at the gas station you can use to call a cab to pick you up and take you to the airport, if you ask real nice. Of course, you'll have to get a plane ticket back yourself. That shouldn't cost you too much, though." He stretched his arm out toward the door. "Go ahead. We won't stop you."

Davis stared at him. "I don't really have a choice, do I?"

"No."

"But don't worry, Mr. Davis," Jonathan cut in. "You'll be well compensated for your trouble."

Davis shrugged. "In that case," he said, and sat down in one of Jonathan's lush chairs, facing the desk.

The office door opened, but it wasn't Jonathan's secretary who walked in, leading the way for the mysterious Peter; it was Mr. Cox, looking bound and intent, followed by a wary Hoshi.

Hoshi had not said much of anything since the moment Justin had called and told him Alex was in trouble. His deeply troubled expression had not altered since then, either.

"Good, we made it," Mr. Cox stated, looking around the room. Then he walked directly to Justin by the window. "Hey, Justin," he said, putting out his hand. There was a brief, single shake between the two of them; then Cox pointed his thumb over at Davis. "Who's this guy?"

"The one who was hired to find Alex," Justin said. "He's going to tell us if it was Peter who hired him."

"So you still haven't heard anything from her yet?" Hoshi asked. He glanced at Justin, then looked at Mr. Bentmoore. Both of them shook their heads. "Not good," Hoshi murmured. "Not good."

"Who're you?" Davis asked, narrowing his eyes up at Mr. Cox. Davis must've had more mettle than any of them were giving him credit for, Justin thought, to look at Mr. Cox like that.

Mr. Cox looked down at Davis and said, "I'm the guy who's going to hurt anyone who's hurt Alexandra."

Davis paled.

At that moment, the office door opened again; and this time, a specter of lush beauty floated into the room, followed by an anxious, jittery young man. He was well dressed in a pair of crème trousers, a yellow button-down shirt, and a dark grey suit jacket. His hair was perfectly coiffed to the side; it looked like he had locked it in place with a dollop of hair gel. But his eyes shifted nervously, and when he entered the room and saw all the people inside, he stopped.

"Mr. Bentmoore, I thought my meeting would only be with you," he said, becoming flustered by all the eyes looking upon him. "Who are these people?"

"Friends and associates," Jonathan said. "I don't believe you've met my brother, Justin."

"No, I haven't." Peter automatically stuck out his hand, and Justin shook it. "It's nice to meet you, Justin."

"You too."

Recalling why he was there, Peter said, "Mr.

Bentmoore, I don't mean to be rude, but there is something rather urgent I must talk to you about—in private."

"I think we know what it's about," Jonathan said. "Alexandra Wellington?"

"Yes!" Peter exclaimed. "How did you know?"

"Before I go any further—Mr. Davis?"

Davis shook his head. "This isn't him," he said. "Doesn't sound anything like him at all."

"Thank you," Mr. Bentmoore said, giving Justin a direct look. "Mr. Trowlege, will you please escort Mr. Davis—"

At that moment, Mr. Cox came forward and, facing away from everyone else, whispered something into Mr. Bentmoore's ear.

"Please escort Mr. Davis to the lobby, and stay with him," Mr. Bentmoore finished. "We might have need of him again."

"Very well, Sir. Come along, Sir." Trowlege held his arm out for Davis to lead the way, and Davis, giving Cox a pointed stare, took his cue. A second later, he and Mr. Trowlege had both disappeared out the door.

"Mr. Bentmoore, what is going on?" Peter asked, confused and uneasy. "Why are all these people in your office?"

"I'm sorry, Peter," Jonathan said, sitting down in the chair behind his desk. "We had to be sure."

"Be sure about what?"

"That you don't have Alexandra."

"We still can't be sure," Justin interjected, his voice raised. "Just because Davis doesn't think this

is his client doesn't mean he's not in on it somehow."
With two quick strides, he walked up to Peter, grabbed
him by the shirt with both fists, and gave him a little
shake. "Where's Alex? Where?"

"Justin, *let him go,*" Jonathan yelled, standing
up from his chair. Mr. Cox stepped over and quickly
separated Justin's grip from Peter's shirt. Peter
cowered away, while Cox held Justin back from trying
to make a grab for him again.

"I don't know!" Peter cried, covering his chest
with his hands. "That's what I came here for, to tell
Mr. Bentmoore I'm worried!"

"Justin, keep your hands off him," Jonathan ordered.
Then, in a more conciliatory tone, he motioned to the
chair across his desk and said, "Peter, have a seat. I'm
sorry about my brother, he's just very worried about
Alexandra. Please, tell us what you know."

Peter studied Justin nervously for a moment. Justin
took a step back, sending Peter a clear message he
wasn't going to attack him again—at least, not yet.
Peter smoothed down his shirt and took a seat.

"I'm assuming everyone here knows who Alexandra
is," he said, speaking to Jonathan directly.

"Yes," Jonathan said. "And we all care about her
very much."

"I'll have to take your word on that." His eyes
narrowed. "You know Alexandra has kept up contact
with me over the last few years."

"The same way she's kept up contact with me,
I'm assuming."

"I have no idea," Peter said. "I speak to Alexandra

two mornings a week, every week, like clockwork. Sometimes we'd speak more often, especially if there was something big going on at Wellington Enterprises. But always, *always,* we'd have those two weekly phone calls, no matter what." He paused. "I was supposed to talk to her two days ago. She never picked up."

"And you think she's in trouble."

"What else am I supposed to think?" Peter said, putting his hands up. "But what am I supposed to do? I have no way of contacting her except through the phone number I've always used. She's mentioned to me she talks to you regularly, too...Mr. Bentmoore, have you heard from her?"

"No, I have not. Peter, we have reason to think Alexandra is in danger."

"What kind of danger?"

"We think she's been abducted again."

"Oh Jesus." Peter put his hands up to his face. "Wait—that's what that guy Davis was in here for, wasn't it? You thought *I* might've taken her." He looked at Justin and said, "I swear, I would never hurt Alexandra, ever. She's like a sister to me. She's the one who gave me the job at Wellington Enterprises, and made me chairman of the board. I would never betray her—never."

Looking into his eyes, Justin had to accept the fact that his brother was right: Peter was telling the truth. But that left Justin with a bigger problem: where, and how, to find Alex.

"Can you think of anyone who might want her out of the way?" Cox asked.

"Not really, no," Peter said, shaking his head. "I mean, why would they? Unless they think they can get her money....Maybe they think she left them something in her will?" He looked at Jonathan. "Do *you* know anything about that, Mr. Bentmoore?"

"No," Jonathan said. "As far as I know, Alexandra's plan is to leave all her money to charity, and somehow I doubt it's a charity organization that's behind this."

"What if it's not about the money?" Justin piped up. "What if it's about her connection to Wellington Enterprises?" At Peter's confused look, he said, "If someone found out Alex was still controlling the company from afar, and didn't like what she was doing, they'd do their best to try to stop her, wouldn't they?"

"It would have to be someone who wields power behind the scenes at Wellington Enterprises," Cox said, "and it would have to be someone smart. Whoever this guy is, he was smart enough to give Davis the impression the guy we're looking for is you."

"There's no one that calculating working behind the scenes," Peter said, looking vaguely away as he thought it through. "At least, not as far as I know. The board members know how to be calculating, of course—we all have to make our backroom deals, to make sure our pet projects get funded...although everyone's projects have taken a back burner the last few weeks."

Mr. Bentmoore's eyes furrowed. "What's been going on the last few weeks?"

"A vote is coming up on a new contract," Peter replied, brushing the question away. "Routine stuff for a conglomerate our size, except this company deals with stuff we normally don't get into. Alexandra is against the partnership though, so it won't go through."

"Why is she against it?" Justin asked, feeling the hairs on the back of his neck begin to prickle.

"I don't know," Peter said. "She didn't share that with me. She gets these feelings sometimes...oh Jesus. Oh man." He leaned back in his chair. "Oh my god."

"What?" Justin said, striding over to stand before him. Everyone crowded around the chair.

"Hector Carmine," Peter said, his eyes staring off into space. "Hector Carmine."

"Who's Hector Carmine?"

"He's the head of Acquisitions. He's been trying to push this deal through for a long time. He's very determined." He rubbed his face with his hands, lost in thought. "This isn't the first time Hector's tried to orchestrate this deal. The first time was about six months ago, but Alexandra called all the board members, individually, and asked them to vote against it. Hector was livid when it fell through."

"How livid?"

"If you're asking me if Hector is the kind of man who would take drastic measures to make sure Alexandra wouldn't interfere with the vote a second time, my answer would have to be...yes," he said. "Hector is hell-bent on Wellington Enterprises partnering up with this company, DSV Corporations. If Hector is getting some sort of kickback on the deal...we're not talking here millions; we're talking billions. He could leave the country a happy man."

"Leave the country? Why would you mention that?" Justin asked.

"I seem to remember Hector saying he was born in Sao Paulo," Peter said, tilting his head. "He told me that a few years ago. I remember thinking, when DSV Corp approached him for the contract, that he probably felt a sort of affinity towards them, since they're based in Brazil. They could all speak Portuguese with each other."

"Portuguese...." Justin's mind cast back to what Alex had told him. *Joshua's whole world was the company. He wouldn't have known how to hire three foreign guns-for-hire to set up an abduction....He must have had an associate, a trusted friend, who knew how to get it done, and give the orders in Joshua's place.*

"This Hector, how long has he been with Wellington Enterprises? Did he know Alex's stepfather?"

"Oh yeah," Peter exclaimed. "Hector's been there for years. He was actually vice-president of the company, back in Joshua's days, ruling the wheel as Joshua's right hand man. Of course, that was all before. After Joshua died, Hector stepped down, and moved into Acquisitions. We all thought he couldn't bear the idea of being vice-president without Joshua being the one giving him orders. What?" Peter looked around the stunned faces. "What did I say?"

"Hector was in on it three years ago," Justin said, looking at his brother. "And he's in on it now, too."

"Peter, this Hector Carmine, where would he be now?" Jonathan asked, leaning over his desk. "Where could we find him?"

"I guess he'd be working over at the main branch, except…." He gave them his far-away look again. "He hasn't come into work the last few days. I thought it was odd, with the board meeting being so close, but then I just assumed he was attending private meetings off-site."

There was a pause of silence. Mr. Cox asked, "This board meeting. The vote for the contract happens then?"

"Yes."

"Will the board members be expecting another phone call from Alexandra before that happens?"

"I…I would think maybe so, yes," Peter said slowly. "If they thought she might have changed her opinion on the matter, and they should vote the other way. Otherwise, they would probably assume she'd still be against it, and vote no."

"What are you thinking, Cox?" Jonathan asked.

"I'm thinking Hector will need Alexandra to call all the board members soon, and tell them to switch their votes," Cox replied. "Which means he must be keeping her alive, at least for now…until he can get the votes through."

Justin's mouth went dry. It had not occurred to him until then—he had not been able to contemplate the very thought until then—that Alex might have already been killed.

"If we're right, and it's this Hector," Cox continued. "We might be wrong."

"We're not wrong," Justin said. "It fits. Can't you feel it?"

"Yeah, I feel it," Cox said, moving his tongue

around his mouth. "It's him." To Peter, he said: "This vote. How long do we have? When is it supposed to happen, exactly?"

"Tomorrow evening," Peter said. "The meeting is scheduled for tomorrow at five."

"And when would the board members be getting a phone call from Alexandra, to tell them to approve the new contract?"

"Tonight."

There was a moment of shocked silence. Then Jonathan asked him, "Does anyone else know you're here?"

"No one, not even my secretary," Peter said.

"Good," Jonathan said. "And I take it you'd be included on this list of board members Alexandra would call, right? As chairman of the board, you're supposed to be at this meeting tomorrow to vote?"

"Absolutely."

"Excellent. Peter, we're going to have to borrow your phone."

"Why?"

"We're going to have to trace the phone call."

"You can do that?" Peter asked, amazed. "You have that kind of technology?"

"No, we don't," Jonathan replied. "But I think we have someone here who does." He picked up his phone and said, "Please send Mr. Trowlege and Mr. Davis back in. Thank you."

Justin watched him, leery. "Jonathan, what does Davis have to do with this? He doesn't have anything on Hector. He's just a PI."

At this point, Hoshi interjected with, "No, he's not." It was the first time he had spoken since Peter had walked in the room. Hoshi glanced at Cox, and they shared a laden look.

Justin turned, saw their expressions, and said, "He's not? Then who is he?"

Hoshi didn't have a chance to reply; the office door opened once more, but this time, Trowlege merely held the door open as Davis walked through, and quickly shut it again as soon as Davis was well inside.

"What's going on?" Davis asked, looking around. His eyes zeroed in on Jonathan and held there. "Why'd you ask me in here again?"

"We need your help," Jonathan said. "We think we know who has Alexandra. It's a man named Hector Carmine."

"Hector Carmine?"

"Yes, and we need to find Alexandra before Hector decides he has no more use for her."

"Um, sure," Davis said, looking amiable. "How can I help?"

"We need to put a trace on Peter's phone here. We think Alexandra will be calling him sometime in the next few hours. We need to know where the call is coming from so we can find her."

"Mr. Bentmoore, with all due respect, I don't see how I can do that," Davis said with a titter of laughter. "I can't put a trace on anyone's phone. I'm kind of a one-man act; I don't have access to that kind of technology. But I'll tell you what: I can make some phone calls, and see what I can find out for you about this Hector Carmine. I'll be right back." He started backing toward the door as he pulled his cell phone out of his pocket.

Hoshi stepped over to block his path before Davis could reach the door; Davis bumped him in the chest. "Sorry man," he said, turning around. "Just going to step out and make these phone calls."

"So you can tell your boss you know where Alexandra Wellington is?" Hoshi said. "I don't think so. Sit down, Mr. Davis."

Davis let his phone drop back into his pocket and put his hands up. "Okay, obviously I missed something here when I was locked outside under guard, because you all seem to have the wrong idea about me. I do not have a boss. I'm a PI, a *private investigator.*" He said the words slowly. "I work on my own. No behind-the-scenes action going on."

"Enough." Mr. Cox's gruff voice echoed around the room. "Sit down." When Davis merely looked at him, Cox said, *"Now."*

Davis sat.

"We know you're not a PI, Mr. Davis," Jonathan said.

Davis made a sound like a half laugh, half grunt. "I'm not?" He said. "You want to check my info again? Cause my business cards seem to think I am."

"We don't have time for this," Cox said. "Alexandra is in danger, we need your help, and by god, you and your people are going to help us, or...."

"Or what?" Davis said, his voice turned suddenly sharp. "What'll you do?"

Jonathan said, "It's actually very simple." He picked

up his phone again, and said into it, loud and clear: "Please call Detective Paulson and have him come over. Yes, Detective Paulson. I have someone here we caught trespassing, taking nonconsensual pictures of our guests, and engaging in lewd behavior. We think he might be in possession of child pornography on his phone. He'll have to be questioned, and his phone will have to be checked. I'm sure they'll want fingerprints, too, in case he's in the sexual predator database."

"NO!" Davis cried, standing up and making a lunge at the phone. "Don't!"

Jonathan held the phone out of his reach. "You want to help now?" He asked.

"Fine! Damn it!" Davis sat back down hard. "Just don't call in other law enforcement. They'll blow my cover."

Jonathan pulled the phone back to his mouth and said, "Scratch that order, we won't be needing Paulson after all." He returned the receiver to his desk and peered at Mr. Davis. "Now then. I think it's your turn to come clean."

Davis looked at Mr. Cox. "It was you, wasn't it? You knew."

"Yes," Cox stated simply.

"Will someone please tell me what's going on?" Justin's voice rose. "Who is this guy?"

Davis sighed. To Justin, he said, "I'm a CI. A criminal investigator." To clarify, he added, "I'm with the Feds."

As he spoke to Justin, his whole demeanor changed: where an affable, jovial, and slightly dim-witted guy once was, now sat a sharp, tenacious man with keen eyes and a cagey smile. Justin was amazed at the change in him. The Davis of a minute ago had been nothing but an act, a façade; now that his cover was blown, he had shed it off like snakeskin.

"For Christ's sakes," Justin said. "Why didn't you tell us?"

"Hello? Cover? Blown?" Davis answered him. "I thought I did a pretty good job with my story. I may need some brushing up on my act," he murmured to himself. He looked at Cox and said, "I might've gotten away with it, though, if I hadn't run into you. The infamous Mr. Cox, standing before me in the flesh. So this is where you ended up, huh?"

"Yup. Don't regret it for a minute."

"After seeing that downstairs floor, I can understand why."

"No," Mr. Cox said coldly. "You can't."

"Let's steer this back to the issue at hand," Mr. Bentmoore cut in. "Mr. Davis—your name *is* Mr. Davis, right?"

"Yeah. That much is true."

"Can you ask your associates to put a trace on Peter's phone here, so we can know where all incoming calls are coming from?"

"Yeah, I can do that," Davis said. "But are you guys sure it's Carmine who has her? Cause he wasn't even on our radar."

"So you *do* know who he is?" Justin said.

"Yeah. Head of Acquisitions. But it's a fluff title; he's a nobody. At least, we thought he was. If he's behind this," Davis shook his head, "then we were *way* off."

"What a surprise," Mr. Cox sneered. "Now get your people working. Put that trace on the phone. We don't have much time left."

The next few hours saw all six men—Justin, Jonathan, Hoshi, Cox, Davis, and Peter Ames—pacing and waiting inside Mr. Bentmoore's office in a state of anxious anticipation. They didn't talk unless they had to. The hours ticked by.

Peter's phone sat on Mr. Bentmoore's desk. There were no wires coming out of it, no added chips or cards to help them trace the phone call. All the technology they needed was being provided from an outside source, one of "Davis's people," who would likely remain anonymous now and forever, hallelujah, amen.

Peter sat in Jonathan's chair, right next to the phone. When it rang, he would be the one picking it up, and he would be the only one talking. They had to make the conversation sound as natural as possible; Hector might very well be listening to Alexandra speak, to make sure she didn't drop any hints. Peter would also keep the conversation going for as long as possible, to give them more time.

But for now, they had nothing to do but wait.

Justin took the opportunity to ask Davis why he had been trailing Alexandra in the first place.

"Your girlfriend's been living a shady life the last few years," he said. "Did you know that?"

"I know she's been travelling a lot from place to place. Since when is that a crime?"

"Since she's got linked bank accounts to Wellington Enterprises, keeps an account in her mother's maiden name, travels incognito, and still maintains secret contact with the chairman of the board of her company. Even you have to admit it all looks fishy."

"That still doesn't explain to me why the Feds started looking for her in the first place."

"It's the DSV Corp deal," Davis said. "Peter told you about it, right?"

"Peter told us Hector's been trying to get a contract between DSV Corp and Wellington Enterprises for a while. He said last time it was up for a vote, Alexandra called all the board members so it wouldn't go through."

"Yeah, well, we started looking into the DSV-Wellington deal back then."

"Why?"

"DSV makes petrochemicals and thermoplastics," Davis explained, "while Wellington Enterprises has some delicate subsidiary deals."

"What kind of subsidiary deals?"

"Let's just call them defense contracts and leave it at that," Davis said. "With DSV Corp on one side, and Wellington on the other...anti-trust laws suddenly became an issue—among other things."

"Other things? What are we talking about here? Espionage?"

"No, no," Davis was quick to retreat, making Justin realize that was *exactly* what it was. "But trade secrets were a concern. Let's just say, we felt like we had enough to be worried. We saw some red flags, not enough for us to stop the deal, but enough for us to take a second look. The deal fell through anyway, though, so our concerns were moot."

"It fell through because Alex put a stop to it," Justin pointed out.

"We didn't know that," Davis said. "At that point, we didn't have any inside contacts at Wellington. But our concerns did not go away. We learned that the contact between DSV Corp and Wellington was not completely dead. So we decided to look further."

"And what did you find?"

"Nothing we could pin down...nothing we could use as evidence...but there were signs of cooperate embezzlement, security fraud, and...worse."

Justin had a feeling that "worse" had something to do with those defense contracts Davis didn't want to talk about. "Holy shit," he murmured. "Alexandra doesn't know anything about that."

"We know that *now,* but look at it from our point of view. Six months ago, we saw signs of some really shady back-room deals being made, information trade going on, and meanwhile, the sole major shareholder of the company is off living a secret life, travelling around God knows where, with access to money accounts nobody knows about. Our natural assumption was that she was calling the shots from behind the scenes, acting as a go-between for the two sides, Wellington and DSV Corp."

"Okay, I get it," Justin said through clenched teeth. "You're right, it does look shady, but Alexandra would never do that."

"We didn't know that. And then a couple months ago, a new RSV Corp-Wellington Enterprises deal was leaked," Davis said. "This time, our contact inside the company moved in on it right away, and I was brought in to find Alexandra. It was easier said than done... man, that woman knows how to get out of Dodge in a hurry—and she leaves no tracks."

"This is true," Justin said, feeling a measure of pride that Alex had managed to outsmart Davis for so long.

"I finally caught up with her in your store, and started trailing her. But she wasn't meeting with anyone from DSV Corp *or* Wellington Enterprises. She didn't even own a fucking computer. All she was doing was living a quiet life, working for you."

"So you must've stopped suspecting her."

"No, because we knew she was still in regular contact with Peter," Davis said. "We put a trail on him, too."

"Does Peter know that?"

"No, and I don't see a reason to tell him. Let's just say, when all this is over, he'll have to find himself a new secretary."

"Ah."

"But we couldn't pinpoint Peter doing anything too suspicious, either. And meanwhile, the new deal with DSV Corp was on the fast track. We had to find something we could use against it being finalized. I took a chance, and broke into Alexandra's apartment." He shook his head, chagrined. "It was a stupid mistake. I didn't find anything, and she figured out I'd been there. I have no idea how. I made sure not to disturb anything."

"Alex has been living the life of a fugitive for a long time," Justin said. "She knows what to look for."

"I guess so. When I realized my little foray into her apartment had been discovered, I thought for sure she'd leave town again. But she didn't: she ran to you. Then lo and behold, a former FBI agent shows up, and I thought I was about to crack the case. If Hoshi was helping her, he could have been the missing piece to the puzzle we were looking for. But that's not how it turned out." He looked away and shook his head again. "I looked into Hoshi, looked into you, hell, I even looked into your coworker Adam, and that girlfriend of his. I found nothing. All of you were clean."

"Must've driven you nuts," Justin said, his fingers twitching with annoyance. He'd been spied on. He didn't like it.

"Yeah, it did," Davis said, unapologetic. "The contract vote was put on the calendar. We were running out of time. I ordered Alexandra's accounts looked into, hoping something would pop out at us."

"You must've known she had enough security in place that she'd be told you guys tried to get access."

"Yeah, but we had no choice. And again, it didn't make a difference: we didn't find anything," Davis said. "I started to think we'd been wrong about her all along. That maybe Peter was the real mastermind."

"Not once did you look at Hector Carmine?"

"No, we didn't. I'm beginning to wonder about that,

too." Davis rubbed his cheek, deep in thought. Then he snapped out of it and said, "I lost Alexandra for a while after that. I thought she'd run again. But then I saw her by your shop on Main Street...or at least, I thought I did. Of course, you know the rest: *that* girl wasn't Alexandra at all. It was your coworker's girlfriend. You guys trapped me, and here we are."

"You gave us this whole story about being hired to find Alex."

"Hey, I thought it was good thinking on my feet."

"It was." Justin's brows creased as he remembered. "*You* led us to Peter. You wanted us to confront him."

"When you told me Alexandra was missing, and you thought she was in trouble, I realized we'd been wrong about her all along; that whoever wanted this DSV Corp deal to go through, they also wanted her out of the way, so she couldn't mess it up. I thought for sure it was Peter."

"Then why didn't you go after him yourself?"

"My cover, remember? I thought you guys would call the police or something, and I could slip away and get in contact with my people. But you didn't just let me go: you wanted me to come here with you. When I overheard you talking to your brother, I realized you had a better chance of getting to Peter than I did without tipping him off, so I decided to come along, to see how things played out."

"So we ended up doing your work for you. We were the ones who figured out it was Hector." Justin made a sound like a grunt.

It dawned on him that Davis had been the one

who'd been after Alex all along. The problem was, Davis had never been any *real* danger to Alex. Hector Carmine was the real danger...and nobody had been looking at him at all.

"I hope you're right, and it is Hector Carmine," Davis said. "For Alexandra's sake."

"We are," Justin replied. Softly, he added, "We have to be."

At that point, Davis put his hand on Justin's shoulder, gave it a squeeze, and walked away.

More time went by.

It was six o'clock.

Then it was seven.

Justin kept his post by the window, gazing out at the horizon. The sun had set long ago and it was impossible to see much of anything outside, but he wasn't really looking, anyway.

The glass reflected his face, pale and gaunt. He tried not to drown his mind in thoughts of what he could have done differently, what he might be doing differently right now to find Alex faster. He tried not to look every second at the clock on the wall, or the phone on the desk.

He tried not to think about what he would do if Alex was beyond his help.

The others left him alone.

Food was brought in. Justin could smell it. But he didn't partake, and nobody pushed him to it. Jonathan put a mug of tea in his hand. Justin took a few sips and put it down on the desk, giving a subversive glance at the phone.

At sixteen minutes past nine, it rang.

Peter let it ring twice before he answered. They had rehearsed what he would say, how he would respond. As he picked up the cell phone and put it to his ear, Justin saw it trembling in his hand.

"Alexandra, hi, I'm so happy to hear from you," Peter said a little too loudly. Jonathan pressed his palm downward in a "tone it down" motion, and Peter gave him a small nod.

Davis, who had stood watching for a moment, now quickly walked out of the room, pulling out his own cell phone as he quietly exited.

None of the others got close to Peter. They didn't want to spook him. Justin stood like a statue from his spot by the window, working hard to keep his breathing slow and silent.

Hope swelled in his chest. His Alex was alive.

"I was surprised I didn't hear from you for so long," Peter said. Jonathan nodded, showing a nervous Peter he was doing well. Jonathan had decided it would be better for Peter to act concerned over Alexandra's long silence; it would look more natural.

"Ah," Peter said into the phone. "Yes, I see. Well I'm glad you're keeping yourself busy. What can I do for you?" He was quiet for a while. "Aha…okay…yes, I see…yes, I understand…but Alexandra, are you sure you want to go in this direction? You were so adamant the deal not go through before." He kept up his vocal acknowledgements to whatever it was she was saying, even nodding into the phone a few times. "Well, that's all true, Alexandra, but I'm wondering if you've really thought this through. The contract has some major provisions in it…uh huh…yes I see….”

Peter kept going for as long as he could. But he stuck to what he had been told: keep Alexandra on the phone for as long as possible, but quit when it started to feel wrong. They wanted Alex, and by extension, Hector, to think she had done her job, delivering orders to Peter he would follow whether he agreed with them or not. That was what Peter had always done in the past; he had to make Alex think he would now do it again.

Deviating from normal would put Alex at risk.

“Okay then,” Peter said with a sigh. “I understand. Have you called the rest of the board yet? No? You might want to hold off on calling Jeff. He’s at his son’s music recital.”

Justin and the others tensed as they stared at him. This had not been part of the script.

Peter continued, “Yeah, his son’s in third grade already, can you believe it? No, sure, I understand, you have to go. Yeah, I’ll remember. Listen, it was good talking to you. Don’t make me wait so long for your next phone call, okay? Okay. Bye now.” He hung up.

“What the hell was that?” Justin roared. “You might’ve just tipped Hector off!”

“No, I didn’t,” Peter said. “I gave Alexandra more time. Jeff does have a son who plays piano, he brags about him all the time. Hector will believe Jeff is off somewhere where he doesn’t want to be bothered. He’ll let Alexandra wait the hour before she calls him.”

“He’s right, Justin,” Cox said, stepping in from the

sideline. He looked at Peter and said, "You did good."

Justin clenched his jaws closed. If Cox thought it went okay, Justin would have to trust his opinion.

Davis pounded in, swinging the door open with a bang. "We got her," he announced to the room. "We have her location."

"Where is she?" Justin yelled.

"You're never going to believe this," Davis said. "She's at a ranch—about four miles away. We can be there in a few minutes." Quietly under his breath he added, "She's been under our noses this whole time."

"Then let's go get her," Justin said, making his way to the door.

"Justin, wait!" Davis called after him, making him stop and turn. "This is not up to you anymore. My people know where she is. They're getting a warrant and making up a plan to go in and rescue her as we speak. They know what they're doing. Let them handle this one."

"The last time Alex trusted 'your people' to save her, she almost got killed," Justin said. "And none of you bothered to figure out who was really behind the kidnapping three years ago. If you had, this wouldn't be happening again. And now you want me to sit on my ass and wait while your people worry about *warrants* and *plans?* I don't think so. I'm going to get my Alex back—as soon as you tell me where she is."

"I can't," Davis said. "I'm sorry."

"Yes, you can," Cox growled. "And you will, because if you don't, and something happens to Alexandra Wellington, I am going to personally blame you, Davis." He pointed a finger into the other man's chest. "Think about that one for a minute."

Cox stared at Davis, his eyes clear and cutting. Davis, to his credit, did not flinch or look away, but Justin detected a tick in his jaw.

"Fine, I'll tell you," Davis finally said. "But I'm coming with you."

"I thought you had to get your warrant first," Justin sneered.

"Yeah, well, you need someone official on this trip," Davis said.

"I think I should stay here," Peter piped up, his voice high. "Just in case Alexandra calls back for some reason."

"That would be a good idea, Peter," Jonathan said. To Davis, he said, "I just need one more thing."

He reached down to his bottom desk drawer, opened it up, and pulled out a Glock-22 9 mm handgun. He checked the magazine, nodded, and tucked it into his belt behind his back.

He looked at Hoshi and said, "You?"

"Covered," Hoshi replied.

To Cox: "You?"

"Covered."

"Good," Jonathan said, giving them all a single hard nod. "Then let's go."

The drive to the ranch took longer than Justin thought it would, with Jonathan driving all of them in his black SUV. Some of the turns they had to take didn't lead onto any marked roads, and some of the driving wasn't done on roads at all, just graveled dirt. It was hard to see in the dark.

Davis, studying the file he had been sent on his phone, took them around wide instead of leading them straight up the front of the property. As they got closer, he ordered Jonathan to cut the headlights completely, so they would be undetectable in the dark.

"Why would he bring her *here?*" Justin asked, keeping his eyes on the view outside the windshield. It was hard to see anything; he had to trust Davis was giving them the right directions, and Jonathan was leading them the right way. "Seems kind of foolish to keep her so close to the Hotel Bentmoore."

"Wouldn't have mattered where he hid her if we didn't know where to look," Cox pointed out. "But think about it: if the police find a body on someone's property, and discover the owner of said property has access to a bank account worth millions belonging to the deceased…who do you think they'll be looking at for murder?"

Justin's whole body went rigid as understanding came to him. "Hector found out Alex shares an account with my brother," he whispered. "And he was going to pin the crime on him."

"Bingo," Davis murmured, studying his phone. Louder, he instructed, "Slow down to a crawl. We should see it up ahead any second."

A moment later, they saw it: a small ranch house, single level, planted next to a rocky hill. Light was coming out the window by the back.

Somebody was home.

Jonathan got as close as he dared, then killed the engine. "Suggestions," he said.

"There are five of us and one of Hector," Justin said. "I say we go in and take down the bastard."

"Even if you're right, you're still putting Alexandra's life at risk," Davis said. "He only needs a second to put a bullet in her head. He might kill her before we can stop him. Plus, we don't know that Hector's working alone."

"Recognizance," Hoshi said with a sigh. "I guess this is where I come in." He opened the door and stepped out of the car before anyone could stop him. "I'll be back."

"Goddamnit Hoshi," Justin hissed, watching the man slink away into the dark. Hoshi disappeared and was gone.

He returned a few minutes later. "One guy," he said, climbing back into the car. "Looks to be about sixty years old, between five foot seven and eight, about a hundred ninety pounds. Has a gun on him. I saw Alexandra: she's tied to a chair. There's a cell phone next to her."

"Did she look okay?" Justin asked.

"She looked scared," Hoshi said, "but unharmed so far. There are two doors: one in the front, and one in the back, leading into one of the bedrooms. There are five windows, but none of them are open."

"That leaves the doors," Davis said. "How close is Hector to Alexandra?"

"She's in the south side of the house, sitting at

a small table off the kitchen. Hector is keeping her in his line of vision. If he hears us coming, he'll go straight to her, and we'll have a hostage situation on our hands—if he doesn't kill her."

"So we need to distract Hector somehow, long enough for us to get between him and Alex," Justin said. "How?"

They were all quiet for a moment. Then Cox said, "There's one thing, but Justin's not going to like it."

"What is it?" Jonathan asked.

"A fire," Cox said. "We start a fire in the back of the house. Carmine will have to choose between putting the fire out, or hightailing it out of there."

"Alex will have a heart attack!" Justin yelled. "You know that's a trigger for her!"

"I said you wouldn't like it."

"Think up something else!"

"Got any ideas?" Cox asked with raised brows. Justin scowled.

Davis looked at him and asked, "How would we make your plan work?"

"Mr. Bentmoore always keeps a couple two-gallon jugs of gasoline in his trunk," Cox answered, looking at his boss, who nodded. "We use them to light the place up."

"Okay then," Davis said. "Cox, you and Bentmoore senior here get the fire going, and wait in the back. Hopefully, Carmine will come straight to you. Hoshi and I will wait by the front, in case he tries to escape that way."

"What about me?" Justin asked.

"You're staying in the car," Davis said. When Justin opened his mouth to protest, Davis continued, "I'm not risking you doing something stupid to save your girlfriend and getting yourself killed. It's why I didn't want you here in the first place. You're a liability, Justin."

"No," Justin stated.

"Yes," Davis answered back. "If you don't trust me, at least trust your own people to get the job done."

"No fucking way."

"Then trust *me,* Justin," Jonathan implored. "We'll get her out of there. I promise." He opened the driver's side door. "Just stay in the car, no matter what happens. We'll be back soon with Alexandra."

Cox had already gotten out and retrieved the gas containers from the trunk. "Let's go," he said. He held a gun in his other hand. It was then Justin realized, he was the only one of them not carrying a gun.

They all got out, everyone but Justin, and carefully slipped away into the dark.

"Shit," Justin seethed under breath. He squeezed his eyes shut.

Sighed, blinked, looked out the window.

Blinked again. "Shit," he repeated.

Then he got out of the car and ran.

He went wide around the house toward the front, keeping his body as low and as silent as possible. He caught sight of Cox, crouching next to his brother, lighting up the back porch; saw the flames leap up and begin to strain toward the night sky. The noise of the crackling fire was surprisingly loud.

He kept going around the house before the acrid scent of the black smoke made it to his nostrils. There, just ahead, were Hoshi and Davis, crouched by the front door, guns drawn.

Before he could reach them, a scream came from inside the house. It was a woman's scream.

Justin sprinted the last few feet to Davis and slid down next to him.

"What the fuck are you doing here?" Davis whispered, his eyes concentrated on the door.

"I'm saving my girlfriend," Justin whispered back. Another scream came from inside, then another. Beneath the screaming, gruff swears could be heard.

Justin could smell the fire now, sharp and pungent. He had a feeling if he stood up, he'd be able to see it from the other side of the house. Meanwhile, the screaming turned into a single, long, high-pitched shriek.

"Shouldn't we go in yet?" Justin whispered.

"Not yet," Davis replied. "Carmine might still be too close to her."

A window exploded, somewhere in the back; the screaming paused, then started again. Justin could hear the fire now, burning the wood fueling it. It was spreading too fast.

The screams turned into hysterical braying.

"For all we know Hector's already gone out the back," Justin said. "We need to get her out of there before the fire reaches her."

"For all you know he might charge right at you

the moment you walk in the door," Davis hissed. "Stay down."

"I don't care if Hector comes at me. I need to get Alex out of there. If he shoots me, get her out."

"Justin—Justin!"

Justin had sprang up and kicked open the door. Smoke tendrils immediately wafted out from the ceiling. Davis and Hoshi both jumped up a second after him, covering his path.

Justin ran to the other side of the house where the screaming was coming from. He had to stop when he got to the next room; his breath locked in his throat.

Alex was there, tied to a chair, just as Hoshi had described. Her head was twisted over her shoulder; her eyes were fixated on the dancing flames coming from the room behind her.

Right next to her stood Hector Carmine, looking down at a fire extinguisher in his hands, swearing loudly.

Alex saw Justin and stopped screaming. Her face was a mask of terror, but no sound came out of her throat. Hector, sensing something was amiss, turned around to see what was going on.

He saw Justin, dropped the extinguisher, and pulled out his gun.

"Don't take a step closer," he said, pointing the gun toward Justin.

"It's over, Hector," Justin said, putting his hands up in surrender.

Hoshi and Davis entered the room, guns drawn. Hector saw them, looked at Justin, and realization spread across his face: he was trapped. His eyes widened, and his face took on a sort of wild desperation, like those of a cornered buck.

He shifted the nozzle of the gun away from Justin… and straight at Alex's head.

"Any of you move, she dies," he said, stepping closer to her seated body. Alex recoiled in the chair, trying to move her head away from the tip of the gun. Hector pushed it into her hair. "I'll kill her right now, I swear I will."

Justin stopped, keeping his hands up. "It will gain you nothing, Hector," he said. "We already know everything."

"At least I'll have my revenge," he rasped.

"You'll die for it," Justin replied.

"Look around you," Hector said. "We're all going to die here."

"How about a Plan B," Justin said calmly. "You run out that door." He pointed his thumb behind him. "None of us will stop you. Just run. You'll live to see another day."

"And then what?" Hector laughed; it was a harsh sound, full of madness. "I won't be able to show my face again. My life will be ruined. I'll lose everything! And she will *still! Be! In! Control!*" He shoved the gun against Alex's head with each word, making her flinch and cry out. "No, I don't think so. If I'm going down, she's coming down with me." He moved the nozzle to Alex's temple. Alex closed her eyes and whimpered.

"Going down, huh?" Justin said, his voice smooth as silk. He tilted his head. "Then we're *all* going down. You, me, Alex…and Judy." He directed his piercing stare straight at Alex, who stared back at him in horror. "That's right," he said, "poor Judy's going down."

"What the hell are you talking about?" Hector yelled.

Justin's stare was locked on Alex. "You ready babe?" He asked her. With wide eyes, she gave him a tiny nod. Justin yelled: "NOW!"

Alex shoved her entire body weight to the left, making the chair tip and fall. At the same time, Justin lunged for the gun in Hector's hand.

He never made it. A shot rang out from behind him; Hector fell back and dropped his gun to the floor.

It all happened so fast, Justin still instinctively tried to grab the gun before it hit the ground; but even as his hands clasped around the thing, he knew there was no point.

Hector was dead on the floor. Davis had shot him.

Justin scurried over to Alex. She didn't move. Her body was contorted inside the chair. "Alex," he said, shaking her shoulder. Her head sagged against the floor; her eyes were closed. "Alex!" Justin shook her face. She was out cold.

Hoshi and Davis knelt down next to him. "We've got to get her out of here," Hoshi said.

"Find something to cut the rope," Davis said.

"Fuck that, just help me carry her," Justin said, picking up the back of the chair with Alex still tied inside. Hoshi grabbed the front chair legs, and together, he and Justin carried her out of the burning house, with Davis only a step behind them.

They didn't stop until they were a good distance away. The fire was now raging out of control; the blustering flames had engulfed the back of the house.

A moment later they were joined by Cox and Jonathan, who both reeked of fire and gasoline.

"You guys all right?" Jonathan yelled, dropping down to his knees next to Alexandra, who was still unconscious and tied to the chair.

"We're fine, but Alex is stuck," Justin yelled back. "We need to get her out."

"Here." Cox pulled a pair of curved sheers out of his back pocket. He handed them to Justin, and in minutes, Alex was free.

But she was still inert. "Let's get the hell out of here," Justin said, picking up Alex's body in a cradle hold.

"You go," Davis said. "I'll stay behind. My people are on their way. I'll need to explain what happened here."

"Are you sure?" Justin yelled over the noise of the fire.

"Yeah, I'll handle it from here," Davis yelled back. "You go, get her safe. I'll meet up with you later."

"Okay. Davis: thanks."

David nodded in response, and motioned them away. Justin, carrying Alex against his chest, walked briskly back to the car, followed by Mr. Cox, Hoshi, and Jonathan. He got Alex into the back with him, and the rest of them piled in.

A second later, they were gone.

The drive back to the hotel took longer, because Jonathan wanted to avoid the roads they had taken before. Within a few minutes, Justin heard sirens coming their way, but the sounds soon passed them from a different road, and quickly ebbed into silence.

Once they got back to the hotel, they carried Alex to the medical room, where the hotel's registered nurse examined her. The only things the nurse could find on Alex were a bruise on her arm and a tiny bump on her head; nothing that would explain Alexandra's blackout.

So they brought Alex downstairs to the dungeon floor, got her inside one of the small bedrooms the hotel used to house new initiates, put her on the bed, and carefully began the process of waking her up. They wanted to do it gently, and not agitate her. But in the end, they had to use smelling salts to get the job done.

After a few quick shakes of her head, Alex's eyes finally opened.

"Hey beautiful," Justin said.

She began to thrash; he and Mr. Cox held her down.

"Alex, it's okay, you're safe, you're at the hotel, you're safe...."

She stopped her thrashing, looked up at Justin, and began to cry.

"It's okay sweetheart, you're safe, it's okay."

"I thought I'd never see you again," she cried. "I thought you'd believe that note I left. I thought...."

"It's okay, Alex. I've got you...I've got you. My Alex, my love...." Justin folded her into his arms, his voice choking on his own tears.

CHAPTER SEVENTEEN

MORNING. JUSTIN KNEW IT WAS morning when he saw the sunlight streaming in through the window of his brother's office.

He had been spending most of his time on the dungeon floor the last few days, and time passed differently on the dungeon floor. It was marked not by minutes, but by cries in the dark.

He used his brother's private elevator to get from the dungeon floor to the ground floor. He'd been doing that a lot recently. Jonathan hated it, which was precisely why Justin kept doing it. Every time Justin came upstairs and managed to catch his brother unawares, Jonathan would scowl, and Justin would give him a bemused smile.

It was normal brother rivalry stuff, still awkward, but much different from what Justin was used to. It felt...good.

This time, when Jonathan saw Justin come through the elevator door, he tried a different tactic, and acted nonchalant about his brother's sudden appearance. "Where's Alexandra? Not with you today?" He asked politely.

Justin grinned. "She's with Mr. Cox right now," he said. "He's preparing her for a scene with me."

"Oh? I'm glad to hear she's up for that."

"Me, too." Justin said. "It's amazing how fast she's come through this whole thing."

"Well, this time is different from last time," Jonathan pointed out. "This time, she has you." Justin looked away, embarrassed, and Jonathan said, "Did I just make my little brother blush? I think I did!"

"Well." Justin let out a noise that ended up sounded like a snort, and shrugged. His face grew serious as he said, "Listen, Jonathan, it's been nice, you letting us stay here for so long, but Alex and I are thinking it's about time for us to go. We need to get back to real life."

"I didn't *let* you stay here, Justin," Jonathan said quietly. "This is your home as much as it is mine. You can stay here for as long as you want."

"I know," Justin said, "and I appreciate it. But Alex and I have a lot to figure out, and it's time for us to get out there and do it."

"Where will you start?"

"At my store, I think," Justin said. "I've spoken to Adam; I'm giving him full control. He and Khloe might take over there...or maybe not. He'll be finishing up his degree in a few months, and then I don't know."

"Does this mean I'll have to find someone else to make our toys?"

"It does indeed, at least for a while," Justin said, grinning at his brother's distraught look. "I'll set up shop somewhere else eventually, but Alex and I are headed to Los Angeles for now. She needs to get back to Wellington Enterprises, and reestablish herself over there."

"How long will you two be in L.A.?"

"I don't know. Why?"

"Alex isn't the only one who needs to reestablish herself in her family's business," Jonathan said. "I'm wondering how long it'll take you to come back here and do that yourself. The Hotel Bentmoore belongs to you, too, Justin."

A look passed between them. They had talked about this: Jonathan wanted Justin to have a bigger presence now at the Hotel Bentmoore, and Justin was eager to reclaim his birthright.

But right now, the needs of his sub had to come first.

"We'll figure it out," Justin said. "Maybe we'll divide our time, half in L.A., half here. Or one of us will fly out more. The distance isn't so far."

"No, it's not."

"But until Alex finishes cleaning house over at her company, and feels comfortable enough that she has things running the way she wants, I need to be there for her."

"I understand."

"I know." Another moment of silence passed between them, but it was a comfortable sort of silence, filled with understanding.

It had been a long hard road for both of them, but they were finally there.

Justin asked, "Anything from Davis?"

"It seems he's keeping his word, and taking care of

everything on his side," Jonathan replied. "Alex won't be bothered again. As long as she does her part, the Feds will back off."

"Good."

Davis had shown up at the hotel the next day, filthy, bone weary, and smelling like barbecued pork. He'd warned Alexandra some agents would be showing up soon to take her statement, but it was just standard regulation stuff, nothing she had to be worried about. Nobody suspected her of anything anymore.

What we really need, Davis said, *is help looking into all the deals Hector Carmine had a hand in at Wellington. Your company's got some shady business going on, Alexandra. We could sure use you on our side, throwing your influence around in there.*

The agreement wasn't spelled out, but it was made clear none the less: if Alexandra helped the Feds figure out anyone else who might've been involved in Carmine's schemes, they wouldn't ask too many questions about his death, and they wouldn't publicize her part in it. They would back off, and leave her alone.

Alexandra was happy to go along. She told Justin, she'd decided it was time for her to return to Wellington Enterprises anyway, to get the business functioning the way her mother would've wanted her to.

Alexandra was tired of running.

So she answered all their questions, and made sure the Feds had all the information they needed, so they wouldn't have reason to bother her again.

Justin remained by her side the entire time she gave them her statement. He was amazed at the story she told them. Hector Carmine, it seemed, had found a way to follow Alexandra's journey all along.

Three years earlier, back when Joshua was acting the devoted stepfather, Alexandra had signed some papers for him, giving him his own backdoor access to her accounts. The problem was, his backdoor username and password had not been magically deleted when he died.

Hector had been using them all along to track Alexandra wherever she went. But he'd never had reason to bother her before, not until she managed to thwart his first attempt at a deal between Wellington and DSV Corp. After that, he'd bided his time, and waited until the moment was just right.

He decided he had to act before the contract was up for another vote; he could not have Alexandra torpedoing his plans a second time. Too much was at stake now.

His first idea had been to kill her. But when he saw all the checks starting to come into her account from Justin's shop, and realized Alexandra was now working for Jonathan Bentmoore's brother, he thought up a new plan: keep Alexandra alive, and use Justin as leverage.

"He called me at Justin's house, and told me he'd kill Justin if I didn't do exactly what he said. That it wasn't just my life I had to worry about anymore," Alex said. "Hector was happy he'd found a way to keep me alive, under his control. He gloated about it. It was what he'd wanted last time." She looked up at Justin and said, "He was the one who helped Joshua abduct me three years ago."

Justin squeezed her shoulder, kissed her head, and whispered in her ear, "He's dead, my love. He's never going to hurt you again."

She smiled, but the smile never reached her eyes. She was healing...but it would take time.

"What about Hoshi, is he still here?" Justin asked his brother now.

"No, he left a couple hours ago," Jonathan replied, shuffling some papers on his desk and moving them from one pile to another. "But I have a feeling he'll be back."

"Really?" Justin asked. "Raven told me he didn't meet with any of the hotel mistresses. I have to tell you, that kind of surprised me, that you allowed someone to enter and exit this hotel without an ounce of hedonistic pleasure."

"It is true, Hoshi did not meet with any of the mistresses," Jonathan said. "However, I understand he did spend some *quality* time with Mr. Bone."

"Wait. *What?*"

"You mean you didn't know Hoshi is...?"

"No, I didn't...." Justin's eyes went wide as he digested this bit of news. Then a smile spread slowly across his mouth as the last shred of tension he felt toward the other man finally melted away.

Jonathan stopped readjusting his papers and peered at Justin. "Are you going to spend all morning in my office, keeping me company?" He asked. "Or is there somewhere you need to be?"

Justin grinned. "I'll see you later, big brother."

"I don't wonder," Jonathan replied with a sigh. He watched Justin get back on his private elevator to return to the dungeon floor below.

By the time Justin walked into the activity room, Alex was already arranged the way he'd requested: bound to the St. Andrew's Cross, legs and arms spread wide, wearing nothing but a simple sleeveless dress supplied by the hotel.

Her dark hair was piled up on her head and cinched in one those velvet-covered hair bands she sported. Her long neck and reedy arms were well exposed.

She stood still against the cross, her head slightly bowed, her hands clenching the pieces of chain that bound her wrist cuffs to the solid wood. She was like a beautiful piece of art come to life, displayed for his pleasure alone.

But there was still one other man in the room: Mr. Cox. He may have been the one to prepare Alex for this little exhibit, but it was time for him to leave.

"Thank you, Mr. Cox," Justin said, his voice formal. "Did she give you any trouble?"

"None," Mr. Cox replied. "She's eager to get this over with."

"Is she?" Justin took a step forward and ran the tip of his index finger down Alex's back. Alex jerked into the Cross. When his finger continued down her sloping back, over the curve of her ass, Alex let out a tiny shiver.

"Everything you requested is on the table over

there," Mr. Cox said.

Justin looked over, and took note of the small rolling table sitting next to the bed, covered with all the toys and tools he had requested.

"Thank you," he said. "It looks like I have everything I need. Could you please hand me the knife on your way out?"

Mr. Cox reached over, grabbed the single-blade knife, laid it across both his palms, and with great ceremony, walked it over to Justin.

With both arms outstretched, Mr. Cox handed it out slowly. "Good luck, Mr. Bentmoore," he said. "Enjoy her well."

"Thank you, I will," Justin replied, taking the knife. He gave Mr. Cox a single, curt nod. Mr. Cox nodded back, turned around, and left the room.

Justin held up the knife and ran his nail across the blade. It was sharp.

Good.

He began to take off his clothes. Alex barely moved.

"Do you know why you're here, Alex?" He asked from afar. Her eyes, rimmed with their thick dark lashes, were closed.

"I need to be punished," she said. He could see a tiny grimace flitting across her profile.

"Yes," Justin said. "Do you know why?"

"Because I made you worry. Because I left that note for you in your house after Hector called me, when what I should have done was tell you what was going on. Even though Hector told me he'd kill you if I told you, or anyone...."

"You still should have told me." He grabbed her dress by the back of the neck, eliciting a soft cry from Alex.

Justin slipped the knife between the dress and Alex's tender skin, pressed the blade into the fabric, and was rewarded with a satisfying *rip.* He pushed the knife down, and the dress began to tear in two.

"You don't get to make unilateral decisions like that," he said, cutting her dress into shreds. "You don't get to shut me out like that, even if it's to try to keep me safe."

He kept cutting up her dress until it fell in strips onto the floor. Within moments, Alex stood naked against the Cross, pale and vulnerable.

But Justin wasn't done with the knife yet. He ran the blade around her arms, across her thighs, down her back...he never left a mark, never cut through the skin...but Alex shivered and moaned nonetheless, feeling that blade slide merrily along her flesh. She quivered on her feet, afraid to move—afraid to breathe.

"Next time we play, I might just stick this knife up your cunt, and you'll know what it means to not be able to move," he whispered in her ear. "But this time, I'm not doing a fear scene. This time, you're going to feel some pain."

He went back to the table, put down the blade, and picked up a flogger. It was a lovely piece, and would work well in his hands. He knew, because it was one of his own; he had made this flogger himself.

"Twenty-strand rubber flogger," he said out loud. "Not too bouncy, not too thick. This should work."

He slapped the flogger into his other hand, making it smack. "Oh, yes."

"But he told me he'd kill you!" Alex blurted out. "I couldn't let him hurt you, not for my sake."

Justin strode over to her splayed body, grabbed a great fistful of her hair, and yanked her head back. "You don't get to decide," Justin whispered into her ear. "You come to me first. Those kinds of choices aren't yours to make anymore. Understand?"

"Yes...yes, Sir."

"Good." He released her hair, and her head fell forward. "Now, I understand why you did what you did. You thought you were doing the right thing. You weren't given enough training yet to know better. That was my fault, a mistake I intend to rectify."

Alex took a quick, deep breath.

"But while I am not without mercy," Justin said, "Your actions had severe consequences. You must pay amends...and so you shall." He ran his finger down her back again, tickling her bony spine. "Are you ready?"

Alex took a long, ragged breath. "Yes, Sir."

"Good girl."

Justin stepped back to just within striking space. He got into position, adjusted his arm for a clean distance, and said, "Oh, and Alex?"

"Yes Sir?"

"This isn't going to be over with anytime soon."

"I...I understand, Sir."

"Good." With that, he swiped the first blow of the flogger across her back, and Alex's whole body convulsed into the Cross.

Justin flogged her for almost an hour. He had purposely chosen to use only one flogger to swing, instead of a matching pair, so the scene would take longer, and he could give one of his wrists a break while the other was working.

He wanted to take his time, because he knew this scene wasn't just about punishment; it was about renewal, too. They needed this scene to begin healing the bond between them that had been tested so harshly. It would be a cleansing, cathartic ritual for both of them.

The beating he gave her ebbed and flowed, and he gifted her with short breaks now and then. But he pelted her long and hard, and by the time he was done, Alex's shoulders, back, and thighs blushed a beautiful red, while her ass, bearing the brunt of the flogging, was a kaleidoscope of crimson, purple, and blue.

Her face, no doubt, was a mess now. He couldn't see it, but he had been listening to her cry for the last twenty minutes, punctuated now and then with a loud sob or a high-pitched shriek.

But she did not beg him to stop, a fact he noted with pride.

When both his arms were too tired to continue, Justin put the flogger back down on the table. Then, thinking carefully, he picked up the cordless Hitachi wand. He had meant to use a paddle and cane on her as well, but decided those tools could wait for another day.

His cock could not.

After giving it another moment's thought, he grabbed the bottle of lube from the table, too.

He opened up the bottle and began to liberally lube up his cock while he stepped up behind her. Leaving the Hitachi wand on the floor by his foot, he spread open her ass cheeks wide.

"I lubed myself, cause I'm nice," he breathed against her cheek as he slid his cock up and down her ass crack, finding his target. "Aren't I nice?"

"Yes, Sir, very nice," she said, shaking.

Justin, locating his target, stopped, took a breath, and pressed home. Alex's sharp intake of breath was like music to his ears. He slid into her asshole slowly, inch by inch, just the head, holding her ass cheeks apart as he pushed. Alex strained against the Cross.

Once the head was in, he stopped. Her asshole was hot, tight, and clenched around his cock like a satin vise.

"This is for making me think you were breaking up with me." He shoved his prick into her, just an inch, and Alex shrieked.

"This is for making me worry about you." He shoved another inch, and Alex shrieked again, her buttocks squeezing against his groin.

"And this is for making me think I might lose you forever." He pumped his hips, pummeling his cock into her until his thighs slapped against her ass, and Alex howled.

Letting go of her ass cheeks, he grabbed her hair in one hand and her waist in the other, and began to fuck her ass with long, pounding strokes.

"You will never scare me like that again, do you hear?" He growled against her face, pumping his cock into her throbbing, squeezing asshole.

"Yes Sir, Yes Sir, yes Sir," she repeated in a litany of benediction, her voice choking on her words.

"Good." Then, he yanked out of her ass, getting a bray of surprise from the buggered woman, grabbed up the Hitachi wand from the floor, turned it on…and pumped his cock right back into her, punching through her tiny gate like a battering ram. Alex's shocked cry was loud, but cut short when Justin put the Hitachi wand against her cunt lips.

As he continued to fuck her ass, he spread open her pussy lips from the front, so that the Hitachi wand could nestle right against her clit. Alex stood up on her tiptoes and tried to sway from side to side, but it was no use; there was no relent from Justin's pounding cock from behind, or the hum of the vibrator against her swollen clit.

"This is how I'm merciful," Justin said, smoothing the hair back from her face with his free hand. "I'm going to let you come, too. What do you say?"

"Thank you Sir. Thank you Sir, thank you Sir, THANK YOU, SIRRRR…." Her voice escalated into a shrill legato as she came; she grabbed onto the chains that bound her wrists and pumped her hips against his prick and the magic wand.

Justin could feel her body tense, her bottom squeeze against his thighs, her churning asshole clamp down on his cock in the throes of her own orgasm. He began to pump furiously into her, grabbing her around waist to hold her still with one hand while he pressed the Hitachi wand against her sopping pussy with the other. Just as her piercing cry began to recede, he felt her come again, and this time, her scream was filled with exquisite torment.

"Oh God oh God oh God oh God—" She came a third time, bucking her hips behind her, slapping her ass against his cock as she slid across the Hitachi wand.

Justin held back as long as he could, relishing the feel of her burning asshole gripping his entire length, pulling him ever deeper into her with each contraction. But it soon became too much for him; his balls tightened and tingled, his cock strained inside her, and a moment later, it erupted within her searing, pulsing ass, shooting jets of liquid come up her back channel.

He pulled out slowly. It took him a moment to regain his balance and get his breath back. But once he did, he began to release her from the Cross.

He carried Alex to the bed, climbed in with her, and pulled her into the crook of his arm, right were she belonged.

In a soft voice she asked him, "Am I forgiven?"

"Yes," he said, smiling into her soft hair. He took a deep breath of her scent, lilac and midnight breeze.

Alex wiggled into the spot between his arm and chest, burrowing in, and Justin's smile widened.

She whispered against his side, "Thank you for coming after me, Justin."

"That's my job, babe. I'm your Dom. I will *always* be there when you need me."

"I know. I love you."

"I love you too." He kissed her head. "You relax now. Everything is going to be okay." He kissed her head again and hugged her tight. "Everything is going to be okay now."

An echo of a scream could be heard from somewhere down the hall, but they ignored it. It was just another satisfied guest, having another glorious fantasy fulfilled.

But what Justin and Alex shared was pleasure of a different sort.

Theirs was a fantasy come true.

Printed in Great Britain
by Amazon

33344601R00191